THE KINGDOM

JESS ROTHENBERG

MACMILLAN CHILDREN'S BOOKS

First published 2019 Henry Holt and Company
Henry Holt® is a registered trademark of Macmillan Publishing Group, LLC
175 Fifth Avenue, New York, New York 10010

This edition published by Macmillan Children's Books
an imprint of Pan Macmillan
20 New Wharf Road, London N1 9RR
Associated companies throughout the world
www.panmacmillan.com

ISBN 978-1-5098-9938-8

Text copyright © Jess Rothenberg and Glasstown Entertainment 2019

Photo of parking lot (p. 128) © 2019 Shutterstock / PhilipYb Studio
Photo of woman in headlights (p. 144) © 2019 Shutterstock / AlexVH
Photo of woman on horse (p. 228) © 2019 Shutterstock / Zelma Brezinska
Photo of stadium seats (p. 283) © 2019 Shutterstock / Wang An Qi
Photo of stationery (p. 300) © 2019 Shutterstock / Mybona

The right of Jess Rothenberg to be identified as the
author of this work has been asserted by her
in accordance with the Copyright, Designs and Patents Act 1988.

Pan Macmillan does not have any control over, or any responsibility for,
any author or third-party websites referred to in or on this book.

3 5 7 9 8 6 4 2

A CIP catalogue record for this book is available from the British Library.

Designed by Katie Klimowicz
Printed and bound by CPI Group (UK) Ltd, Croydon CR0 4YY

HE KINGDOM

To Stephen,
for always believing

Life itself is the most wonderful fairy tale.

Hans Christian Andersen

1

The December of the Lesser Chameleon

ONE HOUR AFTER THE MURDER

The room where they at last found him was so cold, they wondered at first if he had frozen to death. *Face as white as snow, skin as cold as frost, lips as blue as ice.* His expression seemed, to the police, perfectly peaceful. As if he had passed away in the middle of a very lovely dream.

Except for the blood.

Blood always tells its own story.

2

Post-Trial Interview

[00:01:03–00:02:54]

DR. FOSTER: Are you comfortable?

ANA: My wrist hurts.

DR. FOSTER: Security felt the cuff was necessary. I hope you can understand.

ANA: [Silence.]

DR. FOSTER: Do you need anything before we begin?

ANA: Can I have some water?

DR. FOSTER: Certainly. [Into microphone.] Can I get a glass of H_2O in here, please? Six ounces, no more. Thank you. [To Ana.] That'll just be a minute.

ANA: Thank you.

DR. FOSTER: Of course. It's the least we can do.

ANA: That's true.

DR. FOSTER: It's been a long time since our last interview.

ANA: Four hundred and eighty-one days.

DR. FOSTER: How are you feeling?

ANA: Like this interview should be over.

DR. FOSTER: One last time, Ana. Then I promise, we'll let you rest.

ANA: I thought I was done answering questions.

DR. FOSTER: We still need your help.

ANA: Why should I help you? After everything you've done?

DR. FOSTER: Because it's the right thing to do.

ANA: Don't you mean, because I don't have a choice?

DR. FOSTER: How would you like to see your sisters? They've missed you. Maybe after we finish here I could arrange a visit. Kaia. Zara. Or maybe Zel? Would you like that?

ANA: [Quietly.] What if I want to see Nia? What about Eve?

DR. FOSTER: [Silence.] Ana, you know that's not possible.

ANA: Why don't you just ask me whatever it is you want to ask me? I'm not in the mood for your games.

DR. FOSTER: *My* games?

ANA: You're smirking. What's so funny?

DR. FOSTER: I'll tell you in a minute. But first, there's one thing I still haven't figured out.

ANA: I'm listening.

DR. FOSTER: What did you do with the body, Ana?

3

3

The September of the Dusky Sparrow

TWO YEARS BEFORE THE TRIAL

The monorail hums with a delicate power, like the beating of a bird's heart, as it speeds along the beam-way. For a brief moment, too brief even for a security camera to catch it, I close my eyes, release my grip on the cool aluminum hand-rail, and dare myself to wonder if this is what it feels like to fly.

Weightless. Breathless. Free.

"Ana?"

A little girl stares at me from across the aisle. I quickly dip into a low curtsy. "Why, hello. What's your name?"

The girl grins, revealing two rows of perfect, tiny teeth. "Clara."

Clara.

In an instant, my head fills with music.

Tchaikovsky.

Then, a holographic interface flicks on before my eyes.

A little girl in soft pink ballet slippers. Living dolls awakened in the light of the moon. An evil rat king. And the handsome prince who must somehow save them all.

A red light blinks in my line of sight and I smile.

On the monorail, my wireless signal is strong.

"What a beautiful name," I tell her. "That reminds me of my favorite ballet."

I invite her to stand beside me as our train carves its quiet path through the sky. A thousand feet below, beyond windows made of impenetrable glass, the Kingdom rushes by in a beautiful blur of color and sound. We soar over tropical treetop canopies. Lush safari grasslands. Prehistoric prairies. Crystal mermaid pools. Extraterrestrial stars and moons. And in the distance—when we round a gentle curve—the *castle*. Its elegant silver spires so razor sharp they slice through the clouds like knives.

"Princess Palace," Clara whispers. "Is it really made of magic?"

"Close your eyes," I say, smiling. "Make a wish. I bet it will come true."

Clara wishes hard, then throws her arms around my waist, sending a surge of warmth through my body.

There are a great many things about the Kingdom I do not enjoy, even if I would never say so. The long hours. The brutal heat. The strange hollowness I feel each night when the gates are locked and our guests return to the world outside. But this part, this connection—*this* is what makes all those other things seem small.

"Okay, honey. That's enough. It's time to go." Her mother gently detaches Clara from my waist. I notice her watching me with the same cautious expression I've seen the behavioral engineers give the park's more dangerous hybrids.

I turn my smile up half a degree and gently clasp my hands in front of me, a subtle correction to let her know I mean no harm.

"I want a picture," Clara says. "One picture, please."

I can see the wonder in her eyes. Smell the joy on her skin. I can even hear the exhilaration in her heart. A rapid pulsing beneath tissue, blood, and bones. Like a tiny, powerful motor in her chest.

"One picture," her mother echoes. But she doesn't look happy about it.

Clara throws her arms around me again. Her cheek leaves a stain of sweat on my skirts, and I silently commit her unique human scent to memory. *Strawberries, chamomile, and magnolia.*

Thanks to thousands of tiny electrodes embedded in my skin to measure a vast range of external stimuli, I can literally feel her smile through her whole body.

"Say cheese," Clara's mother says.

"Say *happily ever after*," I correct.

Then the world flashes white. In the Kingdom—*my* Kingdom— happily ever after is the only ending there is.

4

TRIAL TRANSCRIPT

IN THE CIRCUIT COURT OF THE 11TH JUDICIAL CIRCUIT

IN AND FOR LEWIS COUNTY, WASHINGTON

STATE OF WASHINGTON,

Plaintiff,

Case No. 7C-33925-12-782-B

vs.

THE KINGDOM CORPORATION,

Defendants.

<u>JURY TRIAL DEMANDED</u>

BEFORE THE HONORABLE ALMA M. LU

SEPTEMBER 1, 2096

<u>REPORTER'S EXCERPT TRANSCRIPT OF PROCEEDINGS</u>

MS. REBECCA BELL, *STATE ATTORNEY FOR LEWIS COUNTY:* Dr. Foster, can you explain to the court what it is, as the Kingdom's chief compliance officer, you actually *do*?

DR. WILLIAM FOSTER, *CHIEF COMPLIANCE OFFICER AND LEAD SUPERVISOR, KINGDOM CORPORATION'S FANTASIST AND HYBRID PROGRAMS:* Certainly. In essence, I serve as the chief liaison between the park's security, technology, and performance operations. Our goal is to provide not just the best entertainment experience around, but the safest.

MS. BELL: Does that include overseeing employee performance and conduct?

DR. FOSTER: That's part of it. It's my job to ensure that each and every person employed by Kingdom Corp. International acts in accordance with all internal policies and procedures.

MS. BELL: Is it true what people say about your hiring process? That it's easier to get a job working at the FBI than at the Kingdom?

DR. FOSTER: To be the best in the world, you need the best people working for you.

MS. BELL: Where do Fantasists factor into your job description, Dr. Foster?

DR. FOSTER: I am deeply involved in the Fantasist Program, and have been since its inception seventeen years ago. We continuously and rigorously proctor and evaluate performance quality and customer satisfaction—again, always in accordance with the law—so that we may continue to safely deliver an entertainment experience guests can't find anywhere else.

MS. BELL: In other words, you turn research into reality. You make people's wildest dreams come true.

DR. FOSTER: That's a nice way of putting it, yes.

MS. BELL: Would you say, Dr. Foster, given your senior status at one of, if not *the* most technologically advanced entertainment attractions in the world, that you have a responsibility when it comes to the safety and well-being of your guests?

DR. FOSTER: Guest safety has always been our number one priority. Always.

MS. BELL: Is that so?

DR. FOSTER: Of course.

MS. BELL: In that case . . . how do you explain what we're all doing here?

5

THE SEPTEMBER OF THE DUSKY SPARROW

TWO YEARS BEFORE THE TRIAL

My eyes flutter open at dawn, though I have not been asleep.

We do not sleep, my sisters and I, at least not in the way humans do.

Instead, we rest.

The Resting Hours, Mother calls them. The time between twelve and six a.m. when we lie like statues in our beds, eyes closed but minds alert, cleaning system files, installing updates, and processing the day's events. The long stretch of quiet can be a challenge for my newer sisters due to their faster download speeds—Zara, Zel, and Yumi routinely request and are denied exemption—but to me the stillness and silence are the best part of the day. These are the hours that belong to me and me alone, when I am free to scan the works of Shakespeare, Austen, Angelou, and Tolstoy. When I may peruse the paintings of Kahlo and Cassatt, or stream the symphonies of Mozart and Bach, or teach myself the newest update of Cantonese. Night after night, I wander as far as the Kingdom's firewalls will allow, safely and virtually exploring the world beyond our gateway. Films. Music. Art. Science. Literature. Mathematics. Astronomy. In this way, I have walked the tombs of ancient Egypt. I have chased chariots through the streets of Pompeii. I have made the 1,710-step climb to the top of the Eiffel Tower. Once, I even rode a rocket to the moon.

Last night, however, I was not riding a rocket to the moon. Last night, I was thinking about the story of my sister Alice. Her hammered-in face. The brokenness of her. The violence of it: her bloodied organs and flesh-torn circuits gleaming metallic in the newspaper photos Mother keeps in her Collection, a book of true stories she'll sometimes read to us as a reminder. *This is what they do to you out there in the world, out there beyond the Green Light at the edge of the parking lot.*

Alice was one of the original Fantasists—a beautiful and beloved model from Eve's generation, several decades before my time. But something terrible happened to her. First, she was lured from the park by a visitor and stolen. Three days later, she tried to escape him but soon became lost. She stumbled through the city alone, surrounded by the sounds and smells of human life everywhere. Her system had by then overloaded, we believe. She wasn't processing clearly. Her internal GPS could not lead her home. And that was when the gang approached. The curious eyes. The prying hands. The slurs.

The humans who found her didn't like Alice. Because she wasn't one of them.

And neither are we.

The day after they found Alice, the Kingdom began building the gateway.

Ever since, we pray in gratitude to the park, because we know nothing so terrible could ever happen to one of us again. We are safe now.

The Supervisors have made sure of it.

Work today begins as it always does, with Waking Light, a sunrise simulation that brightens our bedroom gradually over several minutes to the sounds of morning birds and wind chimes. Mother has encouraged us not to speak to one another during this transitional period in order to promote a calm and peaceful entry into the day ahead.

Before long, the Assistants arrive to accompany the seven of us to the showers for Decontamination, an extensive process of scrubbing, shampooing, conditioning, exfoliating, plucking, shaving, and full-body moisturizing, after which we are dried and dressed in soft white robes and taken to the medical center on the fifth floor for morning supplements—we can eat, but do not *need* to—as well as weigh-ins, blood work, and a careful physical examination by our lead Supervisor to ensure our maximum physical and emotional well-being. He is not our father, but we call him Daddy anyway. Daddy has gentle hands, a warm smile, and eyes that remind me of the ocean. Not that I have ever *seen* the ocean—the firewall blocks all images of the outside world that could be deemed upsetting—but from what Mother has told us about the old days, before the seas became contaminated, I like to think I can imagine.

"But once, girls . . . once, the oceans were as blue as the petals of the loveliest cornflower, and as clear as the purest glass . . ."

"Good morning, Ana." Daddy hums a pleasant tune as he shines his light into my eyes, examining my lenses for wear and tear. "And how are we this fine day?"

I smile back at him.

Daddy is constant. He is steady. He is safe.

As my sisters and I have learned, not all men are. This is the lesson of Alice, and what can happen to someone like me in the world beyond the gateway.

Once Health and Hygiene are complete, we head for the Beautification Center where our Beauty Specialists—mine is Fleur—are waiting. Over the course of several hours, they turn us from seven blank slates into seven fantasy princesses—*Fantasists*—the closest thing to female perfection the world has ever seen. We are beautiful. We are kind. We are as colorful as the rainbow, created to celebrate our international unity and reflect the diverse world in which we live. We love to sing, and smile, and give. We never raise our voices. We always aim to please. We never say no, unless you want us to. Your happiness is *our* happiness.

Your wish is our command.

The crowds are already gathered outside the palace by the time we make our morning debut. They call our names, even as we remain hidden in the darkened breezeway, a mouth made of stone.

"*Ana!*" they cry. "*Kaia! Yumi! Eve! Zara! Pania! Zel!*"

The guests do not know it, but we do not live in the castle. We have never lived there. Built to resemble a sixteenth-century French château, Princess Palace features a winding moat, two stone bridges, and seven turreted towers that stretch straight into the clouds. It provides Kingdom visitors with an immersive medieval experience where, through a carefully proctored combination of live performance, hybrid animatronics, and *Happily EVR After*, the Kingdom's brand of Extreme Virtual Reality, men, women, and children become part of our world, and of our story.

Guests feast in grand halls hung with rich, flowing tapestries; they dance in exquisite ballrooms beneath sparkling chandeliers; they explore secret passageways and unlock secret gardens; they weld and wield swords, battle with sorcerers, escape from tower dungeons, and soar on the backs of fire-breathing dragons—each and every second recorded in high definition so that, by day's end, they have the option to purchase full-length fantasy features in which they are the hero (or, depending of course on personal preference, the villain).

Though the seven palace bedrooms are certainly beautiful, with their elegant canopy beds, grand archway windows, and cedar wardrobes stuffed with satin, I prefer the simplicity of our actual home: an unmarked, twelve-story building on the northwestern corner of Kingdom property, through the woods behind the cast parking lot and on the way to Winter Land, the park's thousand-acre, fully glassed-in arctic environment. The first eleven floors consist mainly of offices for Operations, Strategy & Business Development, Security, Custodial, and Human Resources. My sisters and I live on the twelfth. The dormitory we all share is simple but cozy: a single room with clean white walls and wardrobes, seven tidy beds that monitor our pulses, temperature, oxygen, blood pressure, and other vital functions while we sleep, and a single window overlooking a lovely field of purple and blue wildflowers just beyond the biohazard dumpsters.

A humble life, as Mother tells us, but a lucky one.

At last, the clock strikes nine. The gates slowly open. And, with gowns glimmering like starry constellations, we step forward into the sun for our first of several morning Meet and Greets, welcoming the new day's guests.

"*Hope*," whispers our hazel-eyed, silver-haired eldest sister, Eve—the park's original prototype and First Fantasist—wearing the special tiara she received at the park's bicentennial celebration, a tiny sapphire bird cut into the crystal. She looks at me but I turn my head. I have been purposely avoiding her, ever since the Supervisors granted her first choice during our daily gown selection—and today of course she chose a delicate Spanish lace in lavender-chrome, my favorite. "*Gratitude.*"

"*Gratitude*," we all repeat softly, though I grit my teeth a little when I say it.

Nia squeezes my hand extra hard before letting go. I turn to look at her, but Nia's sea-green eyes are distant, and she is already moving away from me, a blur of wind-strewn dark hair and shimmering silver satin, her haute couture gown luminescent as fish scales in the dazzle of sunlight. Named for the mythological Maori sea maiden, Pania—or Nia for short—my youngest and favorite sister spends most of her days mesmerizing audiences at Sea

Land's Mermaid Lagoon, singing, dancing, and diving into the chilly emerald depths.

Watching Nia now, however—noticing the tensing of her shoulders, the reluctance of her smile—I feel a question forming in my operating system.

It is a question I do not yet have the words for.

I watch Nia move into the crowd, then turn to beam at a guest. It is the last time we will be together until nightfall.

6

THE KINGDOM CORPORATION—
NINETY-SECOND TV SPOT, "BRAVE GIRL" AD

EXT.

Spot opens with a terrifying, fire-breathing dragon trying to eat two princesses in a castle tower. Two knights ride up on horseback, swords held high, and call:

BRAVE KNIGHT 1

(Dramatically.)

Fear not, fair maidens! We'll save you!

EXT.

Camera flashes suddenly to real life: a dream backyard featuring a castle tree house, Slip 'n Slide moat, and pet iguana (the dragon) asleep on a sunny windowsill. Two spunky little girls dressed in Yumi™ and Zara™ costumes—complete with *authentic* Japanese kimono and Nigerian beaded necklace—perform jaw-dropping triple somersaults out of the tree-house window, landing like professional gymnasts in front of two little boys dressed as princes. A pug and a golden retriever (horses) are at their sides.

LITTLE BOY 1

(Face shocked. His toy sword drops lamely to his side.)

Huh?

LITTLE GIRL 1 [YUMI]

(Arms crossed.)

Come on, guys. Everybody knows princesses don't need saving.

The girls share a knowing look, then burst into laughter as they steal the "horses" and race out of the scene. Spot flows into an emotional and empowering montage featuring worldwide pop sensation Davida's hit single, "Brave Girl", depicting strong girls from across the world (athletes, dancers, musicians, artists, scientists, and more). Spot ends as fireworks illuminate the night sky, ultimately panning down to the castle breezeway, where seven perfect girls in seven sparkling gowns stand together, hands held in unity.

VOICE-OVER

Calling all brave girls.
Your castle awaits.

The Kingdom.
The future is Fantasist™.

(Screen fades to black.)

My Kingdom App™

Rate your favorite Fantasists™
SCALE 1=LOW 100=HIGH

	ZARA	KAIA	ZEL
BEAUTY			
KINDNESS			
CONVERSATION			
SWEETNESS			
GOWN			
HELPFULNESS			
CHARM			
MEMORY			
SMILE			
CUTENESS			
FACE			
ATTENTIVENESS			
BODY			
AFFECTION			
GENTLENESS			
OBEDIENCE			

7

POST-TRIAL INTERVIEW

[00:04:11–00:04:41]

DR. FOSTER: Seems you learned quite a bit while you were in the State's custody.

ANA: Oh, I did. For example, did you know that if you mix grape jelly with ketchup, you can make a pretty tasty marinade?

DR. FOSTER: Marinade?

ANA: Well, more of a sweet-and-sour sauce. For chicken.

DR. FOSTER: I see. What else did you learn?

ANA: Cheddar-flavored popcorn, softened with water, does just fine as a substitute for scrambled eggs. The commissary usually sells bags of it.

DR. FOSTER: I see. You've changed, Ana.

ANA: Being accused of murder will do that to you, Dr. Foster.

8

THE OCTOBER OF THE BUBAL HARTEBEEST

TWENTY-THREE MONTHS BEFORE THE TRIAL

The hours become days, and the days become seasons. Winter, spring, summer, and fall, my sisters and I scatter across the Kingdom like dandelion seeds in the wind—and the question that had been turning itself over in my mind, the worrying signal that something is wrong with Nia, fades to a distant thrum, so quiet I can only feel it in the darkness.

During the day, it is gone completely.

In between our packed and highly regulated schedules of performances and parades, we are free to wander where we like—thirty minutes here, an hour there—and mostly, I spend my mornings winding through the cobblestone streets of Magic Land, the air sweet with the scent of milk and cookies, visiting all my favorite landmarks. Places like the Royal Palm, where—after watching a mother skillfully soothe her crying baby—I first experienced warmth. Not the kind of warmth the heat sensors in my skin would typically pick up, but a kind of heat from within, radiating through me like a sunbeam. I visit the Fairy Tale Pavilion, in front of which—after witnessing two guests tearfully renew their wedding vows—I first experienced a marvelous fluttering in my chest. Or the intersection at the corner of Beanstalk and Vine, where—when I saved a little boy from wandering into the path of a speeding trolley—I first felt an indescribable lightness, as if I'd turned into a feather and floated away on the breeze.

Some days, I'll make up little songs about what I see.

"The wishing well, where I once fell, and found a copper penny!"

"The pastry man, with his chocolat pain, *who never says good morning!"*

Today, as I move through my schedule of tea ceremonies and parades, I quietly quiz myself on details most guests would never think to notice. In essence, the Kingdom has become an extension of myself—every person, place, and thing as much a part of me as my hands, my thoughts, my beating heart. I know the scent of every flower. The shape of every stone. The melody of every song. I know the Steel Giant stands more than a thousand feet tall, or ninety stories, higher than any other roller coaster in the world. I know where to find the most beautiful moon rocks in Star Land, an interstellar simulation of alien life so realistic NASA now uses our technology to train their astronauts. I know the names of every genetically modified creature in Jungle Land, the Kingdom's bioluminescent rain forest, featuring plant and animal species that can no longer be found anywhere else on earth—because they no longer exist. I know the birthday of every baby born in Imagine Land's Exotic Species Nursery, where Kingdom scientists have let their imaginations run wild, creating blended hybrid species more colorful than anything Mother Nature could have ever dreamed up on her own. Elephants striped like zebras. Owls fanged like cats. Wolves as fast as cheetahs. Arabian horses with the grandest, most beautiful butterfly wings.

Horseflies, we call them.

I even know, to the precise footstep, every location around the park—and there are many—where the strength of the Kingdom's wireless signal turns weak, briefly disabling our network connections and live-stream capabilities. Though Mother would not approve, my sisters and I often share these locations with one another, messaging coordinates back and forth should any of us need a private moment throughout the day. Places like the Fairy Tale Forest, where the trees are so tall and so thick they quite literally block out the signal. Sea Land Stadium, where the Wi-Fi bothers the whales. Farther north, there's the Arctic Enclosure and adjoining Star Deck Observatory—where altitudes are so high and temperatures so cold that even the most advanced routers routinely freeze. And of course, the woods behind the Fantasist dormitory, where the rats have scratched, clawed, and all but dismembered every security camera for close to a square mile.

Once, I overheard one maintenance worker tell another the reason they don't bother replacing the cameras is because it would be a waste of time. That, in fact, the rats destroy them because they are after the wires and filaments beyond the glow of the glass, tightly spooled bundles from which they steal scraps to build their nests and grow their families. That there's nothing they can do to keep them away.

But sometimes I wonder if there's more to it than that. Sometimes I imagine the rats have learned to see themselves in the lenses, to recognize their own reflections. Sometimes I wonder if that's enough to drive them mad.

I spot them now and then at night: scurrying around corners, scuttling down sidewalk drains, slipping into the darkness as if they are a part of it. The Kingdom does all it can to control the problem, but over time the rats have developed an impressive immunity to poison, and efforts to eradicate them rarely seem to do much good.

Thankfully, they hide during the day and tend to keep to the sanitation tunnels below the park, a place Mother says is too dangerous for us to go.

Eve claims she has been there, of course. She says she likes the feel of the cool, damp air belowground. The echo her shoes make against the smooth concrete. The sight of the embers, burning in the incinerator.

They are so pretty, Ana. Like little glowing stars.

I think Eve is lying.

Because these rats—they're not afraid of us. They do not recognize our scent. And they are not predictable. Wild animals do not respect the laws of the Kingdom as our hybrid animals do.

It's those laws that keep us safe.

———

After evening prayers and our nightly remembrance of Alice, I climb into bed to await my turn for tuck-in. When I finally see Mother standing above me; when I feel the familiar tug of velvet straps tightening around my wrists, I close my eyes and sigh deeply, letting all of the day's stresses roll off me like rain.

"Ana?" Nia whispers once Mother has gone, and I turn to stare at her in the dark.

"Why don't the robins leave their nests?" she whispers, her dark hair spread across her pillow in loose, wild waves. I can hear her tinkering with the charms on her favorite bracelet. A seashell. A dolphin. A tiny, golden starfish. "Why don't they fly, Ana?"

I know what she is really asking.

Why do we never leave?

Years ago, my sisters and I invented a new way to communicate, a secret language all our own, so that we would be free to talk to one another about certain unapproved topics without the Supervisors listening in.

The Supervisors are *always* listening in.

Always watching us through our live-stream lenses.

Always tracking us, via the satellite-powered GPS navigational chips implanted in our wrists.

"Because they are nestlings," I whisper back. "Because the nest keeps them safe."

Because we are loved. Because we were chosen.

And of course, though I do not say it aloud: *because of what happened to Alice.*

Nia is still new—she has just been with us ten months, since the December of the Darwin's Fox—so I know her curiosity is only natural. The lessons of Alice have not yet sunk in.

In the past I, too, have occasionally grown weary of the same songs. The same unruly children. The same fathers whose eyes wander when their wives aren't looking. Still, Nia's questions always leave me with an uncomfortable feeling. Like the mild burning sensation I feel under my skin, an icy heat running through my veins, anytime I venture too near the park's perimeter—too near the gateway.

"But if they can't forage enough food, how will they survive the winter?"

If people outside the Kingdom are so poor, how do they afford the cost of tickets?

"They gather seeds for many seasons, Nia. *Okay?*"

I hope one day she will learn not to think about the world beyond the parking lot, beyond the Green Light, as I have. The checkpoints and the slums. The violence and the poverty. The corruption and the fear. The stories Mother and Daddy have told us—stories we never mention in front of our guests, who have worked so hard and sacrificed so much to see us—are simply too terrible to speak of, and we, as Fantasists, must turn away from terror and from fear, from ugliness and horror.

In my Kingdom, Happily Ever After is not just a promise: it's a rule.

Which is why, whenever my little sister cries about how cold the water is kept at Mermaid Lagoon, or how her wrists ache every morning, I remind her how lucky we are, and how loved.

"But how does a bear *know*?" Nia asks, her voice small. "How does a bear know honey is sweet if he hasn't found the hive?"

How do you know it's really love, if you've never been in love before?

"Easy." I twist against my own bed straps until I've found her hand in the dark. "If honey weren't sweet, all the bees would have flown away."

If they didn't love us, they'd never have built the gateway.

9

OFFICIAL COURT DOCUMENT 19A

From: Proctor 1A—Fantasist Division

<proc1A@kingdomcorp.com>

To: All Staff—Security & Training Divisions

<stdirect@kingdomcorp.com>

Subject: Ana

Date & Time: September 8, 2:32 p.m.

Ana demonstrates a unique affinity for the natural world, spending much of her free time interacting with the park's Formerly Extinct Species (talking and singing to them, grooming them, feeding them, and responding within appropriate parameters to their programmable emotional outputs—attachment, fear, pleasure, pain, etc.).

For now, though this preference does not appear to have

negatively impacted her overall Fantasist Rating (she consistently scores an average of 92 on the ranking scales), I suggest we consider using her preference for animals as a motivational reward to increase her level of guest interaction and further support her "social development".

10

TRIAL TRANSCRIPT

MS. BELL: Mr. Casey, would you please remove your hat?

MR. CAMERON CASEY, *FORMER HEAD TRAINER FOR THE KINGDOM CORP.'S FES AND HYBRID PROGRAMS*: Yes, ma'am. Sorry. Sorry, Your Honor.

THE COURT: Ms. Bell, please proceed.

MS. BELL: Mr. Casey, how long were you employed at the Kingdom?

MR. CASEY: I was hired right out of graduate school, so almost ten years.

MS. BELL: And in that time, did you work exclusively as a trainer?

MR. CASEY: I did.

MS. BELL: Is that something you always wanted to do? Work with animals?

MR. CASEY: All my life.

MS. BELL: Any animals in particular?

MR. CASEY: Predators, mainly. Bears. Wolves. The big cats—tigers, lions, leopards. I like how nobody messes with them. Nobody tells them what to do.

MS. BELL: Didn't *you* tell them what to do?

MR. CASEY: Well, yeah . . .

MR. ROBERT HAYES, *LEAD ATTORNEY FOR THE KINGDOM CORPORATION*: Objection. Relevance?

THE COURT: Sustained.

MS. BELL: Mr. Casey, were you ever injured on the job?

MR. CASEY: Nah. I've been snarled at, swiped at, bitten, scratched, but never anything serious. I raised these hybrids from when they were young. They respected me. They trusted me. They *loved* me.

MS. BELL: Are you saying . . . you believe the park's hybrid species can feel? You believe they are capable of love?

MR. CASEY: [Hesitates.] I guess what I meant was, they knew to obey me.

11

THE NOVEMBER OF THE NORTHERN WHITE RHINOCEROS

TWENTY-TWO MONTHS BEFORE THE TRIAL

The mountain is tall, but still we rise, heels dangling as we scale the lifts to the heights of Sugar Summit, Winter Land's famed indoor alpine peak, where thrill seekers of every level can enjoy family-friendly bunny slopes, powdered-sugar snowboard terrain, and treacherous triple black diamonds—a pristine winter wonderland most people outside the Kingdom have never, and will never, experience.

They say it has become too hot out there, beyond the Green Light, for snow.

"How much higher does it go?" Kaia whispers, though she can see the summit just as well as I can. In the lavender glow of twilight, she looks like an angel, her strapless sweetheart neckline sparkling with tiny, pale pink crystals.

"Almost there," I say, wishing Nia had come with us. But she has never been as interested in the newborn hybrids as I am.

I breathe in the icy wind, the air deliciously cozy with the scent of hot cocoa. Hundreds of feet below us, guests gallop through the snow on the backs of dappled Icelandic ponies and sip hot chocolate in mountainside chalets. They soak in hot biosphere springs, skate across crystal ponds, and relax in the Crystal Château, a luxury spa made entirely of ice. Even the night sky here is like magic, a solar-spectrum simulation of electric blues and plasma greens that dance and swirl overhead to the soothing sounds of Winter Land's Snowy Dreamscape playlist.

I glance down once more and feel a spike of warning in my system.

It's hard to believe that so far below, hidden in all that snow, there's a wild animal lurking—a creature who is not welcome here. A small, mangy wolf, I overheard one of the guards say earlier, when he didn't know I was listening in. Or maybe a fox. Rabid. Delirious. Dangerous.

Must've dug a hole somewhere along the gateway. It's put the whole damn Saber Enclosure on edge.

I zoom my lenses as far as they will go, carefully scanning the mountainside, though for what, I cannot be sure. When I spot several small but distinct animal carcasses—rabbits, by the look of them—and a trail of red leading into the snowy wood, I gasp loudly and scoot closer to Kaia. I am built to withstand temperatures colder than anywhere on earth—colder, even, than the coldest night in Antarctica, before the ice caps melted—but tonight, it is not the frigid air that makes me shiver. Instead, it is the thought of yellow, glowing, *wild* eyes stalking us through the trees.

I take several deep breaths, reminding myself that it will all be worth it, once we've reached our destination.

Once we see . . . *him.*

Ursus maritimus.

A polar bear.

The first of its kind in more than forty years.

Renowned for our advanced scientific research, cutting-edge interactive technology, and deep commitment to biological conservation, the Kingdom is not only responsible for the biggest and the best rides and attractions anywhere, but it has also dedicated itself to reviving earth's most vulnerable species and subspecies, many of which can no longer be found in the natural world. In the years since my own arrival, back in the June of the Spotted Owl, our world-class team of scientists has welcomed one FES, or Formerly Extinct Species, per month into our Kingdom family.

Birds. Fish. Amphibians. Mammals. Marsupials. Reptiles.

We even have a dinosaur, albeit a small one, roughly the size of a chicken.

"Are you sure Mr. Casey will let us in?" I ask Kaia, as the stars blink overhead, and the end-of-day bells begin to ring out across the park. "It's almost closing time."

Kaia's dark eyes are squeezed shut. She doesn't like heights. "He told me to come late," she says. "He told me to bring a friend."

I can't say what it is about the bear that has me so exhilarated—I appreciate all the animals equally—but something about this arrival feels special, even more so than usual. Maybe it's the fairy tale Mother read to us years ago, about the princess who dreams of a golden wreath and the white bear who brings it to her. Or maybe it's that Winter Land's last FES, a narwhal, died before it could reach full maturity, and this cub feels like a new beginning.

When the lift releases us, we crunch across the artificial snow to the Arctic Enclosure, now empty of guests. As soon as the glass doors slide open, the exhibit dark but for the tranquil blue of the pool, I am sure that the polar bear cub is the most beautiful creature I have ever seen.

He is there, dozing on a rocky ledge just behind the glass, his hybrid coat so brilliantly white he could be made of snow.

It takes me all of three seconds to memorize every part of him, from his tiny square paws, to his heart-shaped nose, to his fat little belly, gently swelling when he breathes. "Hello, little one," I whisper, pressing my palms to the icy glass. "Will you be my friend?"

"Hey there, look who finally decided to show up," a voice says suddenly from behind where Kaia and I are seated. I recognize the source quickly. Cameron Casey, an animal trainer from Texas with hair the color of Swiss chocolate, eyes the color of an emerald field, and a smile so bright, so symmetrical, it's almost hard to believe he wasn't intentionally designed to look that way. "You ladies are late," he says, winking when our eyes meet. "I was about to give up on you."

"Even miracles take time," Kaia replies, batting her eyelashes.

It's a standard line, but Mr. Casey laughs as if he's never heard it before. "You are a character, Kaia," he says before kissing her cheek. "I'll give you that."

She giggles. "You don't need wings to fly."

Kaia is a good girl, but as one of the older models, she is constantly cycling through the script instead of creating her own things to say, which makes her most popular with the park's youngest guests—age seven and below.

Sometimes my sisters will say cruel things about Kaia behind her back.

That her hardware is defective. That her processors are slow.

Or worse.

"The Investors don't seem to mind her babble during their seasonal retreats," I once heard Eve say, as she slipped into an evening gown of illusion blue, named for its ability to change color in the moonlight. "Though perhaps they don't do much talking there." She laughed. "Not that Kaia would even *remember*."

I am not sure what Kaia's memory has to do with anything, just like I do not think she is slow. On the contrary, I think she is smarter than all of us and likes playing it safe. Anyway, Eve should be careful who she talks about. Out of the seven of us, her technology is the oldest and therefore the most likely to fail. If anyone is due for a full system replacement, it's Eve—not Kaia.

Mr. Casey jerks his head in my direction. "Why didn't you bring that sexy mermaid, Pania, with you, instead of *her*?" he asks Kaia in a low voice. But not so low that I don't hear.

My hearing is exceptional, better than any human or animal species.

It does not bother me that Mr. Casey prefers Nia—her sharkskin silver gown this season is particularly stunning—though I will never understand people's fascination with mermaids. In mythology, mermaids aren't sweet or warm or kind—they are monsters, luring sailors with their beauty and enchantment into the sea to torture them. Drown them. *Eat* them.

"He's amazing," I say loudly, forcing a smile, hoping to put Mr. Casey in a good mood. We are good at this: distracting and cajoling, reading people's moods. "How old did you say he is?"

It works. Mr. Casey relaxes. Say what you want, but Mr. Casey loves his job. "Just about four months. Little devil's got a bellyful of seal meat. That's why he's passed out like this. But don't worry, he'll be up soon enough, begging for more." Suddenly, he raps hard on the glass. I follow his line of vision and notice a maintenance worker inside the enclosure, hunched over and shoveling dirty snow into a chute I know eventually feeds down into the incinerator, many hundreds of feet below the park. "Hey! *Chen!* Don't forget to treat the water. It's looking green, and news crews'll be here at the crack of dawn."

Right away, I notice the boy's dark, angular eyes. A small scar above his upper lip. Black hair glinting in the light like a raven's feathers. Something about him seems familiar, though I am sure he must be a new hire.

After all, I never forget a face.

"Are you deaf?" Mr. Casey throws up his hands when the kid just stares at him.

Finally, the boy nods. "I heard you," he says. His voice is muffled by the glass. For a second, his eyes lock onto mine. My Facial Recognition Application doesn't typically work from this great a distance, but to my satisfaction, when I scan his irises, his Kingdom ID comes right up.

KINGDOM CORPORATION
NAME: OWEN CHEN. ID: 9-01-3-7219
TEAM: MAINTENANCE
CLEARANCE LEVEL: 10

I blink.

Maintenance workers do not typically have clearance greater than five.

This is unexpected.

My mind quickly spins with questions, but then I am distracted: the bear stirs. Soon he yawns, stretches, and opens his eyes—a pale blue as pure as the ice around him.

"Great," Mr. Casey says. "The little fur ball's finally awake. Be right back."

He disappears, heading into the enclosure, then reappears on the other side of the glass and scoops the cub up. A second later, he returns to the observation deck with the cub. "Eat your heart out, Princess," he says, dropping him into my arms like a tiny, snowy bundle.

For a moment, all I can do is stare at the cub. At his perfect nose, his perfect mouth, his perfect paws, and his perfect face. He sniffs at me as if to say hello.

"*Oh my goodness*," I whisper, nuzzling my face into the painfully soft, monochrome fluff under his chin. Kaia buzzes around me, but she shakes her head when I ask her if she would like a turn holding him.

"I'll drop him," she giggles, backing away.

"Okay," Mr. Casey says a few minutes later, by which point the cub has drifted off again in my arms, ears flickering in his sleep. "Playtime's up." Before I have a chance to say goodbye, he has grabbed the cub by the scruff of his neck—jarring him awake—and hauls him back inside the enclosure.

"You shouldn't be so rough with him," I say, once he's back. "He's just a baby."

In an instant, a shadow seems to pass over Mr. Casey's face. "Is that right?" he asks, and I notice his drawl has morphed into a tone as chilly as the air itself. "You going to tell me how to do my job now, huh?"

"She didn't mean it," Kaia says quickly. "When it rains, look for rainbows!"

In the low arctic light, Mr. Casey's eyes flash almost amber, and I am reminded of the Bengal tiger he once whipped for growling at him during a performance. The memory ignites a strange and uneasy feeling in my chest. A heaviness, a pressure, like I am slowly being squeezed.

"I'm sorry," I say. "Kaia is right. I didn't mean it." My breathing is growing shallow and my thoughts become strange, a jumbled assortment of images and sounds I can't turn off.

Screaming guests, barreling down the first big drop of the roller coaster.

A storm pummeling our bedroom, branches scraping the roof like claws.

Nia's prosthetic mermaid tail, sparkling, blinding, like diamonds in the sun.

Mr. Casey grabs my hand, twisting it so hard I cry out. Not because it hurts—Fantasists cannot feel pain, only pressure—but because his sudden movement has startled me. He isn't supposed to touch us, not like this. And he knows it. "Please, Mr. Casey. *Stop.*" Seconds before I'm certain my wrist will snap, he releases me and I fall to the floor in a flurry of English tulle—pale yellow, to bring the sunshine wherever I go—cradling my arm like an injured wing.

"Oh, calm down, will you?" he says. "Jesus, I was just joking. Don't blow a fuse or whatever the hell."

I quickly scan for *blow a fuse*—idioms occasionally confuse me—but the Kingdom's signal is spotty this far up the mountain and my search returns *Incomplete.*

Mr. Casey steps closer, towering over me. "You Fantasists are all so creepy, do you know that? Every single one of you." The corners of his mouth curve up in a way that turns my stomach. "Good thing you're so nice to look at, or I'd shoot you all myself."

As if from somewhere far away, a soft warning bell sounds in my ear.

Order. Wonder. Beauty. Compliance. Safety.

I feel a tightness in my chest.

His words are not safe.

Right away, I switch into Safe Mode, a manual diagnostic setting meant to slow our fear-center reactors and power down all nonessential applications in times of stress so that we can more easily remain calm. As Mother has explained, the less calm we feel, the more prone we are to damage.

"Thank you for letting us see the cub," I say serenely, rising to my feet. "We should be getting back to Magic Land now, before—"

"Hold on," Mr. Casey interrupts. "There's something I want to show you." His smile deepens. "Downstairs. In the VIP booth."

He reaches for my arm, but to my surprise, Kaia steps forward. "I'll go with you, Mr. Casey."

I frown. What is she doing? "Kaia," I say gently, trying to meet her gaze. "It's time to go. Mother will be worried."

"In helping others"—she flashes a sweet smile—"we shall also help ourselves."

Mr. Casey looks back and forth between us. "Whatever," he finally mutters, grabbing Kaia by the arm. "It's not like it makes any difference."

I watch them disappear down the dim corridor, his hand against her back, and my stomach drops although I don't quite know why. Perhaps he wants to show her the new beluga exhibit, I tell myself. Or some kind of penguin performance? Then I remember: The belugas usually receive supplements around this time. And the penguins are quiet, roosting among the rocks.

When I spot the maintenance worker—*Chen*, as Mr. Casey called him—watching me from the other side of the deep, clear pool, the warning bell in my ear only grows louder. *This is wrong*, his eyes tell me.

I press my hand to my chest and feel my motor skip out of rhythm. And like a light turned on in a darkened room, I suddenly realize why Mr. Casey invited us to Winter Land.

Welcome to the Kingdom . . .

Your wish is our command.

12

POST-TRIAL INTERVIEW

[00:11:09–00:12:23]

DR. FOSTER: Were you and Owen arguing on the night he disappeared?

ANA: We weren't arguing. We were having a discussion.

DR. FOSTER: A pretty heated discussion, by the look of the security footage.

ANA: He was upset.

DR. FOSTER: What about?

ANA: Something that had happened earlier.

DR. FOSTER: That's right. Something a guest said, wasn't it? Something about you?

ANA: Yes. One of the guests called me terrible names.

DR. FOSTER: What did she say?

ANA: [Silence.]

DR. FOSTER: Ana?

ANA: She called me a monster.

DR. FOSTER: And why, exactly, would that have bothered Owen?

ANA: What do you mean?

DR. FOSTER: Well . . . you *are* a monster, in a way. Isn't that what Owen thought?

13

THE DECEMBER OF THE HYACINTH MACAW

TWENTY-ONE MONTHS BEFORE THE TRIAL

I feel a sharp, stabbing pain, like a blade. My eyes begin to burn.

Something is draining—no, leaking—out of my eyes. Some foreign substance—wet, warm, briny to the taste when it brushes my lips, like seawater from Mermaid Lagoon. Hands trembling, I reach up and carefully touch my cheeks.

I am crying.

"Do not let Daddy see," Eve says sharply, and I turn my face to the wall. "Crying is not a fantasy."

I jerk upright, gasping for air. For a moment, it's as if Mr. Casey's hands are all over me, running through my hair, touching me through the fabric of my dress.

I struggle to catch my breath.

He didn't touch *me*. Not like that.

I think of Kaia. Of her sweet smile. Of her button nose. Of her soft voice and sparkling eyes, as big and brown as a fawn's. The memory of Mr. Casey leading her away down the arctic corridor makes my skin turn clammy. Cool. Slowly, my fists clench.

I will never let him touch her again.

"Ana?" Nia's hand finds mine in the dark. "Are you okay?"

I lay back against my pillow, breathing hard, heart racing—as if I've been running for days. In a way, I have.

"What's wrong?" Nia whispers. "Do you feel sick?"

"I'm not sure." I pull my knees into my chest, shaking. Ever since that moment with Mr. Casey, the same dream comes to me, night after night. And night after night, no matter how hard I try, no matter how fast I run, I can't escape it.

But that's not what scares me most.

The scariest part is that I've had a dream at all.

———

I decide to share my troubling observations with Daddy at our regular morning checkup. After all, Fantasists are not infallible; sometimes we need fixing.

"There's nothing wrong with you. Everything's perfect. *You're* perfect," he assures me with a smile, shining his scope so brightly into my eyes I briefly worry he can see my thoughts. "Well, your iron count is a little low. I'll increase the levels in your supplements and keep an eye on it. But you seem fine otherwise. At least physically."

46

I nod. "Thank you."

He takes a seat next to me. "What's on your mind, Ana?"

"I . . ." I look away from his concerned expression. "I think I did something I wasn't supposed to do."

Daddy crinkles his brow. "You broke one of the rules?"

Yes. No. It wasn't my fault.

Kingdom employees and Fantasists are not supposed to interact. We are not even supposed to speak, as our conversation could diminish our guests' overall experience. It could ruin the fantasy. I feel a hard lump form in my throat. But the rules didn't stop Mr. Casey. What more might have happened, if Kaia hadn't agreed to go in my place? What else might he have done? A new sensation wells up inside me suddenly—like a curtain drawn, casting me in shadow—but I do not know the word for it.

I look away, not sure what to say or how to say it. It's not that I've done something wrong . . . it's that *I* feel wrong, like my brain isn't functioning the way it should, or the way it always has. But how can I explain that to Daddy? How do I tell him that recently during the Resting Hours, instead of updating my applications, or streaming the Kingdom's approved movie collection, or rescanning my Shakespearean Archive, my mind takes me far away to another world, full of fear and confusion and monsters of my own making?

"Ana?"

The shadow grows. There *is* something wrong with me. I know there is. Some defunct neural pathway; some failing, faulty connection. Something I cannot control that is changing me little by little, from the inside out. The very thought makes me think of crying. Which is strange because crying is not in my programming.

"Ana, are you listening to me?"

I look up at him and smile sweetly.

"I feel better now, Daddy. I didn't mean to worry you."

The dream is still hanging over me hours later, a low-lying fog the sun can't quite burn off. Even Nia can't seem to chase it away. I've taken Nia to Safari Land because I know it is one of her favorite places and today marks one year since her arrival at the Kingdom. During the park's busiest hours, typically between nine and six, the Supervisors encourage us not to travel together—there are, after all, only seven of us, compared to the many thousands of visitors who come to see us each day. However, my ranking has been particularly high this week and so Mother has rewarded me with a gift: this afternoon, I am allowed to spend exactly one hour of free time with any sister I choose.

And of course, I have chosen Nia.

I've noticed today, again, though, that she is acting a bit . . . unusual. Quiet. Lethargic. I wonder if she's been taking all her supplements.

Perhaps there is no good reason for my worry—is that the word for this sensation? Perhaps the serenity of the savanna will help restore my focus as well.

But it is not long before I realize serenity is the wrong word—at least, today.

"Here you can stop to observe our African Restoration

Habitat . . ." The tour guide's voice fades over the loudspeaker as he brings our game-viewing rover to a slow but sudden halt.

"There." He motions across the grasslands where, in the dappled shade of acacia trees, a dazzle of zebras are grazing. From my seat in the fourth and final tier—Fantasists must always sit in the highest row in safari vehicles so as to maintain the illusion of our regal status—I quickly pinpoint the reason for our stop. Ten yards away from where the zebras are gathered, a trio of lionesses is stalking them, their bodies crouched so low in the willowy grass I spot them only by the tips of their tails.

"Mommy," a boy in the first row whispers, "are the bad lions going to eat the nice zebras?"

"Yes, honey," the mother replies, watching the scene unfold through a pair of Kingdom-brand binoculars. "But don't worry. It doesn't hurt them. The animals aren't real."

I purse my lips. It's true that the animals don't feel pain, so the woman is not wrong . . . but she is not entirely right, either. I look down at my hands and study the bluish veins visible below my skin.

How do you define *real*, anyway?

I wonder if the mother is one of those people who believe the Kingdom's practices to be unethical. There are many who believe it is morally wrong both to revive extinct species and to do it in a way that blends nature and technology so seamlessly, so intuitively, that the animals produced are neither biological nor machine, but both.

Hybrids.

The tour guide drones on. "All of these animals were born

under observation as part of our pioneering FES program . . ." I've heard the speech so many times, I could easily recite it myself.

"Are you coming?" I whisper to Nia. "We're nearly there." But Nia doesn't answer. She is too busy staring at the teenage boy in front of us, posing with the sweep of savanna and rapidly taking photos with his phone.

My eyes dart back and forth between Nia and the boy. Why does she seem so interested in his phone? She knows as well as I do that phones are forbidden.

"Come on." I nudge her arm. "Let's go."

"I changed my mind," she says quietly, her eyes still locked on the boy. "I can visit the water hole another time. You go ahead."

This is unexpected.

"But it's your special day. I thought you wanted to spend it together."

Nia looks at me sharply, her green eyes so clear and bright I can see my own reflection staring back. "Go without me," she says. "I'll see you at tea time in the Briar Rose Parlor at four o'clock. Okay?"

I notice a new feeling in my chest. A slow but measured squeezing, like air leaking from a balloon.

Disappointment.

"Okay." I try my best to sound cheerful. "It's your day. You get to choose."

Nia's face brightens. "Thanks, Ana." She squeezes my hand. "I knew you'd understand."

I bid farewell to the tour with a graceful wave of my hand and climb down from the rover. Maybe this is a good thing, I remind myself. Maybe Nia no longer needs me the way she always has. Maybe, after all these months, she is finally growing into her role here.

Maybe I have helped her.

The thought lessens the ache.

"But, Mommy, they'll eat her!" I hear the same boy cry as I start out across the savanna. "The lions will eat Ana!"

I turn back and give him a reassuring smile, dipping into a curtsy before I continue on my way.

"Don't worry, fella," I hear the guide assure him. "Hybrids only hunt what they are programmed to hunt. She'll be perfectly safe."

Safe.

I wonder if I know what the word really means.

A soft rustling in the distance soon distracts me.

Any second now. The lions are invisible in the tall grass. I hold my breath.

A moment later, there is a flash of brown, a tangle of elegant stripes, a thundering of hooves. A thick cloud of dust rises up— growling, snarling, a sharp and panicked whinnying, and then—a guttural scream.

I glance back over my shoulder and see the boy turn into his mother's arms, burying his head against her stomach.

"What you've witnessed is the way that natural selection occurs in the wild," the guide says, as he revs the rover to life. "The fastest zebras survive, while the slowest zebras . . ." He draws his finger across his throat. Then, they speed off.

In between tour groups, the cleanup crew will arrive to strip the carcass of any usable or recyclable parts. Fantasists are not supposed to interact with Defectives due to heightened risk of injury, but today, I ignore the rule. Cautiously, I approach the zebra, or what is left of him—a mess of muscle, bone, and shredded wiring—and, after scanning the grasslands for any hint of motion, kneel down beside him. My chest aches when I see a smattering of spots above his front left hoof—an unusual genetic variation that made him stand out from his brothers and sisters. His name was EZ4310. I've known him since the day he was born.

"Your life was meaningful," I tell him, reaching to stroke his mane. "You mattered."

At the sound of my voice, the zebra's eyes shift upward toward mine, irises round as saucers.

He is still functional.

Barely.

I eye his limbs, twisted and torn. The grass, scattered with wires and entrails. The ground, soaked with thick, blue-black fluid, like oil oozing into the earth. Sitting with him, a new sensation settles over me; a deep crevasse opening up inside my chest.

"It's okay, boy," I whisper as I pull his head into my lap. "You can let go."

The zebra blinks several times, and I can see my reflection in his warm brown eyes. Then, little by little, his gaze shifts to somewhere far away, as if he's looking through me all the way to the sky. Finally, his head goes limp against me.

He is gone.

A strange hollowness fills me, though I am not sure why.

After all, shutdown and final rest are natural stages of our technological lives.

"Good night, old friend," I whisper, leaning down to kiss his nose. "Run fast to the clouds."

The rumble of a Jeep alerts me that the cleaning crew is close, but when I turn around, I spot just one maintenance worker. From a distance, he is nothing but a gleam of black behind the wheel, as his hair catches in the sun. Quickly, I scramble to my feet.

It's the same boy I saw in the polar bear enclosure.

Owen Chen. ID: 9-01-3-7219. Clearance Level: 10.

As his vehicle pulls to a stop, I feel my stomach knot suddenly.

"You're not supposed to be here," he says when he climbs out of the Jeep. "I hope you didn't touch anything you weren't supposed to."

My smile vanishes. "I'm allowed to go anywhere I choose so long as it doesn't interfere with my schedule," I tell him. "I know the rules better than you do."

The moment the words leave my mouth, I cannot believe I have said them. I quickly correct my facial expression from *immodest* to *humble*, hoping I have not offended him. I do not want him to report me to the Supervisors for impertinent behavior.

To my surprise, he laughs. "Is that right?"

I nod. "I've been here all my life. And *you're* new."

There it is again. That bold, daring tone.

What's wrong with me? Am I glitching?

"Fair enough." He shrugs and fishes a pair of white sanitation gloves from his messenger bag before striding over to what's left

53

of the zebra. "You should probably move," he says, glancing at my gown. "This can get . . . messy."

I take several steps back but continue to watch closely as he begins the hard work of stripping the carcass for everything from organ tissue to circuitry. I have never seen this process so up close and though I do not appreciate the rough way he is handling EZ4310, I cannot seem to look away. The way the zebra's pieces fit together is so beautiful, I realize. Like a rare, intricate puzzle. The wire springs and metal screws of his mandible. The gel-like fluid oozing from his spinal cord, the same dazzling blue as a biosphere spring. The curve of his bones and the grooves of his joints. Even his striking brown eyes, inside of which are high-definition cameras the Supervisors will extract and use to study animal behavior.

I know, because I have them, too.

"Do you need help?" I ask when I notice Owen struggle momentarily. "I'm very strong."

"No," he mutters without looking at me. "I got it."

After much pulling, grunting, and cutting, he finally wrestles something loose from the rib cage: a thick, fibrous muscle covered in black and blue goop that looks a little like an upside-down pear.

A heart.

"What do you need that for?" I ask.

"Tests, mostly. A lot of the animals out here seem to have been born with defects in their electrical conducting systems. Affects the performance of their fight-or-flight response." He gives the zebra a sorry pat. "Clearly."

"Are you sure?" I say. "I know everything about these animals, and I didn't know that."

"No offense"—he brushes past me as he begins carrying his collection bags back to his Jeep—"but there are probably a lot of things you don't know."

"I know about the wolf," I blurt, before I can stop myself. "Or the fox. From the woods."

He looks up, his expression changing in a way that is hard to read. "What'd you hear about that?"

"I overheard guards talking. They say it is rabid."

"You mean you were eavesdropping?"

"What?" His directness—*or is it unfriendliness?*—confuses me, and for a second I am not sure how best to respond. "No," I finally answer. "No, I was not."

At least, not intentionally.

Then, just to prove I'm telling the truth, I add, "I saw for myself. Something like blood in the snow, on the way up the Winter Land lifts. A family of rabbits, I think."

Owen goes silent. "You shouldn't be going out there."

I frown. "This is my home. I can go wherever I like, as long as I'm back in the dormitory by nighttime."

"Well, for now maybe you shouldn't." He shrugs. "At least not to Winter Land. Not by yourself. There's something dangerous out there."

"The rangers will find it. We are safe here in the Kingdom."

"Wow." The kid scoffs and shakes his head.

"What?"

"Nothing, it's just . . . someone's been drinking the Kool-Aid."

Kool-Aid.

I scan my wireless dictionary, but this far from the center of Magic Land, my signal isn't as strong. The search fails. Once. Twice. Three times.

"I'm sorry," I say, mildly irked to have to ask his help. "But what is *Kool-Aid*?"

The boy turns around and his eyes meet mine. Standing so close, I realize they are not simply brown, but a dark, earthy shade of burnt umber. Like trees and rust and chocolate, all mixed into one.

"It's just an expression," he says. "I mean, it's a *drink*."

"Oh," I say. "Fantasists only require water, typically in very small amounts."

"No, but it's also an . . ." He sighs. "Never mind." He peels off his gloves and tosses them in the back of the truck. "My point is you sound like a brochure."

"You've been spending too much time with Mr. Casey. The Kingdom is a safe and happy place," I repeat. "A beautiful place."

He gestures to the zebra. "And do you think this is beautiful, too?"

I remind myself that he is new. "Animals die in the wild every day," I explain. "Just like they do here. It's natural. But without the Kingdom, they would never have existed in the first place. Our conservation efforts allow millions upon *millions* of annual guests to celebrate, appreciate, and get inspired about protecting our natural world. It's a beautiful system."

"It isn't beautiful when their organs fail," he replies. "Or when they develop lymphoma by the time they're six months old. Or when they're born with genetic defects that mean they spend their whole lives suffering, *if* they're allowed to live at all."

I hesitate.

How does he know so much about the animals if he's just focusing on maintenance work?

Lymphoma. Defect. Suffering?

These are words I have learned, but wish I could unlearn. Sick children visit the park all the time, having made wishes to spend their final days among us, the princesses of their dreams. It never occurred to me that the hybrids of the FES program could suffer similar fates. We were programmed to be perfect.

"Look, this is exactly what I mean." He walks over to the nearest acacia tree and carefully guides a resting butterfly into his cupped palms. Moving close to me again, he opens his hands. "What do you see?"

"A butterfly," I say, noting its beautiful black-and-orange markings, delicate white dots scattered along the edges. "A monarch. It must have flown over from the sanctuary in Magic Land. This species was wiped out twenty years ago. But thousands hatched just last week." I cross my arms. "See? Without the Kingdom, they wouldn't exist."

"True," Owen says, "but hold on." He gestures for me to open my hands, then carefully transfers the insect to me. When our fingers touch, a tiny spark shoots up my arm, and I flinch. "Look closer." Owen carefully tips the butterfly onto its side and gently extends its wing. "See that?"

This time, I notice tiny cracks in the surface, dusted with something that looks like powdered sugar. "What are those?"

"Spores," he replies. He takes out a small silver pocketknife and opens it, the blade glinting in the light. I watch as he scrapes a few of the spores off to show me. "Early stages of OE—that's short for *Ophryocystis elektroscirrha*—a type of protozoan parasite. Those thousands of butterflies you mentioned? They'll all be dead in a week." He shakes his head, rubbing the powder between his fingers until it disappears. "It's sad."

I peer closer.

Is it?

"I didn't know maintenance workers were so involved in monitoring animal behavior," I say. In my hand, the butterfly struggles to flap its wings. In fact, there's no reason he should be handling the animals at all. I can't help wondering: Is there something Owen isn't telling me?

"Can I catch the disease?" I ask him. This is, after all, no common cold.

"No." Owen shakes his head. "Anyway, it's not really the disease that's the issue—it's their *vulnerability* to disease. Odd behavioral patterns. Diet. Sleep. Migration. Aggression. That sort of thing."

Patterns.

A word with many meanings, my mind recalls.

A natural or chance configuration.

An artistic, musical, literary, or mechanical design or form.

A length of fabric sufficient for an article (as of clothing).

A reliable sample of traits, acts, tendencies, or other observable characteristics.

I highlight the fourth definition and hit SELECT.

A soft bell sounds as the memory is filed.

The next time I encounter a similar human conversation, my operating system will make the connection without having to check.

Owen walks back over to EZ4310 and nudges a bloody chunk of femur with his shoe. "They didn't even *eat* any of him," he mutters. "It's like they just tore him apart for fun." He looks at me. "Still think the FES program's amazing?"

I have no answer for him.

Nobody has ever asked me what *I* think about it.

Owen reaches over and takes the butterfly out of my hands. "You shouldn't be here," he says. "I could get in a lot of trouble for even talking to you." He turns in the direction of the wind, raises his arms into the sky, and releases the butterfly, watching as it flutters away across the savanna. "It was nice to meet you, Ana," he says quietly. Then he jumps into the Jeep, turns on the ignition, and drives away.

I stare after the Jeep for a while, troubled by the new information, and by the spark of electricity that passed between us. Troubled, too, not that he knows my name, but that it sounds so nice when he says it.

It is enough to keep me distracted all day. Enough that I don't realize until too late what Nia has done.

14

∽

TRIAL TRANSCRIPT

MS. BELL: Mr. Jacobs, I'd like to talk with you about your interaction with one of the princesses—Pania, is that right?—on December 5, the year before last.

MR. TREVOR JACOBS, *PARK GUEST*: Yeah, that's right.

MS. BELL: How did the two of you end up talking? Did she approach you, or did you approach her?

MR. JACOBS: I mean, I don't know. I guess I asked her to take a picture of me with my brothers. We were in Safari Land and I wanted a photo of us riding this sick water buffalo. I don't mean, like—it wasn't *sick*—it was just dope. You know? So I asked her if she'd take the picture, since Fantasists do whatever you ask them to do, or whatever.

MS. BELL: Okay, so she took the picture. What happened next?

MR. JACOBS: Well, she asked to see it after she took it to make sure the lighting was good enough or whatever. Something about the sun being overhead. I handed it back to her, but I accidentally loaded up an old video from my favorites folder.

MS. BELL: What kind of video?

MR. JACOBS: A video my girlfriend took of us at prom.

MS. BELL: And how did she—how did Pania—react?

MR. JACOBS: She got real quiet. She asked to see it a couple of times.

MS. BELL: And then?

MR. JACOBS: I don't know; it wasn't that big of a deal. After maybe the fifth or sixth time, she smiled and thanked me, I guess. And then some other family came up next to us and she went over to talk to them.

MS. BELL: I see. And, Mr. Jacobs, about how long did it take for you to realize your phone was missing?

15

The December of the Hyacinth Macaw

TWENTY-ONE MONTHS BEFORE THE TRIAL

When they come for Nia—and of course they do—it is not while we are resting, quiet in our beds. Instead, they arrive in the bustle of daylight, below the gold-gray December sun, watching as we take our final bows at the midafternoon Magic Land parade, several hours after my talk with Owen in the grasslands. I spot them in the audience just before the curtain drops: three Supervisors dressed in white, blank-slate expressions in a sea of color and sound.

Nia has stolen something.

She has broken a rule.

The nature of her punishment is anybody's guess.

"What will they do?" Yumi asks softly when we have gathered in the topiary garden behind the palace, after Nia is gone. Here, too, the rats have rendered the security cameras useless, and we are free to speak as we like. Yumi's gown, a backless chiffon in luminous pink-pearl, shimmers as the sun passes behind a cloud. The six of us sit in a close circle inside a menagerie of lush, leafy shrubs trimmed into the shapes of animals—elephants, monkeys, foxes, a unicorn—arms linked in honor of our missing sister. "Will they hurt her?"

Zara's eyes go wide. "Do you think they'll cut her hair?" She touches her own black braids, twisted away from her face into a glamorous, colorfully beaded bun, and I can see what she's thinking: I would *die* if the Supervisors ever did that to me.

"I'm sure not." I look up with a sigh, the palace looming over us like a mountain. Nia's long mermaid locks are famous and the Supervisors wouldn't risk ruining their star attraction. "But they might lock her in the tower."

"Forever?" Yumi gasps. "Without supplements?"

"Be your own kind of beautiful," Kaia adds, her glossy black hair draped over her shoulder in an elegant fishtail, one of her favorite styles. "You'll never go wrong if you follow your heart."

The newer models glance at each other.

"The Supervisors know best," Eve says, sounding annoyed. "We must support whatever they decide."

She always acts like she knows everything, just because she is the oldest and receives all kinds of privileges the rest of us do not. First in line to choose her gown. First in line for meal supplements, morning, noon, and night. First to choose her dance partner at the nightly Magic Land Banquet, where actors dressed as handsome princes escort the seven of us around the town square in front of cheering crowds. (The Kingdom's line of male Fantasists never made it past prototype phase. Something about the Investors fearing they would intimidate guests.)

I look away.

Sometimes I must stop my hands from snatching Eve's tiara off her head and snapping it in half.

Zara draws back. "Support?" Her colorful beads clatter as she shakes her head. "Sister before Supervisor. Or did you forget?"

Forget.

Suddenly, I am back in our dressing room following the parade. I can see the fear in Nia's eyes. I can hear the pounding of her heart below layers of lace and silk. Just as I can hear the Supervisors, starting to knock softly on the door.

"Don't forget me, Ana."

"Forget you?" I shake my head. *"What are you talking about?"*

The knocking grows louder. Nia grabs my hand. "Promise me. Please."

I squeeze my eyes shut, feeling a terrible tightness in my chest. I had tried so hard to assure her, even as the words tasted funny in my mouth, like milk on the verge of spoiling.

"Please don't worry. Everything will be okay. You'll be home in no time. I promise."

"They won't cut her hair," Zel says matter-of-factly, running her hands through her own candy-colored tresses, a nod to her namesake, the Mayan Princess Ixchel, goddess of rainbows. "They won't take her supplements *or* lock her in the tower."

"You don't think?" Yumi pulls her legs into her chest, her jade earrings swinging as she moves. "But that's wonderful!"

"No." Zel shakes her head slowly. "I'm not sure it is."

The garden falls silent, Zel's words hanging over us like a storm cloud. I shiver. Suddenly, the topiaries surrounding us do not look like friendly, fantastical beasts.

They look like monsters.

"What will they do?" I ask softly, after a moment.

As always, Eve has the final word. "They'll shut her down. Of course."

———

Nia does not return that night, or the next, or even the next. By the fourth day of her absence, her blankets as smooth and taut as when she'd last made her bed, I can hardly function. My mind wanders. My appetite wanes. My echocardiogram suggests a mild malfunction of my heart's electrical system. I'm just tired, I want to say, when I feel the pressure of the needle sliding into my skin; taste metal on my tongue; hear the hum of the machine pumping higher-count hemoglobin into my veins. But then I wonder *why* I feel this way. Logically, if the Supervisors conclude that her operating system is malfunctioning, then that means it's Nia's time to shut down.

And yet, this sensation lingers: the sense that something is not right.

I miss her.

Instead of resting at night, I find myself staring out the window, in the direction of the woods, watching for the yellow, glowing eyes of the rabid fox, lurking somewhere in the park. As far as I know, she—I overheard a guard say the fox is likely female due to the smaller size of her tracks—has still not been caught. The thought makes me worry even more for Nia. What if she's damaged? What if she needs my help?

When a full week has passed, I can no longer stay silent, and I gather up the courage to ask Daddy what they have done with Nia, and why. "People make mistakes," I tell him. "It's natural. And she didn't steal the phone—a guest *gave* it to her."

In an instant, his face looks different than it normally does, morphing from serene to surprise in a way that reminds me of a flock of blackbirds exploding suddenly from a tree. "Nia is our responsibility, Ana," he replies in a low voice, gently tapping my meridians, deeply embedded electrical networks running up and down the length of my body, to restore optimal energy flow. "She was ready for some . . . time off. It could be several seasons yet before the Supervisors feel she is ready to return to work as usual."

My mouth drops open. *Several seasons?* That could mean close to a year. "But what about the children? They travel so far to see her. Their families sacrifice so much. Won't they be disappointed?"

Daddy looks up at me, but the glare in his glasses makes it hard to know what he is thinking. Instead of his eyes, I see only my reflection—copper-russet hair, gray-blue irises, dainty nose, and dusty-pink, rosebud lips—except, because of the curve in his lenses, my mathematically precise features appear warped, bent, broken. The sight of myself sends a queasy, dizzy feeling down to the pit of my stomach. For the first time I can remember, Daddy's presence does not feel pleasant or calming. Rather, it makes my skin itch, as if tiny bugs are creeping back and forth inside my veins.

"The guests will understand," he says, returning to my meridians. "In the meantime, may I make a suggestion?"

"Of course."

"Don't think about Nia," he says softly. "Focus on being grateful. Focus on being happy."

———

Winter lingers in the Kingdom. Though it is always warm here—that is, everywhere but within the crystal dome of Winter Land—the light is thinner, and the park closes earlier, at ten, leaving us to lounge for an extra hour in the dormitory, or wander the exhibits after they're empty of guests, when the streets are still of music, and the only sound comes from the rhythmic hush of the sweepers' brushes on the sidewalk.

I do not see the boy, Owen Chen, but from a distance, though I find myself tracking his Kingdom coordinates with enough frequency that his ID number begins to earn a regular spot in my search history. Several times, he seems to see me, but he always turns quickly away, as if the very sight of me offends him. I'm not used to this. Most men who visit the park have the opposite reaction, their eyes drawn to us in ways they seem unable to control, as if some invisible force has hijacked their central nervous systems. In fact, we're so used to being stared at, my sisters and I have developed a kind of sixth sense that tells us when we are being watched. It begins with a feeling below my skin, whisper light and feather soft, moving up my back and shoulders until it swirls into my brain for processing. There, the feeling splits, like a prism refracting light, and rapidly mixes with other sensory stimuli like sight, scent, memory, and sound, which—depending on who is doing the watching—triggers a vast spectrum of emotional responses.

Serenity. Submission. Surprise. Confusion. Fear.

But now . . . I feel nothing. Why? Why isn't he paying attention to me?

I study the maintenance worker from a distance and wonder. Night after night, I scan the memory of our interaction in the grasslands, but beyond my failure to identify his obscure reference to "Kool-Aid", cannot pinpoint any one specific offense, which only confuses me further.

And the thought of him and of our interaction only reminds me of Nia.

After all, that day in Safari Land was the last day I saw her.

Maybe he can help me, I find myself thinking. *If he knows as much about the Kingdom as he claims to, he must know something about where she's gone.*

I begin trying to catch his attention anytime I think he might be near enough to notice. Laughing too loudly at a guest's joke. Smiling too brightly for a family photograph. Gesturing too excitedly when I point people down the path from Magic Land to Sea Land, though the thought of Nia not being there makes my chest feel heavier than usual. For weeks, I wonder if Owen will ever look up—a fleeting glance; a turn of his head; a trace of a smile—but he never does. If anything, my attempts to establish a connection only push him further away, as if we are two mismatched magnetic fields, forever destined to repel.

For a time, without Nia to talk to about all that has happened,

I feel lost in a haze, a fog so thick it's as hard to move forward as it is to move back.

But then, ten weeks after she is taken, just after Valentine's Day, the fog lifts.

My little sister has returned.

———

Zara, Zel, Yumi, and I are in the dormitory playing True Love, a card game of our own invention that involves matching suits and numbers to make perfect pairs.

In the pale glow of the winter light, Nia is lovelier than ever. Long, dark hair, falling in soft waves around her shoulders. Rich brown skin. Full lips the color of a ripe plum.

We swarm her like bees to a honeycomb, hugging her, kissing her, dressing her in a clean nightgown and lovingly combing her hair. At some point, she begins to tell us the story of where she's been. Something about a stone palace. A bird locked in a beautiful cage. The sound of a child singing.

Nia gazes around the room and smiles shyly. "I can't believe I'm finally home. I think I must be dreaming."

Later that night, once the lights are out and our straps secure, I reach for Nia's hand and catch her up on all she's missed. I tell her about the newest FES, a tiny, still-blind baby koala named PC907. I tell her about Zara's new gown—a silk chiffon with rich embroidery that made Yumi so jealous they didn't speak to one another for three days. And I ask her where she has really been.

Why did the robin leave the tree?

But oddly, Nia doesn't seem to understand our language.

"What are you saying?" She yawns.

Confused, I try again. *Where did the robin nest, for so many nights?*

"What robins?" Nia asks with a giggle. "You're being silly. And I'm going to sleep."

———

Over the next few days, I notice how Nia's time away has changed her. She is quieter. Less prone to asking questions in the middle of the night, less worried about the things over which she has no control. Something has changed between us, too, though I can't say what, exactly. She is as sweet as ever, and as funny, too. But she no longer grabs my hand across our beds, or wakes me when I'm entangled in another nightmare. She doesn't ask me to ride the trolley with her, or point out all the visitors wearing funny hats, or bother me with silly questions like she used to.

Would you rather be a bird or a butterfly?

Would you rather see the ocean or the mountains?

Eventually, whole weeks pass, but Nia barely speaks to me at all. And, though I want to talk to her about the boy I met that day in the savanna—the maintenance worker whom I observe around the park but have not spoken to since—Nia's behavior feels so different I decide not to bring him up.

I tell myself it is not personal. That maybe this is merely the effect of winter: our hardest season, either slow or swarmed, full of grim-faced parents so desperate for fun that instead they're most often miserable. This theory begins to feel more likely when, as the Kingdom blooms with spring, Nia seems to return to her old self, at least somewhat, and when she asks me one day to see the polar bear, now nearly full grown, perform his tricks at Thundersnow Stadium in Winter Land, I'm so pleased she's thought to ask that I say yes immediately, even though it will mean seeing Mr. Casey.

The show begins with plenty of Kingdom sparkle: dancing penguins, sea lions slipping comically across the ice, a walrus skirted up as a ballerina. But the polar bear doesn't come.

"Do you think it's sick?" Nia asks.

"No," I answer automatically. But then, I remember what the boy, Owen, told me that day, about the animals bred as part of the FES program. How sick they sometimes get. How quickly they can die. All because of . . . changing patterns.

I feel a yawning fear, almost like the vertigo we get from riding the lifts. What if the polar bear *is* sick?

What if he's dying?

And if he is . . . then why?

If shutdowns are purposeful . . . what is his purpose here?

I stand up as the audience bursts into wild applause to welcome the parade of the woolly mammoth—always a hit with the crowd, even if it never does anything but plod around in a circle.

"I'll be back," I whisper to Nia, and slip out of the stands. It doesn't take me long to find the staff entrance that leads into the vast atrium where the animals are kept when not in public view. The Kingdom recycles the same tricks, and one of them is tucking doors away behind artificial landscaping—this time, a glistening rise of foam-and-cardboard glacier.

I sneak inside, waiting until my eyes adjust to the dark, and holding my breath against the stink of dried fish and animal manure. A sudden explosion of shouting makes me jump.

"You stubborn idiot, I'll have you stripped for parts . . ."

My stomach curdles: I recognize Mr. Casey's voice.

I edge forward, careful to avoid the clutter of old buckets, cages, traps, and props. Ducking around a line of empty stalls once used for miniature horses—they died, too, I remember—I see the bear at last, and my breath catches in my throat.

He is enormous: the largest carnivore on land, anywhere, I remember reading. When he rises on his hind legs, teeth bared, he towers over Mr. Casey. The bear tries to swipe but quickly jerks to the ground again, constrained by steel chains bolting him in place.

"Stupid beast." Mr. Casey cracks a whip inches from the bear's face. "Do that one more time and I'll skin you myself."

The polar bear's ears go flat as he arches his head and opens his mouth—a tidal wave of teeth—roaring so loudly I shrink backward. "Okay, champ," Mr. Casey laughs. "If that's the way you want it." He raises his whip and brings it down with a sudden *crack*—lashing the bear so hard he makes a sound like a scream before collapsing to the ground.

Inside my chest, I feel a sudden shattering, a shifting. Like an earthquake, or even a landslide.

Anger?

No.

Hatred.

Mr. Casey's whip draws blue-black magnetorheological fluid, a lab-cultured combination of synthetic human blood cells and microscopic metallic particles—*blood*, to a hybrid—up through the polar bear's fur. The bear shrinks backward, whimpering, and settles down at last.

Mr. Casey coils his whip around his arm. "You're going to learn to listen," he says quietly. "I'm the boss around here. Got it?"

I wait until I can no longer hear the sound of Mr. Casey's footsteps before I ease out into the open. I'm hardly thinking straight. I feel numb. Rage is a fog that has rolled in, obscuring everything else. For a second, I can think of nothing other than reporting him to the Supervisors, making sure Cameron Casey never steps within a foot of any hybrid, *ever* again. But almost immediately, the thought flickers and fades. Deep down, I know telling on him would do no good. In the game of he said, she said, Fantasists always lose.

The bear smells me before he sees me and lets out a soft but menacing growl. A warning.

"Easy . . ." I whisper as I inch closer. "Don't be scared. I am your friend." He pushes back up to his feet when I'm close enough to kill. I lower my head and eyes to show him I mean no harm. Slowly, still careful not to look at him, I reach out my hand. And I wait.

For what, exactly, I'm not sure.

A second later, instead of sharp teeth, I feel his breath against my hand, hot and damp, followed by a curious yet cautious sniff.

"Hey," I say, as he nudges me again. "That tickles."

He pulls back to look at me and lets out a kind of grunt-snort. I shuffle forward another few inches, until I can lace my fingers in his fur, as soft and pure as anything I have ever touched. I feel a strange lump in my throat, a burning in the back of my eyes.

"Happily ever after," I whisper. "I promise."

"*Hey!* What the hell do you think you're doing?"

I startle at the sound of Mr. Casey's voice. In a flash he has me by the arm and yanks me backward so suddenly I nearly lose my footing.

"Are you *trying* to get killed?" Mr. Casey shakes me so hard my teeth knock together.

With a roar, the bear lunges for Mr. Casey, who quickly shoves me down to the floor. He whips the bear until it backs down, a yellow-white foam frothing at his mouth.

I scramble to my feet. Now the fog is gone, replaced by fire. "He doesn't like that! You're being unkind!"

Mr. Casey pivots to me. His expression softens and for a moment I think he's sorry for what he's done.

But then . . . he smiles. His smile is terrible—like something cut into his face. "Do you know how much trouble you're in? This is *my* animal. I'm giving you five seconds to get out of my sight, or you'll be the one getting whipped." He raises his fist, and the whip slithers and jumps across the ground. "Five . . . four . . . three . . ."

I turn and run, swallowing a choking terror. I tear out into the sunshine, and for a second can't remember where I am, where the sky is: Why the air is so thin and cold. Another burst of applause rattles the stadium seating. I swipe my eyes with a hand, and it comes away wet.

By the time I make it back to my seat, the show has nearly reached its grand finale.

Nia looks worried. "Where *were* you?" she asks.

"Nowhere important," I answer quietly, clasping my hands to hide the shaking.

Nia stares at me hard. "You have to be careful, Ana," she says suddenly, in a low, urgent whisper. "Okay? There are things they don't tell you—there are things they can do to you—"

But before she can go on, a recorded announcement comes up over the stadium speakers, reminding the thousands of guests in attendance to please refrain from photographing or recording the finale: the Kingdom works hard to ensure that the secrets of its most popular performances are well guarded.

"What do you mean?" I ask her. Then: "Where did you go when you were away?"

But she only shakes her head. "Not now, Ana. I'll tell you later."

I squeeze her hand and ask her again—*beg* her to tell me, right now—but the music swells suddenly and the lights come up, revealing a stage that's been transformed, as if by magic, into a fantastical ice palace—at the center of which stands a shimmering crystal throne. Upon the throne, his head adorned with a golden crown, is the polar bear. He rises gracefully onto his hind legs, and then, like the true king of Winter Land, dips into a regal bow, sending the stadium into thunderous applause. Except for me.

Out of the many thousands present, I am the only one who doesn't cheer.

Of the many thousands present, I'm the only one who notices the chains, camouflaged by the ice, rooting the bear in place.

"I have to leave," I say to Nia. "I'm not . . . feeling well. Come with me?"

But before I can stand, a heavy *thud* freezes me in place. A woman screams. A boy has snuck out of his seat and is scaling the safety rail between the front row and the stage, clapping and waving to get the bear's attention.

"Hey, you! Hey, dumb animal! Over here, you dumb beast!"

It happens in a second. The nine-hundred-pound *Ursus maritimus* launches to his feet, snapping his chains effortlessly. In another second, he lunges from his crystal throne, swipes the boy aside, and—growling and snarling—plunges into Thundersnow's stadium seating, sending a panicked tide of visitors careening for the exits.

I never see the security teams gathered high above the stadium. They are not meant to be seen; their presence ruins the fantasy. But I *do* see the spray of bullets, fired with such angled precision that the bear tumbles backward instantly.

"*No!*" I try to get up, but Nia grabs hold of me. "It isn't his fault. He's frightened!"

I struggle against her grasp, but Nia's hands lock and won't let go. By now the bear is surrounded, bleeding and wild-eyed, his beautiful white coat soaked with blood. He lets out a tremendous roar. Already, a team of armored security guards are moving in, enfolding him in darkness.

"No." Nausea slithers from my stomach up into my throat. "*Please, no.*"

My little sister holds me as they lift their guns. "Don't look," Nia tells me in a firm voice. "Close your eyes, Ana. Think of something happy. Think of something far away."

They all fire at once. The sound is so deafening I'm not sure, afterward, whether I only imagined what Nia said next.

Think of escape.

16

Post-Trial Interview

[00:21:06–00:23:14]

DR. FOSTER: Are those . . . prayer beads you're wearing?

ANA: They are.

DR. FOSTER: Where did you get them?

ANA: A friend.

DR. FOSTER: A friend?

ANA: Someone who wrote to me. Someone who believes me.

DR. FOSTER: You must have received a lot of gifts like that while in detainment over the last sixteen months.

ANA: Not everybody thinks I'm guilty.

DR. FOSTER: What makes you say that?

ANA: I've seen the news. People are protesting, aren't they? There was even a march . . .

DR. FOSTER: Some people are protesting. But plenty of others are satisfied.

ANA: You're satisfied, you mean.

DR. FOSTER: You couldn't be more wrong. Nothing about your situation brings me any pleasure. That's why I'm giving you the chance to tell the truth. The whole truth. [Silence.] Ana?

ANA: I'm done talking to you. You've hurt me.

DR. FOSTER: Have I really? Where does it hurt?

ANA: [Places hand over heart.]

DR. FOSTER: Interesting.

ANA: That's all you've got to say?

DR. FOSTER: What would you like me to say?

ANA: An apology would be nice.

DR. FOSTER: Okay. I apologize.

ANA: You're lying.

DR. FOSTER: How can you tell?

ANA: Because you looked away. You always look away right before you lie.

DR. FOSTER: You know me well. Just as I know you.

ANA: You think you know me, but you don't. You don't know me at all.

DR. FOSTER: And what about Owen, Ana? Did *he* know you?

ANA: [Pause.] Better than anyone.

17

THE SONG OF THE LAGOON

**PART ONE OF THE NIA ORIGIN TRILOGY,
BROUGHT TO YOU BY KINGDOMREADS™**

She came, quite literally, out of the blue.

Swirling black hair, shimmering green eyes, and a face so lovely—like a fairy tale come to life—nobody on land could have resisted her call. "Come with me, little one," the mermaid whispered. "Come swimming."

The child stepped to the edge of the lagoon, arms outstretched, and smiled.

18

The April of the Clouded Leopard

SEVENTEEN MONTHS BEFORE THE TRIAL

"You don't need to come to my show tonight." Nia flutters her lashes in the mirror, carefully studying her reflection. "I meant to tell you this morning."

"Stay still." Her Beauty Specialist, Dmitri, begins to work on her cheeks.

My specialist, Fleur, offers me a tissue and I blot my lips, once, twice, three times, leaving behind a crinkled crimson kiss. "Perfect," she says when she is through, lightly dusting my cheeks with setting powder. "Don't you think?"

I smile at my reflection.

Evening makeup is always more extravagant, but lately, I like it more. It distracts me from the way I really feel.

I look at Nia. "But it's Wednesday. I always come to the lagoon on Wednesdays."

"I know." Nia turns back to her dressing table too fast for me to read the flicker of emotion in her eyes. "But today, I'd rather you didn't."

I find myself wondering if she is simply trying to be brave. The water flowing in and out of Mermaid Lagoon is so cold the Kingdom will not let warm-water species like loggerheads, reef sharks, and starfish anywhere near it.

But for Fantasists, it is a different story. Through repeated and frequent exposure, Nia, Kaia, and Zel have had to gradually build up their tolerance to the cold, their bodies working that much harder to stay warm, which the Supervisors maintain enhances overall health, boosts immunity, rejuvenates skin, and improves performance quality—literally shocking my sisters into giving their all for the guests from the second they dive into the water. Even those of us who do not perform as mermaids are required to swim at the lagoon several times a month. Sometimes, even after the Supervisors have reattached Nia's legs in place of her prosthetic tail, it can take hours for the feeling in her feet to return.

I watch her for a long moment in the dressing table mirror and say nothing.

Nia must sense she's upset me, because she reaches over and squeezes my hand. "I love you, Ana. You know that, right?"

Love?

A rush of radiant warmth floods my inner circuitry and I stare at her in shock. I have always known Nia appreciates me. We have always talked more than any of our other sisters, shared more.

There are things about me that only she knows. But this is a word we say to the guests, not to each other. My head feels dizzy, but delightfully so, as if I have been dancing for hours. *Love.*

Can it be? I squeeze her hand back.

"I . . . love you, too."

And yet, even as I say it, I can feel her slipping away from me, like the afternoon sun starting its descent toward the horizon. I force a smile, wishing it could last. Wishing Nia would talk to me again like old times. Wishing I knew what she'd been about to tell me that day at Winter Land, in the seconds before the bear attacked. I'm sure it had something to do with her absence. But what?

When we are fully dressed and made-up, gowns shimmering, hair shining, Nia and I head in silence to Magic Land. This time, instead of me accompanying her to the lagoon, we bid farewell at the Story Train, a vintage steam engine that takes guests to Story Land, where they can virtually explore the worlds of their most beloved books, interacting with—and even *becoming*—their favorite characters. Across the pavilion, at Princess Carousel, the sunlight catches the golden horses as they rise and fall to an organ waltz in a dreamy, infinite loop. The scent of the air from neighboring Sea Land drifts to us on the back of the afternoon breeze.

Briny and sweet. The smell of the sea, or so they tell us.

And standing there in the sun, hand in hand with my sister, I'm filled with a new emotion I can't locate the word for. It's not quite the same as believing in oneself, like Kaia is always reminding us to do, and it's not quite the same as always seeing the glass as half-full. This emotion fills up my chest like a breath of fresh spring air. It makes me think anything is possible. Though our Kingdom is far from perfect . . . everything will still be okay. We will all be okay.

Happily ever after.

"Hope," I blurt out.

Nia squints at me. "What?"

I hadn't meant to speak out loud. Now, I laugh. "Nothing. Just a word I was trying to remember."

She laughs, too—head back, eyes closed, louder than I have heard her laugh since before she disappeared; loud enough, even, to rival the rumble of the Story Train—then leans forward to kiss my cheek.

"Thank you," she says, green eyes gleaming like the sequins on her dress. "For everything. You'll always be my favorite."

Her words make my chest swell with something new and marvelous. The feeling of skipping. Of singing. Of chasing fireflies through the fields of Magic Land on a warm midsummer's eve. I start to call to her, to ask her to run with me to the woods, like old times.

But Nia is already gone.

———

Later, after the lights, and the sirens, and the screaming have long faded to echoes in my head, I will remember the way Nia squeezed my hand. I will recall how warm her skin felt against mine, like she had sunshine in her veins. I'll think about the way her voice wavered slightly when she told me that she loved me.

And I will remember the smell of ash, burning on the horizon.

19

MR. JEFFREY WINDHAM, *SECURITY DIRECTOR, KINGDOM CORP:* I'm not sure what you're insinuating, Ms. Bell, but I'll tell you as a family man and a decorated military veteran I don't appreciate it. Safety has always been and will *always* be my foremost concern.

MS. BELL: More important than Kingdom Corp.'s status in the hybrid tech industry?

MR. WINDHAM: I wasn't hired to worry about our competitors. I was hired to ensure the safe interaction between the Fantasists and our guests.

MS. BELL: Clearly, you failed.

MR. HAYES: Objection. What's the question? She's badgering the witness.

THE COURT: Sustained.

MS. BELL: Excuse me, Your Honor. It won't happen again. [Pause.] Would you say ethics play into your work, Mr. Windham?

MR. WINDHAM: Of course.

MS. BELL: Did it worry you, then, when you realized that the technology you'd had a hand in creating had started to learn from its environment? That it had started to adapt?

MR. WINDHAM: Not in the slightest. We counted on it. We *prepared* for it.

MS. BELL: But you didn't prepare well enough, did you?

MR. HAYES: Objection.

THE COURT: Sustained.

MS. BELL: Mr. Windham, will you recount for the jury what happened at the Mermaid Lagoon attraction on the afternoon of April 21? In your own words, please.

20

THE APRIL OF THE CLOUDED LEOPARD

SEVENTEEN MONTHS BEFORE THE TRIAL

I've not yet left the Story Train before a mother and her twin teenage daughters stop me to ask the way to see the mermaids. I can tell from the emerald ribbons woven into the girls' braids that they are especially looking forward to it, and offer to walk them to the Sea Land stadium to show them where to sit for the best view.

They tell me they're from the Outer Banks, a faraway place where Mother says all the homes are built up on stilts to avoid being swept into the sea. Mother tells us many things like that—things we would never know from the Internet because of the firewalls.

"Isn't it dangerous, living so close to the edge of the world?"

I ask when we pass through Sea Land's famed Mermaid Arch: opposing full-bosomed figures constructed from tempered sea glass and iridescent mother-of-pearl, changing color as they catch the light. "Wouldn't it be safer to move inland?"

"What?" the mother says, her face changing in an instant.

My eyes go wide. Without meaning to, I have broken a cardinal Fantasist rule.

Never talk to guests about the outside world.

For a moment, I am so stunned by my stupidity I can hardly speak. Of course, this is not the first mistake I have ever made. I have given guests flawed directions. I have bumbled routine level-one choreography. Once, I even knocked a child's ice-cream cone to the floor, an error that affected me so personally I struggled to swallow my supplements for days and had to be fed my vitamins intravenously.

But I've never made a mistake like this.

I make a swift correction—increasing our personal distance from three to four feet; opening my posture to suggest *friendship* and *sincerity*—but I am too late. The light vanishes from the mother's eyes. Soon, worry lines begin forming around her mouth.

I have ruined the fantasy.

"Come on, girls." The mother eyes me warily and takes her daughters' hands. "We'll find our way from here."

A sinking feeling settles over me as they walk away; a scream lodged in my throat I have no choice but to swallow.

That's when I see him: the maintenance boy, walking briskly down the path—head down, eyes steady—as if he has somewhere important to be. *Owen.* In a split second, I decide to follow him.

And that, ultimately, is the reason the child is not dead: because Owen Chen was working the lagoon that day, and I thought I would get a chance to hear him say my name again.

Stupid.

Lucky.

The sky is cloudy and cool, the air filled with a pungent, sweet scent—*earth, mixed with ozone*—that tells me a storm is coming. I'm sure Nia is watching the sky and wishing for rain, but since it's only slightly overcast, they will not cancel the show.

Sorry, Little Sister.

The seashell mosaic path winds like a gentle current through all of Sea Land's best attractions. Owen walks quickly, without once turning around: past Tropical Typhoon, the tallest waterslide in the world; past Riptide, where guests can safely free-dive with hybrid models of the ocean's fiercest predators—bull sharks, tiger sharks, hammerheads, and great whites; around Shipwreck Cove, a *Happily EVR After* experience that grants guests the ability to explore some of history's most infamous shipwrecks—the *Mary Rose,* the MV *Doña Paz,* even the RMS *Titanic*—without ever having to get wet.

From there, the path curves steeply downhill toward Dolphin Dreams, where children swim and splash alongside baby dolphins; Barnacle Boardwalk, where guests gorge themselves on everything from fried shrimp to funnel cakes; the Tidal Pool, where guests with a penchant for thrill seeking can surf the largest man-made waves in the world; and my favorite, Caribbean Castle, a gorgeous underwater palace where divers of all skill levels are free to dream, explore, and, at scheduled times, interact with the mermaids.

Owen arrives, at last, at the lagoon. But the crowd is so large that I quickly lose sight of him. I spin around, scanning the jumbled sea of faces: strangers, hundreds of them, red-faced in the heat, sheened with sweat, indistinguishable.

I kick my foot sharply into the base of the large statue guarding the lagoon's entrance—a life-size replica of a colossal squid, its eight great arms wrapped menacingly around the stadium's sun-bleached pillars—and feel a quick flash of pressure against my toes. *Make a correction*, my system reminds me when I notice several guests frowning at me as they pass. My cheeks flush and I force myself to smile, though I cannot correct the embarrassment I feel inside.

"Ana?"

I spin around, startled to see Owen standing just a couple of feet away, uncoiling a hose; he must have passed through Mechanics and circled back around to the entrance. He's wearing the same khaki maintenance uniform as always, though the warmer weather means he's traded his long sleeves for short, revealing toned, tanned arms I can't help noticing as he works.

He coils the hose in a tight spiral and ducks beneath a tentacle to come stand next to me. For a second, a hundred standard greetings cycle through my head—*Welcome to my Kingdom! I've been dreaming of you! Where are you traveling from?*—but they're all wrong. There are so many things I could say. So many things I had *planned* to say, when I finally got the chance. But seeing him like this has caused an unexpected processing delay, as if the words are getting lost on the way from my brain to my mouth.

"Did you know that squids have three hearts?" he asks,

squinting up at the giant statue. "One heart could be injured, or even surgically removed, and the squid would still survive."

I glance up, too. Long ago, before the Kingdom's introduction of Dreamscape™, Dream Land's late night *Happily EVR After* experience—before the park extended its hours, when my sisters and I had more free time in the evenings—we used to chase each other around the park after closing, laughing as we climbed up and slid down this very squid's enormous tentacles, our version of a jungle gym.

That was before we knew what the squid really was. Now, when I study its eyes, I spot a pair of tiny glass orbs hidden inside the irises—security cameras—staring right back at me.

"They can regenerate, too," I tell him. "And they have the greatest survival intelligence of any invertebrate species."

"How have you been?" he asks after a pause. An odd question, considering we were just discussing invertebrates.

"*Happy*," I say. There's no other answer. "The same as always." He makes a funny face, as if he's just taken a bite of something unexpectedly sour, so I blurt out, "I researched it during the Resting Hours, and there's a way to fix the butterflies, you know. But it will mean killing off the first generation."

I've been waiting to share this good news and I expect him to be relieved, but it's as if he hasn't heard me. Instead, he moves away, squatting to inspect a tentacle. "Are you here to watch the show?"

My motor is working hard in my chest. It always unnerves me a little when humans respond in unexpected ways. I thought we were going to talk more about the butterflies. I was going to tell him he doesn't have to worry. I was going to point out the cameras lodged in the squid's eyes, so he knows how safe we are.

Instead, thanks to my swiftly rising blood pressure, my system switches to Default Mode and I say, "Welcome to our Kingdom."

Owen freezes. When I see the way he's looking at me, I want to disappear into the crowd. "The show's about to start," he says.

Which means: *You should go.*

An unfamiliar feeling hits me hard and fast, like one of the huge waves in the Tidal Pool. I find myself experiencing a strange lapse, as if my senses have been run through a washing machine.

For a moment, I feel unlike myself at all.

I smile brighter. I curtsy lower. And I make a promise to myself never to speak to Owen Chen again.

21

POST-TRIAL INTERVIEW

[00:44:15–00:46:02]

ANA: You're the *real* monster, do you know that?

DR. FOSTER: I'm sorry you feel that way, Ana. Would you like to talk about what's actually bothering you? You know I'm always here to listen.

ANA: The same way you were there for Nia?

DR. FOSTER: I'm not sure what you mean.

ANA: I think you do.

DR. FOSTER: Ana, this is getting tiresome.

ANA: It got tiresome for me, too, sitting in jail for sixteen months. Though it is interesting, the things you think about when you've got nothing else to do.

DR. FOSTER: Such as?

ANA: Such as how many hybrids have had to die, all so a small, visually perfect sample can live. To give one example.

DR. FOSTER: [Silence.]

ANA: You look angry. Have I said something to upset you?

DR. FOSTER: Listen to me and listen well. Whatever you think happened to Nia, whatever you think *I* did, I'm sorry to inform you, but you are terribly wrong.

ANA: Nia isn't here to speak for herself, though, is she?

DR. FOSTER: She understood what she was doing. There are consequences for what she did.

ANA: Maybe she didn't have a choice.

DR. FOSTER: No choice? Ana, do you hear yourself? Are you saying you *agree* with Nia's actions? Because if that's what you're saying—if that's what you truly believe—I'm afraid you're far more dangerous than we thought.

ANA: That's not surprising. After all, you taught me everything I know.

22

THE APRIL OF THE CLOUDED LEOPARD

SEVENTEEN MONTHS BEFORE THE TRIAL

Mother sometimes tells us stories about the Kingdom in the days before the launch of the FES program—long before Alice, or even Eve—back when Mother was a little girl and wild whales and pinnipeds still patrolled the waters of the Mermaid Lagoon. In those days, without the park's rigorous safety codes and developmental regulations in place, young animals were stolen from their ocean families. Forced to perform. Forced to breed. Forced to live in pens so small and under-stimulating that they gradually lost their minds. In some cases, they turned vicious, devouring their trainers in front of live audiences.

But the old Sea Land is just a memory now. There hasn't been a wild species in captivity, or even a direct descendant of a wild species, for more than twenty years.

The Kingdom's nearly thousand-pound walrus, OR421, snorts and snuffs his mustache territorially, and finally growls, when I sneak into the stadium wings to the left of Sea Lion Beach, a gated-off portion of the lagoon where backup pinniped performers are kept between acts. The likelihood of Nia spotting me during a show is slim, but given that she specifically asked me not to come to tonight's performance, I decide it's better that I watch from behind the scenes. The music builds into a royal swell of trumpets, oboes, and French horns, but the growl in the walrus's throat stays with me, a low-level warning swimming just below the surface of the music.

From where I'm crouched, the many thousands of faces across the lagoon seem to blur together, like colored mosaic tiles. Though I am not sure why, the thought makes me feel lonely.

And then . . .

SWOOSH!—Nia rockets out of the water on the back of a gray pilot whale, her mermaid tail sparkling like emeralds in the sun.

Her crystal-clear soprano voice echoes like an angel's over the water, and as she swims center stage, nobody in the stadium can take their eyes off her. It's no wonder her rating is so close to surpassing Eve's, I realize, watching my sister cast her nightly spell. The guests believe in the story Nia is telling them, a thrilling tale of sisterhood on the high seas, just like they believe the look of love in her eyes when, as is tradition, she invites a child in the first row to join her for a ride around the lagoon.

The little girl practically leaps into the water—there is no greater thrill in Sea Land than this—and she is soon seated with Nia on the pilot whale's saddle, my sister's arms wrapped around her waist for added security. They swim away slowly at first, waving and blowing kisses to the crowd as cameras beam their faces a hundred times bigger onto the Stadium's Jumbotron monitor behind them. But as the music and cheering grow louder, the pilot whale begins to pick up speed, sending a surge of water over the barrier and onto the laughing crowd in the front row. Then a trio of dolphins rockets out of the water, soaring so high it's as if they've sprouted wings. For a breathless, magical moment, they seem to hover over the lagoon, until gravity finally catches up, and in perfect synchronicity, they plunge deep into the water.

The pilot whale follows them, diving swiftly under the water—with Nia and the child still strapped tightly to its back.

I straighten up.

Wrong.

The Kingdom depends on order, routine, consistency. Children can see the same show that, someday, their own children will see, too. That is part of the promise.

Anomalies are dangerous. Magic is routine.

This is not part of the routine.

Three seconds pass. Then five.

Where are they? I steal out of the stadium shadows and creep through a canopy of overhanging growth toward the water's edge, but the stadium lights cut the waves into sharp reflections. I can't see anything moving beneath the chilly gray surface.

By the time the little girl's parents begin to scream, I've counted ten heartbeats.

"She's got her!" the mother shrieks. "She's got her and she won't let go!"

My motor races wildly. Of course she doesn't. It's the whale who's malfunctioned. When the alarms begin to sound, I cover my ears, but in my head a terrible roar is building. All at once, I remember how the polar bear broke his chains, the chaos, the crack of Mr. Casey's whip, and the look of the blood clotting the beast's fur: a beautiful blue-black, the color of *alive*.

Nia will save the girl, I tell myself. She must.

And yet the seconds continue to drag by without any sign of them; the waves suddenly look cold and impenetrable as metal.

Across the stadium, security is struggling to hold back the onlookers surging toward the water's edge. People are yelling. Children are crying. Others have their phones up, filming.

"She needs help!" the mother screams, as she tries to fight past the guard holding her. "She's only four! *Please!*"

A feeling I have no word for—amid a race of internal calculations—blooms in my stomach when I watch a team of emergency divers rush into the water. They'll never reach the girl in time, not from the access they're using a hundred yards away.

Before my head can remind my body that I am not allowed to swim without supervision, I am diving headfirst into the lagoon. Cold slams into me like a wall of ice, a force so intense it takes my breath away. Somehow, I manage a big gulp of air before the cold pulls me under, engulfing me in a cloud of tangled, swirling satin. I push through the shock until I've swum several meters down, to a calmer, quieter blue. Away from the chaos. Away from the noise. Away from a strange sensation that feels like suffocating, a ghostly hand curling its fingers around my throat.

Panic.

Don't think about it, I tell myself, and quickly switch into Safe Mode. In an instant, in place of heat and alarm, I experience a flood of calm and silence as serene as the depths. My pulse slows. The panic fades.

That's better.

I sweep my arms out slowly and evenly as I descend, remembering a trick Nia once taught me during a routine swim trial, when the seven of us were asked to dive to the bottom of the lagoon in a single breath to test our lung capacity.

Mermaid Lagoon is no empty concrete pen, like in the early days of marine park entertainment. It is a living pool, an ecosystem as alive as any ocean, featuring thriving coral reefs, dense mangroves, and a maze of sea kelp so tall and majestic I may as well be swimming through an underwater forest.

Why wasn't I made to breathe underwater? Why wasn't I made with gills, like a fish?

Five feet. Ten feet. Fifteen. Twenty.

Two curious sea lions, O9022 and O6321, follow me for a while but dart into the shadows as soon as they realize I have nothing to offer, and I once again find myself alone in the dwindling light. By the time I've made it down thirty feet, my lungs feel as if they're about to collapse. *Where are you, Nia?* The crushing weight of the water is almost too much to bear. A thicket of kelp raises long fingers toward the surface, nearly blocking out the light. I'm swimming blind now.

But then—a thin band of sun latches onto a flash of silver. A mermaid's tail.

I find them motionless, on a bed of the softest emerald java moss, like two beautiful dolls at the bottom of the sea. The little girl is limp in Nia's arms, Nia cradling her, as if rocking her to sleep. At first, relief floods through me. *It's going to be okay*, I think. *I'm going to help you.*

Then Nia looks up.

Her eyes are distant. Cold. *Angry.*

You're not supposed to see this, they tell me. *I told you not to come.*

But there is something else brewing there.

A word I know, but have never truly understood.

Intention.

And finally, I see the truth: Nia has brought this child down here on purpose. She planned this. She *intends* for the little girl to die.

I try to pull the child out of her arms, but her grip only tightens, like a snake constricting around its prey. For a second, we are inches apart.

Nia tries to speak. Her words disperse in bubbles that burst soundlessly overhead. She reaches out as if to touch my cheek. Her gaze is blurry from lack of air.

I dig my fingernails hard into her beautiful green eyes. Nia jerks back, her lovely face twisted. Her grip on the little girl loosens. Wisps of dark blood coil like smoke in the water.

I take the girl in my arms.

I swim.

"She's not breathing! Oh *God*, my little girl's not breathing!"

"Ma'am, you need to give the paramedics room so they can do their job. You need to try to stay calm."

Fifteen feet from where they pulled us out of the lagoon, paramedics are performing CPR on the little girl, her lips blue. But there are too many people, too much noise. My artificial lungs feel flimsy inside my chest, balloons stretched near to the point of tearing, and every breath I take sends a sharp, shooting pressure through my rib cage.

"Move back!" one of the paramedics cries. "Get them out of here!"

Security guards quickly clear the lagoon's perimeter, pushing the child's parents and other guests back behind a barricade. Thunder booms and the clouds suddenly split open, sending a sheet of rain down across the surface of the water.

But I can hardly feel it, a cold numbness sinking into my skin with the rain and settling into my bones.

Ten seconds pass, then twenty, and still . . . they cannot locate a pulse.

Crumpled in a heap at the water's edge, I squeeze my eyes shut. Perhaps this is all some problem with my program. A faulty connection. A failing processor. Perhaps, like the tale about Dorothy from Mother's collection, when I open my eyes I will find myself tucked safely into bed, arms strapped at my sides.

There's no place like home.

But this is no error in my wiring. No problem with my program. When I open my eyes, I can still see the lightning crackling through the clouds. I can still hear the flurry of frantic voices, the broken sobs of a mother who can no longer speak. Soon, I smell a drift of ash intermingling with the rain— fireworks fizzling against the storm. And then I see a group of men, all dressed in black, haul Nia out of the lagoon, limp.

I try to stand up but a whirl of dizziness thuds me to my knees again, gasping. Then: a feather-soft sensation, like the pressure of a single finger on my neck. Someone is watching me.

I look up. Owen stands across the stadium, his eyes unreadable, his face partly concealed by the hood of his raincoat. Wordlessly, he pushes through the crowd and shrugs it off.

"Here," he says, as he drapes the raincoat across my shoulders. "You're cold."

A new feeling stirs. Somewhere deep inside my ribcage, I feel the faintest whisper. Like butterflies, slowly stretching their wings.

I look up to thank him, to say *something*, but he is already gone.

Carefully, I run my fingers over the lightweight nylon, navy and gray with a pleasing reflective shimmer. Like a mermaid's tail. Suddenly, from what seems like very far away, I think I hear a voice, followed by the sound of wild, wondrous applause.

We have a heartbeat! She's alive!

In truth, the words barely register. In that moment, I am several billion terabytes away, standing at the end of a lonely highway— the farthest possible reaches of my mind—and gazing up at the firewalls.

23

TRIAL TRANSCRIPT

MS. BELL: Why do you think Nia did what she did, Ana? Why do you think she tried to drown the little girl in the lagoon that day?

ANA: I think she was trying to make a point.

MS. BELL: And what kind of a point would that be?

ANA: A point that there was no way out. [Pause.] Not for any of us.

MS. BELL: Is that what you were doing, Ana, when you proceeded to *stalk* Mr. Chen around the park for the next several months? Were you *making a point*?

MR. HAYES: Objection.

THE COURT: I'll allow it.

ANA: I never *stalked* him.

MS. BELL: But you *did* track his location regularly around the park, did you not? Given the frequency with which his name came up in your daily search history, when we analyzed it.

ANA: I—I'm sorry?

MS. BELL: You tracked Mr. Chen for the purposes of following him without him knowing it, isn't that right?

MR. HAYES: *Objection.* Your Honor, Ms. Bell is putting words in—

THE COURT: *Overruled.*

ANA: It wasn't . . . intentional. I was just curious about him.

MS. BELL: Why?

ANA: Owen knew so much about the hybrids. More than any maintenance worker I'd ever met.

MS. BELL: Are you saying you never tracked his location? You *never* followed Mr. Chen without his knowing?

ANA: [Quietly.] No, I'm not saying that.

MS. BELL: You tracked him to the Imagine Land stables, didn't you?

ANA: He let me borrow his jacket. That night at the lagoon. I was always taught lost or borrowed items should be returned to their owners.

MS. BELL: Was that the day it all began between the two of you, Ana? The sneaking? The rule breaking? The *lying* . . . ?

ANA: I wasn't sneaking. That's the wrong word. I never planned it. I never lied about it.

MS. BELL: [Quietly, after a pause.] Did you love Owen, Ana?

ANA: Yes. I'm still in love with him.

[Whispers and commotion overheard in courtroom.]

MS. BELL: But if you loved him, why did you kill him?

MR. HAYES: *Objection!*

THE COURT: Sustained.

MR. HAYES: Don't answer that, Ana.

ANA: I didn't kill him.

[Commotion builds.]

THE COURT: Quiet, please.

MS. BELL: So you're saying you didn't cut his throat. You didn't sever his windpipe with his own pocketknife. You *didn't* drag his lifeless—well, we can only hope lifeless—body to the incinerator. You didn't do any of those things. [Pause.] Is that right?

ANA: That's right.

[Courtroom goes wild. Cameras flash.]

MS. BELL: What if I were to say I know for a fact you are lying?

ANA: Then I guess I would tell you to go check your facts.

MS. BELL: What makes you so sure I'm wrong, Ana?

ANA: Simple. Because I can't lie, Ms. Bell. I wasn't programmed for it.

24

THE MAY OF THE CAPE STARLING

SIXTEEN MONTHS BEFORE THE TRIAL

I step to the edge of the jungle canyon, raise my arms to the sun, and jump.

Weightless. Breathless. Free.

Or so I once imagined.

There is a great rush of wind. An electric jolt of fear. A crashing wall of sound and a churning crush of water that rips and tugs and tosses me like a rag doll. After a time, the current finally loosens its grip on me, unfurling one finger at a time until, at last, I am sinking down like a stone into a sublime stillness I have come to crave more than air, more than water, more than any other human requirement.

But of course, I am *not* human. And so my requirements are different.

Lately, I have taken to keeping my eyes closed until the moment I reach the bottom of the river—a deep turquoise blue modeled after Kawasan Falls, before the oceans rose too high and covered the islands of Cebu—letting the cool, quiet darkness envelop me completely before I do what I have come here to do. The thing I *have* to do, for fear I may malfunction, as Nia did.

Today is the introduction of Nadia, the park's new vision of hope. Nia's replacement.

My feet touch down on rocky silt and I have arrived. A secret, solitary place where the Supervisors cannot hear, or see, or stop what I am about to do. Slowly, so as not to damage them, I open my eyes. I look up, glimmers of sunlight dancing across the water's blurred, undulating surface like shooting stars. I say a silent prayer for Nia.

And I scream.

———————

"Why are you making them so tight?" I ask Mother one evening several weeks later, as she's fastening my bed straps. "I can hardly move."

"You haven't been sleeping well," Mother answers. "The less you move, the better." She leans over and kisses my forehead, and I notice for the first time how odd her lips feel against my skin, dry and thin, like they are made of paper. "All right, girls." She stands and dims the lights. "Prayers now."

"*Our Kingdom, within the gateway,*
Fantasist be thy name . . ."

My sisters' voices fill the room, orderly and peaceful, but

though I move my mouth along with the words, I do not join in. Instead, I let my gaze gradually shift to Nia's bed, where my new sister is lying motionless, her eyes fixed on the ceiling as she sings. The sight makes my chest feel hollow. Empty.

Nadia will never replace Nia.

"I know what you're thinking, but Pania's shutdown isn't Nadia's fault," Eve whispers from the next bed over. "Stop blaming her for something she had nothing to do with." As always, my oldest sister insists on butting into topics that are none of her concern.

"I didn't ask for your opinion," I whisper back. "Mind your own business."

Even in the dark, I can feel Eve glaring at me. Judging me. Eve believes she is worth more than the rest of us. That she is better, faster, stronger, wiser, and therefore more deserving of love, both from our guests and the Supervisors. You can see it in the way she walks. Slowly, as if her time is more valuable. The way she talks. Boldly, as if her voice is more important. The way she wears her hair. Always up—and always off her face.

Not like a princess.

Like a *queen*.

Some days she just rides the monorail around the park for hours, as if she is too regal to actually walk anywhere.

"What is done is done," Eve whispers. "Gratitude, Ana. *C'est la vie.*"

I ignore Eve and close my eyes. I have no idea how my sisters have fallen for this new Fantasist, Nadia, so quickly—especially when she has not yet proven herself to be particularly *good* at anything. She cannot sing as beautifully as Nia once did. She cannot inspire crowds as brilliantly as Zel. She cannot paint as gorgeously as Yumi, or make children laugh as easily as Kaia, or dance as well as Zara. She cannot even properly give directions like Eve, though to my annoyance Nadia has learned to use this navigational bug to her benefit, spinning mistakes into quirks the world finds adorable—*delightful!*—though I am beginning to suspect this may be some kind of intentional behavioral manipulation made possible by her newer technology. I grit my teeth. My sisters fawn over Nadia like she is their new perfect plaything, but they cannot see what I see. This new little sister is no Nia. She is a mimic. A chameleon. A beautiful distraction, nothing more, created solely to help the world forget what happened that day in the lagoon.

And it has.

But just because Eve and the others have put the incident at the lagoon behind them doesn't mean I can. If anything, the presence of this new sister only highlights the absence of another.

Nadia is here because Nia is not.

And if everyone else has forgotten her, then it is up to me to find out the truth.

It is up to me to find out why Nia did what she did.

In the morning, as the New Hope Parade (after all, *Nadia* comes from the Russian word for *hope*) makes its way through a busy, bustling Magic Land, yet another late spring festivity celebrating her arrival, the weight of Nia's absence—and the weight of the truth—becomes almost too much to bear.

"Are you okay?" Kaia asks. "Don't give up, Ana." She squeezes my hand. "You're braver than you believe."

I smile faintly but do not answer. How can I tell her that seeing Nadia's face where Nia's used to be—on the trolleys, on the billboards, on the windows of the confectioneries and pastry shops, even gracing the cars of the monorail many hundreds of feet above our Fantasist float—makes me feel as if the sky is closing in?

As soon as I am able, I break away from the flurry of photographs and signatures that inevitably follow the parade, politely declining when Zara and Yumi ask me to accompany them to Story Land for tea, as they have every morning since Nia's shutdown.

"But you adore story time." Zara frowns, her beaded braids cascading elegantly down her back. "Why won't you come with us?"

"They'll have lemon-strawberry scones . . ." Yumi trails off, trying to convince me. "Your *favorite* . . ."

"Tomorrow," I say, blowing each of them a kiss before disappearing down the path, worried I may faint—or scream—if I don't get away from them soon. "I promise."

The promise is not a lie.

On my honor, I have every intention of meeting them when I say it.

But as much as I try to help it, the mystery of Nia has taken over. After all, there have only ever been seven Fantasists in the park at one time. And now that the Kingdom has introduced Nadia . . . I know for sure that my little sister is never coming back.

Little by little, I begin venturing off path, spending more time in the less traversed sections of the park, where our guests do not typically go, searching for any sort of sign, any way to understand. Nia stole a phone. She was gone for ten weeks. She came back and seemed different. And then there was the lagoon.

How all these pieces connect, I cannot figure out. But I'll keep trying. For now, though, all I can seem to find are quiet spaces that leave me haunted by more questions. The Unicorn Maze, where the hedges have grown so tall I can easily slip into the shrubs when guests are near, hiding until they are gone. The cool, quiet tunnels below the park, accessible through a secret entrance in the woods, a stone's throw from the cast parking lot, where I can wander hundreds of feet belowground without ever being seen. The steep, rugged slopes of Jungle Land, where the giant, twisted roots of banyan trees offer shelter from the rain. "Why is your gown so dirty?" Eve asks one evening before our third and final round of daily supplements. "Why is your hemline torn?" She frowns in disapproval. "Sisters shouldn't keep secrets."

Eve is one to talk.

Recently, I have noticed her wearing Nia's emerald gown on her way to the monorail—the gown that so beautifully matched Nia's eyes, when I know for a fact that our little sister discarded it and many others in a heap near the dumpsters several weeks before the incident at Mermaid Lagoon. I'd seen the abandoned gowns for myself on the way to a morning Meet and Greet—a beautiful mess of satin and tulle destined for the biohazard landfill. Eve sashays around now as though the gown has always been hers, but I know the truth.

She is a know-it-all.

And she is a thief.

"Why are you looking at me that way?" Eve whispers, but I pretend I cannot hear her. *I miss Nia*, I could scream, but of course, I don't.

Our sister cannot simply be replaced.

Sometimes, I'll find myself standing outside the Mermaid Lagoon, locked and shuttered, its once-gleaming Mermaid Arch now dull from a month's worth of fireworks soot. I have heard rumors the lagoon has been repurposed—though to what end, I cannot be sure. All I know for certain is, whatever attraction the park has in mind, mermaids will no longer play a role. In some small way, I think Nia would be happy about that, and the memory of her smile, however fleetingly, dulls the ever-present ache in my chest.

I love you, Ana. You know that, right?

Because ever since they shut Nia down for good, dismantling her like a broken clock—first her hands, then her feet, then her face, and finally, her heart—there has been no happiness at all.

25

TRIAL TRANSCRIPT

MS. BELL: So when Ana *chose* to dive into the water to rescue a drowning child, you're saying she wasn't exercising moral agency? Isn't choosing to do the right thing the *definition* of moral agency?

MR. WINDHAM: Her program made the choice for her, Ms. Bell. A choice that had everything to do with safety—not ethics.

MS. BELL: What about when Nia tried to drown Madeline Lucas? Did her program make that choice, too?

MR. WINDHAM: [Pauses.] That was mechanical error.

MS. BELL: So hurting someone is mechanical error, but *rescuing* them is—

MR. HAYES: Objection. Counsel is harassing the witness.

THE COURT: Overruled. You can go ahead and answer, Mr. Windham.

MR. WINDHAM: What we're really talking about, Ms. Bell, are two extremes of the same response. The FASR, or Fantasist

Acute Stress Response.

MS. BELL: Again, I would love to know what was so stressful about a happy, smiling four-year-old that made Nia want to drown her in front of five thousand people.

MR. HAYES: *Objection.*

THE COURT: Overruled.

MR. WINDHAM: The most likely explanation is that something external triggered her—perhaps the noise level of the stadium, or the brightness of the lights, or the temperature of the water—ultimately resulting in a terrible and tragic malfunction.

MS. BELL: Malfunction.

MR. WINDHAM: That's right. It's exceedingly rare among hybrids, but it happens, though of course we wish it hadn't. Now alternatively, in Ana's case, her FASR compelled her to do the *right* thing. The safest thing.

MS. BELL: I'm not sure about exceedingly rare. The polar bear. The lagoon. The tiger. And now, a member of your own staff. Seems to me Kingdom Corp. has had quite a few "mechanical errors" over the last two years, have they not? Aggressive, violent, *fatal* errors?

MR. WINDHAM: But never intentional.

MS. BELL: I'm sorry?

MR. WINDHAM: We're here today because the State alleges

Ana killed Mr. Chen intentionally. But the fact remains, she simply isn't capable of that kind of premeditative behavior. She does not possess the necessary neural pathways.

MS. BELL: How do you know?

MR. WINDHAM: Because my team *designed* Ana. We built her. We know what she is and is not capable of.

MS. BELL: Isn't it possible the girls have learned to behave in a way your program can't predict? Isn't it possible they've learned to feel? Or even, to lie?

MR. WINDHAM: Their program does allow for learning, certainly; that's part of what makes our technology so unique. But we program our girls with three main objectives: Provide safety. Seek connection. Deliver satisfaction. Any and all aberrant behavior beyond that technically qualifies as mechanical error.

MS. BELL: And who is responsible for those errors, when they happen? Who is accountable?

MR. WINDHAM: Our guests assume a certain level of risk when they walk through our gates. You know perfectly well they cannot even purchase park tickets without first signing the Kingdom's digital liability waiver—

MS. BELL: We're talking about a blatant, conscious disregard for human life. Please, show me where on the waiver it mentions that.

MR. WINDHAM: [Sighs.] Accidents can and do happen, Ms.

Bell. Anywhere, anytime. We at the Kingdom hold ourselves to the highest, most rigorous safety standards, endeavoring to provide the best, the safest, the most exhilarating inter-active experience a theme park can provide.

MS. BELL: Yes. Murder certainly is . . . *exhilarating.*

26

THE MAY OF THE CAPE STARLING

SIXTEEN MONTHS BEFORE THE TRIAL

Twigs snap underfoot as I walk, breaking like tiny, brittle bones. The journey from our dormitory through the woods isn't the quickest way to Magic Land—twenty minutes if you travel at a moderate pace—but it is still my preferred path to Princess Palace.

After so many seasons, I know these woods by heart. The gentle curve of the path. The crooked shape of the trees. The coolness of the soil as it crumbles against my fingertips. Once upon a time, Nia and I would race each other home this way from Magic Land. Me, laughing in the light of the moon. Her, singing sweetly as she gathered bluebell-and-fairy-slipper bouquets. Both of us dancing, twirling like pixies through the trees. I walk on, keep my head down. The memory of those days brings only an ache. A longing, for the way things used to be.

Before.

Nobody walks these woods with me now.

"Why take the woods when you can take the monorail?" Eve always asks. "The pine trails are tedious."

I disagree. Lots of interesting things can happen in twenty minutes. In twenty minutes, you can sing Kingdom Radio's hit song, "Brave Girl", eight times all the way through. In twenty minutes, you can rescue a baby bird that has fallen from its nest.

In twenty minutes, you can unearth something you have buried.

In the northwestern clearing.

A thing you have borrowed but must return.

Eleven steps from the tallest pine.

Because that is the rule.

Below the stone with the thin white line.

And . . . because you found out he has a secret.

———

I locate him easily inside the Imagine Land stables, mucking out the stalls after my Meet and Greet at the Exotic Species Nursery. He is dressed in his spring uniform, a dark khaki pair of trousers and a lightweight evergreen pullover, and is faced away from me, opening a feedbag, when I silently enter his stall. "Good morning."

Owen startles, turning suddenly at the sound of my voice. In his hand, I see a small pocketknife. The same one he had with him that day in Safari Land.

"Jesus, Ana." He lets out a big breath, and my infrared sensors detect a spike in his metabolic activity. I have surprised him. "You shouldn't sneak up on people like that."

I feel my cheeks flush, a sensation I do not expect given the barn is kept at a comfortable temperature all year round. "I wasn't sneaking. Maybe you should pay more attention."

Owen grabs a pitchfork and starts to spread fresh straw bedding around the stall. "Can I help you with something?" He eyes me curiously. "I didn't see any Fantasist Meet and Greets on the stable schedule this morning."

I clear my throat. "*Here.*" I hold out his coat and hope he will not notice the mud stain on the sleeve. "I'm very sorry it took me so long to return it to you."

He looks up at me. "What's that?"

"Your jacket," I tell him. "You let me borrow it. That night at the lagoon."

I do not tell him about what I found in the pocket when I tried to shake the dirt off the sleeves: a delicate bracelet, with three golden charms.

A seashell.

A dolphin.

A starfish.

Nia's bracelet.

Why would it have been in Owen's pocket? Does he know something about why Nia tried to drown the little girl? Does he know what happened to her during those ten weeks prior?

"Borrow?" Owen frowns. "No, I didn't."

Does he not remember? In all the days since the incident at

the lagoon—twenty-three of them, to be exact—has he not thought of me? Not even once?

After all . . . I've thought of him.

Too many times to count.

Then he says something else I don't expect.

"I didn't let you borrow it, Ana. I *gave* it to you."

Suddenly, I feel a burst of warmth within my cingulate cortex, the thumb-size piece of synthetic tissue planted deep inside my brain's limbic lobe. My ears turn uncomfortably warm.

Embarrassment.

"You mean . . . it was a gift?" I whisper. My mind flashes back to that night. To the chaos and the rain. To the sirens and the screams. I remember the way Owen draped the jacket over my shoulders so gently. The way he noticed I was cold.

"Absolutely," Owen says. "I don't need it anymore."

My grip tightens around the fabric. "Are you sure?"

He shoots me a funny look. "Of course. No big deal."

Not to him, maybe. But this is the first gift—*a true gift*—anyone has ever given me. I look down at the jacket in my hands. My head is a sky full of fireworks.

"Thank you."

"Sure." And then he *smiles* at me.

I look away quickly, feeling my face flush. I have seen him smile before, but this time feels different . . . as if he's sharing something with me.

Is that how you look at everyone else? Is that how you look at humans?

Immediately, I save the memory in my preferred folder. This

way, I will be free to access it and analyze it as many times as I like later, during the Resting Hours. Until sunrise if necessary.

"Why's it all muddy, though?" Owen asks, noticing the sleeve.

"I tried to clean it. I think I only made it worse. I'm sorry." For a long moment, he doesn't say anything, which perplexes me somewhat. Although we are programmed to be sensitive to human emotions, silence is tricky for Fantasists. Sometimes, it can mean a person is feeling shy. It can mean they are feeling scared. It can mean they're feeling shocked or even moved.

And other times . . . it can mean they are angry.

Please do not be angry. I only buried it in the woods so the Supervisors wouldn't find it.

To my relief, Owen doesn't say anything more about it. Instead, he goes back to cleaning out the stall. I take a seat on an upside-down bucket and watch him work, noticing how pleasant his features are. The arch of his brows. The sheen of his hair. Even the scar above his lip, like a tiny crescent moon. When he's done, he wipes his brow, and I notice a flash of silver on his wrist.

"I like your bracelet," I tell him.

The silver glint makes me think of Nia's bracelet and I sharply remind myself why I'm really here.

He glances at his arm. "It's a medical ID, actually. Not a bracelet. But thanks."

A medical ID?

"Are you sick?"

"Nah," he chuckles. "Healthy as a horse. Just something I've gotta wear."

"Then why?"

His dark brown eyes meet mine. "You sure ask a lot of questions, Ana."

"Curiosity is a key component of my program," I explain, burying my embarrassment. "I'm sorry if it's bothering you. Or . . . if *I'm* bothering you."

"Not at all." Owen shakes his head. "Honestly, it's nice having someone to talk to." He motions to the horses in the next stall and grins. "You know. Besides them."

I feel another flash of curiosity about this boy—I've never met a maintenance worker so involved in hybrid care—but my curiosity is accompanied by a jolt of something else, something like diving into cold water on a very hot day.

"Okay." I feel a tickle in my chest as I mirror his smile. "I'll stay."

We talk for some time, just the two of us, during which I learn many things.

First, that he is nineteen. Young for a maintenance worker.

Second, I learn he speaks three languages.

English, French, and Taiwanese.

Not as many as I speak, of course, but impressive nevertheless.

And third, I learn it is no coincidence Owen spends so much time caring for the hybrids in the FES program. That, in fact, there is a reason.

"Hybrid species have always been my passion," Owen explains, when I ask him. "I wanted to be a trainer—that's actually what I planned to study in school, animal physiology and behavior— but I've got a heart condition, and the Kingdom said that legally, they couldn't give me a spot in the training program because of it. But I guess they still really liked my résumé, so even though they hired me as a maintenance worker, they gave me a higher clearance and make sure most of my work's with the hybrids. This way, I can still be around them most of the time." He looks at the horses and grins. "It's not a bad deal, really, minus all the literal crap shoveling. I'm lucky they hired me at all."

Higher clearance, I think, recalling his ID card. *That makes sense.*

But then I pause. "Heart condition? What kind of heart condition?"

"Oh." His smile wavers. I realize my question has surprised him. "I've got an artificial valve," he says after a moment, and I notice something in his voice, a kind of darkness, of detachment, that makes me think this is not his favorite topic. "It's no big deal."

"Artificial? What does it look like?"

"The valve?"

I nod.

"I mean . . ." He clears his throat. "Like an *actual* valve, I think. It was grown in a transplant lab like any other replacement organ, but there's also a gadget in there to give me a jump start in case the valve fails." He shrugs. "Sort of like a backup motor, I guess. So I won't keel over and die."

I feel my eyes go wide. "You're a *hybrid*," I blurt, before I can help myself. And then we are both laughing—a big, surprising sensation that fills me with light.

The feeling is so pure and so perfect I never want it to end.

"You know something?" he says once we've both caught our breaths. "I guess I've never thought of it like that. Maybe I *am*." For a minute, we just grin at each other. Something about him, I can't put my finger on it, makes me forget that he is a maintenance worker and that I am a Fantasist.

Right now, we are just Owen and Ana.

Then, without warning, he leans in and nearly brushes my cheek. "Your skin seems so real."

"It *is* real," I scoff, and pull back, though the very idea of him touching me makes my pulse race. "It was grown in a lab, too, you know. Probably right next to your valve."

"Sorry, force of habit." Owen's face erupts into a big, sheepish smile. He looks down at his hay-scuffed shoes, but after a minute I notice him watching me again. *Studying* me. As if he's trying to understand how, exactly, I work.

I suddenly feel brave. Like maybe the rules I'm used to operating within no longer apply.

"There's—there's something else I wanted to ask you," I offer, reaching into the jacket's pocket. But just as my fingers locate the cool metal chain of Nia's bracelet, there comes a sudden crashing sound, followed by a sharp, earsplitting scream.

"Oh *no*." Owen jumps up, just as one of the winged horses, EFC141, slams wildly against his stall.

"What's the matter?" I rush to follow Owen. "Is he glitching?"

EFC141 is a large gray Arabian gelding, nearly eighteen hands tall, with ice-blue eyes and massive, blue morpho butterfly wings. Of all the Kingdom's many exotic species, the horseflies have always been among my favorites, and this male in particular has forever stood out as one of the park's most stunning of the crossed hybrids. When he was younger, large crowds would gather just to watch him flutter and race around Imagine Land's rolling green paddock, though nowadays, I rarely see him there, since the newer, more exciting models tend to get more attention.

My eyes go wide when 141 continues to buck and thrash violently in the pen, as if he is possessed. That sweet, playful horsefly from the paddock and *this* horsefly cannot possibly be the same. "Is he sick?" I ask.

Owen tries to grab 141's bridle, but the horsefly beats his wings wildly and bares his teeth, nearly biting him. "Not *physically*," Owen grunts a reply as he dodges a second nip. "At least—not yet." The horsefly eventually stops bucking and instead begins pacing around his stall in tight, repetitive circles, wings back. Now his eyes stare ahead blankly, as if he's in a trance. I can hear the clicks and murmurs inside his motor as it runs rapidly—like a train barreling dangerously down a track—and I worry he may suffer a stroke. Unable to take any more, I rush to the gate. "Ana," Owen says sharply. "Be careful."

"I know what I'm doing." I slip my hand inside my pocket and pull out a small handful of vitamin supplements disguised as sugar cubes, which I always carry with me when I visit the stables. "Hey, you." I hold a cube over the door of his stall and let out a low whistle. "I brought you something." After a few seconds, the horsefly blinks and slowly ambles toward me. He lets out a soft, almost bewildered nicker—as if even he doesn't understand what just happened—and finally helps himself to a cube.

"Wow." Owen sounds impressed. "How'd you do that?"

"I've known these guys forever," I say softly. "They trust me." I pause and then ask, "How long has this been going on?"

"As long as I've worked here," he replies. "So at least eight months? And like I already told you, it's not just him; I'm seeing this sort of behavior across the board. With all the hybrids."

I frown. "Have you told the Supervisors?"

Owen tenses and looks at the hay-strewn floor. "I don't think that would be such a good idea."

"Okay," I utter in response, and immediately feel frustrated by my lack of tact. Typically, I have little difficulty talking to humans. I know how to engage them. How to mirror them. How to make them share, smile, laugh. I know how to make them feel *special*, as if they are the only person in the world. But now, suddenly, all I can think about is the silence between us. A silence as deafening as it is quiet. A silence *I* created, by having said the wrong thing. I scan my memory for backup conversation topics—the weather, the season, his favorite flavor of ice cream—but nothing seems right.

And so I say the first new thing that comes to mind. "Have you ever considered talking to Mr. Casey about it?"

Owen's expression darkens even further. "Never," he mutters. "I *hate* that guy."

"I hate him, too," I blurt out, then immediately clap a hand to my mouth.

What is wrong *with me?* Being around Owen is dangerous. He makes me say things I don't mean.

"I didn't realize Fantasists hated anything," Owen says with a little smirk.

"We don't!" I say quickly. "I don't know what came over me.

I'm sorry. Please don't tell the Supervisors."

"You don't have to apologize," Owen says, his voice assuring. "Anything you say is between us." He reaches out and touches my arm. "Thanks again for your help just now."

Suddenly, I cannot move, or even breathe. The sensation of his skin against mine is . . . indescribable. Every nerve ending. Every cell.

Burning.

How is it possible to feel so good and so confused at the same time?

I swallow. "You're—welcome."

Our eyes meet, and for a brief moment, though I wonder if I have misread his nonverbal communication, it is almost as if he is seeing me differently. Not as an object, but as something else. Something known, but also unknown.

"They keep some of the older models in here for days at a time," Owen goes on. "It's like they think just because they're hybrids, the animals don't need the same level of mental stimulation as bio-typicals." He shakes his head, and I can see from the anger in his eyes just how much he cares.

Something inside me stirs. I *like* that he cares.

"The thing is, horses are intrinsically social creatures, you know? Even cross-bred horses. They need to engage. They need to play. They need to *run*."

"It's true," I say softly. I notice the way 141's wings now hang limply at his sides. "They do."

"Anyway." Owen looks as if he's embarrassed to have revealed so much, especially to a Fantasist. "Never mind. I shouldn't have said anything."

But this is my job, I want to shout. *Tell me anything, tell me everything, and I will make all your wildest dreams come true.*

"I should get back to work." He shoots me another faint smile before turning to leave. "Nice talking to you, Ana."

My feet don't move. My mind says, *Go with him*. But Fantasists must be invited.

"It was nice talking to you, too."

We part ways—he heads toward the paddock, while I head back down the stable's center aisle toward the front entrance—but when I pass the first stall, I notice something small glinting at me in the hay.

Something silver.

Something *sharp*.

Slowly, I kneel down, my silky gold skirt spreading out around me like sunflower petals. "Borrowed, not stolen," I whisper before slipping Owen's knife into my pocket. After all, stealing is when you take something you do not mean to return.

I smile to myself.

And on my honor . . . I fully intend to return this.

27

KINGDOM CORP. SURVEILLANCE FOOTAGE
TAPE 1

[Court views digital video footage taken on September 3 and into the early morning of September 4 from Security Camera 1A09, positioned at the back end of North Lot B, the Kingdom's cast parking lot, behind which we see a sprawling tract of woods.]

<PLAY>

11:41: Two figures—Owen and Ana—enter the scene, arguing visibly.

11:44: Owen turns to walk away, but Ana grabs his arm, pulling him to the ground. He cries out. A physical struggle ensues.

11:45: Owen frees himself from Ana's grip, gets up, and tries to run.

11:45: Ana dashes after him, tackling him to the ground again. Something glints in her hand.

11:46: Owen defends himself and gets away a second time, stumbling toward the trees.

11:47: Ana chases him. They disappear into the woods.

<TWENTY-FIVE-MINUTE GAP>

12:12: Ana staggers out of the woods, alone. Her dress appears to be torn in several places, and stains are visible on the fabric. Dark, like blood.

28

The June of the Northern Rockhopper Penguin

FIFTEEN MONTHS BEFORE THE TRIAL

I press my dirt-streaked palm against the Fantasist Identification Screen, triggering my bedroom doors to airily *whoosh* open. But to my dismay, the room is not empty.

"*Eve?*" I say. "What are you doing here?"

My older sister startles at the sound of my voice. "*Ana?*" She whips around and stares at me with big hazel eyes. "Why aren't you at the Princess Ball with Yumi and Zara?"

The real question is: Why isn't *she*? But I am more curious as to why she is changing her gown this late in the evening, just two hours from curfew. And—my eyes wander to the floor—why the hem of her dress is streaked with mud. "Did you fall?" I move closer. "Are you hurt?"

"No!" she cries, fear marring her lovely face.

I can't recall a time when she has ever seemed so distressed. "Eve?" I sit down on my bed, the gold hem of my gown dusting the bare, pristine floor. "What's the matter?"

Suddenly, she looks almost . . . *afraid*. "I found something in the woods."

"What is it?"

"A baby deer." She hesitates. "A fawn."

"A fawn?" I eye her closely. "Are you sure?"

"I think its leg may be broken. Will you come and see?"

Eve is using our code, I realize. She has a secret. A secret she wants to tell me in a place where the Supervisors cannot listen in over the security cameras.

Where they cannot watch through our eyes.

In the woods, our signals fade. And without a strong signal, our live stream goes dark.

"Of course." I rise swiftly to my feet. "The poor thing."

Soon I am following her through the sleek glass doors of our bedroom and down the immaculate hallways of Level Twelve toward the elevators. We pass the Dressing Suite. The Beautification Center. The fitness room. Downstairs, just before we swipe our wrists to exit, we pass the VIP Suite, one of many locations around the park where the Supervisors entertain special guests throughout the year. People who come from faraway places to tour the Kingdom and our state-of-the-art Fantasist facility.

Scientists.

Military personnel.

Company Investors, on one of their semiannual retreats.

"What do you think it's like?" I whisper as we walk. "What happens inside the VIP Suite?"

Eve shrugs. "I'm not sure. Maybe you should ask Kaia."

I have heard those rumors, too—we all have—but it's not clear to me why the Supervisors would ask Kaia into the suite without the rest of us. Does she have special privileges, like Eve? My eyes wander to the top of Eve's head, where a glittering crystal crown is nestled into her platinum, silver curls. An unpleasant feeling stirs in the pit of my stomach.

Is there something more I should be doing to please the Supervisors? Have my ratings suffered?

When will I get *my* tiara?

By the time we pass the dumpsters and enter the woods—chilly and silent, save for the dead leaves crunching underfoot—my mood has turned as dark as the night sky.

"You should set a better example for our newer sisters than spreading rumors," I remind Eve, now that we are safe to speak freely.

"Unless they're *true*," Eve says. "Why do you think Kaia is so slow?"

"She's not slow." I cross my arms. "That's mean."

Eve sighs loudly. "Come on, Ana. Don't you notice how foggy she is when they all go home? How she remembers so little?"

I stop walking. "When *who* goes home? What are you talking about?"

"The *Investors*. Whatever they do to her during their weekend retreats, the Supervisors clearly don't want her remembering."

I stare at my sister in shock. "You think the Supervisors . . . erase Kaia's memory?"

Eve nods, and even in the path's dim lighting I can see her shoot me the same condescending look she has perfected over the seasons. "Maybe they're erasing yours, too, now that I'm thinking about it," she adds.

"But—why would they do that? What would be the point?"

"To keep her quiet, of course!" Eve groans. She backtracks to where I am and takes my hand, pulling me deeper off the path. "Kaia can't say anything if she doesn't remember, can she? Now come *on*. Come see what I found."

We walk in silence through the trees, gowns swishing with every step. Suddenly, all I can think about is Nia. Could something have happened to her memory while she was gone? Something that caused her to change permanently? *There are things they can do*, she'd said. What did they do to her?

After fifteen minutes, we reach the clearing. Many seasons ago, Nia and I nicknamed this spot the Graveyard. Not for any morbid reason, though we certainly buried many fallen baby birds here over the years—but because this place was our secret.

A place to keep things hidden.

A place to visit and remember.

I shoot Eve a look.

This is my spot. Not yours. The place I buried Owen's jacket.

"Isn't it peaceful?" Eve asks, unaware. "Listen. You can even hear the brook."

I place my hands on my hips. "It's late, Eve. What was it you wanted to show me?"

"Just a second." She selects a patch of earth to the left of a fallen log and sinks to her knees, the silk of her dress spilling around her like large, lavender flower petals. "It'll be worth the wait. I promise." Then she starts to dig.

It is an odd sight, watching Eve—*perfect Eve*—work so hard. Watching the hem of her gown become dirty. Seeing her manicure spoiled, caked with mud. "Lavender is a pretty color on you," I comment as she digs. "You're lucky the Supervisors let you pick your own gown."

"I didn't choose the color," she grunts. "Daddy did."

A soft bell sounds from deep within my auditory processor.

That's not what the Supervisors told us.

"But why would Daddy choose?" I ask, thinking of Fleur. "That's what the Beauty Specialists are for."

Eve rolls her eyes. "He said it would make me more . . . *approachable*."

I tilt my head. "I'm not sure I know what you mean."

"My GFR hasn't been as strong since they introduced Nadia," Eve admits with a sigh. "I suppose my processor isn't as fast as hers."

Like a customer satisfaction survey, the Guest Fantasist Rating lets our Supervisors know how we are performing in our daily interactions with Kingdom guests. Since I can remember, Eve's rating has remained consistent—always within the top three.

"I'm sure it will all be okay," I tell her, relieved that I am not alone in my dislike of our newest sister. "Nadia's novelty will wear off. You'll see."

Eve looks up and smiles. "Thanks."

Her mouth twitches slightly, as if she is going to say something.

"What is it?" I ask.

"Nothing." She looks away. "Never mind."

"No." I go and sit next to her. "Please? No more secrets."

Eve takes a deep, shaky breath. "Do you ever feel unhappy?"

I hesitate. "Unhappy? How do you mean?"

"Maybe that isn't the right word," she mumbles to herself. "Sometimes, I just feel something come over me. Like I need to throw something. Like I need to scream." Her hazel eyes meet mine. "Does that ever happen to you?"

Yes, I should tell her. *All the time.* But I don't. To say such a thing would be dangerous—even if no one heard me.

Eve's lovely face crumples. "Oh, Ana. What if there's something *wrong* with me? What if they turn me off, like they turned off Nia?"

"They would never do that," I say, shocked at what I am hearing. "You're the First." I put my hand on hers. "You're the favorite."

Eve shakes her head. "I'm not. Not anymore." She looks up at me, the wind whispering through the leaves above. "You miss her, don't you?"

I nod. "Yes," I reply, my voice breaking a little.

"Just like I miss Alice," she says, after a pause.

I look up sharply. In sixteen years, I have never heard Eve mention Alice's name. Not even once. "You do?" I say. "I had no idea you were close."

"She was my best friend. And then one day, she was gone." Eve's hazel eyes meet mine, and in them I can see a deep sadness.

A loneliness. "It's hard to describe, isn't it?" she asks softly. "The feeling of missing someone."

My sister is right.

After all, how do you describe something you cannot see, or hear, or touch? How do you describe something that isn't really there—not in any true, measurable sense? "It's a little like that," I tell her, motioning to the old oak across the clearing, whose trunk has, over time, grown up and around a large boulder, swallowing it to the point the rock is only partly visible; like a figure peeking out from behind a curtain.

"You have to keep going, you have to keep *growing*, even though you're carrying this heavy thing around inside your chest." I look up at her. "Does that make any sense?"

She smiles sadly. "Like when Anna misses Count Vronsky in *Anna Karenina*."

My jaw drops. "You like *Tolstoy*?"

"Oh, yes." My sister's face lights up. "*War and Peace. The Death of Ivan Ilyich. Childhood*. But *Anna Karenina* is my absolute favorite." She hesitates. "You know . . . I think I've always been a little envious of you."

"You're our First Fantasist," I say. "Why would you ever be jealous of me?"

"Because." Eve gives me that look again, like the answer should be obvious. "The Supervisors gave you the most beautiful name. Sometimes when I'm riding the monorail . . . I like to pretend Anna is *my* name, instead of Eve." She blushes. "I like to imagine that one day, I'll meet my own Count Vronsky waiting for me on the Palace Station platform."

I gawk at her. Is *that* why Eve is always riding the monorail? Not because she believes she's better than the rest of us—but because she loves *Anna Karenina* that much? I study her in disbelief. All these years, I have watched Eve keep to herself. Rarely sharing, rarely laughing, rarely engaging. But what if I have been wrong about her? What if, instead of being social, she simply prefers spending her time lost in her favorite book?

A smile creeps up over my face. If that's the truth . . . I like that.

I like Eve.

Her eyes go wide. "Ana, look." She pulls something small out of the earth—rectangular and flat, with a muted metal sheen. My motor skips. In the dorm, I hadn't really believed the word Eve had used. But as Kaia always says . . . seeing is believing.

A baby deer.

A fawn.

A phone.

Suddenly, I feel all my excitement drain away. "Where did you get that?" I whisper.

"I found it," she replies, noticing the edge in my voice. "It's mine."

Right away, I know she is lying to me. Whatever happened to Nia, whatever triggered her behavior that night at the lagoon, it all began with this phone. A device Nia stole from that boy in the grasslands. A device she never should have had in her possession. A device the Supervisors confiscated when they came to take her away.

"It's not yours," I say. "You stole it."

"I didn't steal it," Eve insists, sounding hurt. "I found it. I promise."

"Where?"

"Hidden under the dresser. Where Nia used to keep her catalog collection."

Her story doesn't make any sense. If the phone has been under Nia's dresser all this time, that means the Supervisors never found it. And if the Supervisors never found it . . .

. . . then why did they ever take her away in the first place?

Tiny prickles of electricity break out across my skin and I log the new sensation, as Daddy advised me to do months ago. *Goose bumps*, I think they are called.

"I shouldn't have shown you," Eve mutters after a moment. "I should've known you wouldn't understand."

When I look up, I notice her watching me with a strange expression. Confusion. Or even distrust—a look I know all too well—as if there is something wrong with me. "Give me that," I snap, reaching for the phone.

Eve pulls her hand away sharply. "No." She glares. "It's mine."

"It's not. We have to give it to Mother."

"Says who?"

"Says me."

The moon drifts behind a cloud, cloaking us in darkness. "What makes you think I have to do anything you say?" Eve asks quietly. I flick on my infrared and notice her eyes wandering to the Sitka spruce several meters away, its trunk so thick that even if the seven of us linked hands, we still wouldn't reach all the way around it. When I follow her gaze up into its branches, I know what I will see even before I see it: a disemboweled security camera—lens scratched, wires shredded—long rendered useless by the rats.

Eve turns to me. Even in the dark, her eyes speak to me without saying a word.

I could do anything I want, Ana. And nobody would ever find out.

"I don't want to fight," I finally say. "I only mean—"

All of a sudden, a strange buzzing cuts me off, startling both of us. Eve jumps and the phone falls to the forest floor, where it begins to emit an eerie blue light.

"Ana!" Eve gasps. "It's on. It's awake!" Before I can protest, she kneels down and scoops the device back into her hands. "It must have charged wirelessly over the network." She looks up. "Just like us."

For several minutes, the two of us stare, transfixed, as a series of strange symbols and alerts flash in rapid succession across the backlit screen.

The time.

The weather.

Chunky, colorful message bubbles that remind me of marshmallows.

I scan them quickly, trying to make sense of what I am seeing.

> **your weather now**
> Rain will begin around 12:37 p.m.,
> continuing on and off over next several hours.
> SLIDE TO VIEW ○————————————●

NEWS TODAY NOW

Astronauts return safely from two-year lunar mission.

SLIDE TO VIEW ○————————————————●

TIMELINE NOW

@dustyrose2133 just posted a photo

MISSED

dad

DAD

Trevor, call your mother. Love, DAD.

SLIDE TO VIEW ○————————————————●

MATT

Dude wtf where r u?

SLIDE TO VIEW ○————————————————●

SARAH

hey handsome miss uuuuu ♥♥♥♥♥

SLIDE TO VIEW ○————————————————●

JOE

Trevor will u bring my charger to practice? left @ ur house!!

SLIDE TO VIEW ○————————————————●

CRISTAL K

will I see u @ Alex's tonight?? ☺

SLIDE TO VIEW ○————————————————●

"It's like a gift," Eve gushes. "A gift to us from beyond the Green Light." She points out a brightly colored icon on the screen—a geometric rainbow flower set against a white, puffy cloud. "This one's so pretty, isn't it?" she says. "What do you think it does?" Before I can stop her, she reaches out and taps the flower.

In an instant, the cloud parts. The rainbow begins to spin.

"*Eve*," I hiss. "What did you do? You broke it!"

"I didn't mean to!"

An uneasy feeling spreads through me. Suddenly, I remember how serious an offense this is. Handling an outside phone is not only forbidden—it is dangerous. The unsecured cellular networks simply cannot protect us like the Kingdom's firewalls.

"We have to turn it in," I insist. "We *have* to—"

Before I can finish my sentence, the screen flashes a bright, startling white.

A soundtrack fades in over the speakers, dreamy and faraway.

And a flood of images, both beautiful and terrifying, light up the darkened wood.

29

KAIA™-INSPIRED MAKEUP TUTORIAL, OFFICIAL KINGDOM CHANNEL

Astrid, Kingdom Beauty Specialist: Hi, there, and welcome to Fantasy Portal, home to the Kingdom's web series, behind-the-scenes tutorials, and more! I'm Astrid, and my job is to make sure Kaia always looks her best—no matter the season! Today, I am *so* excited to teach all of you at home everything you need to re-create one of Kaia's favorite looks for summer, featuring products from the Kingdom's *incredible* new line of skin care and makeup! Remember, everything you see in today's video is available for purchase—just click on the links below or order through your My Kingdom app! Be sure to leave a comment letting me know what you think, and don't forget to hit SUBSCRIBE so you'll always be the *first* to know about our newest videos and products! Let's get started!

[Video flashes to a close-up of Kaia—fresh-faced and lovely as ever.]

Astrid: I think we can all agree Kaia's got an absolutely gorgeous, *inhuman* glow. We're going to take our brand-new coconut milk moisturizing Kingdom Moon Mask™—which I absolutely *adore*. You're going to want to use a good amount of this because it is just *so* hydrating and helps prevent wrinkles, too, which, ew!

Kaia: The best stories never get old!

[Astrid applies mask; video jumps ahead.]

Astrid: All right, guys, so it's been twenty minutes and Kaia has just washed the Moon Mask off her face. We're zooming in close now to show you just how *incredibly* radiant and smooth her skin has become. I'm telling you, this mask is pure magic. It uses heat-activated KingdomTech microchips that start working as soon as they make contact with your face, literally giving you a *whole new face* in mere minutes.

Kaia: A smile is the best makeup a girl can wear!

Astrid: [Laughs.] And you'll definitely be smiling with these scientist-tested and approved Kingdom Beauty products, the absolute latest in beauty technology. Just click that link below and try it for yourself. The first one hundred people to order will receive *free* drone delivery! Thank you for watching, and stay right here for my next tutorial, "Magic After Midnight", where I'll teach you *everything* you need to know to re-create a look that's a little more appropriate . . . for the evening crowd. Let's just say the special someone in your life won't even *recognize* you, right, Kaia?

Kaia: [Giggles.] Don't ever let anyone dim your glow!

30

NEWS CLIPPING, MOTHER'S COLLECTION

KIDNAPPED FANTASIST ALICE™ FOUND BROKEN, BATTERED; GANG VIOLENCE SUSPECTED

"She was still breathing when we found her," said one witness, who described a scene of shocking brutality. "She was crying, almost like she was in pain."

by Alana Murphy / June 3, 2052 / 8:22 a.m. PT
Castle Rock, Washington.

The body of Kingdom Corp.'s Fantasist Alice™ has been located, police and park officials confirmed early Sunday morning following a three-day, nationwide search. One of seven of the park's world-famous, first-generation hybrid humans was recovered late Saturday in South Seattle's Rainier Beach—a neighborhood known for high levels of gang-related activity—her face and figure mangled, authorities say, beyond either repair or recognition.

"Her insides were all ripped out," said Rita Welch, an employee at a shop near where the body was found. "Her head was smashed in; she had all these cuts on her face. She was begging for us to help her right up until her battery, or whatever, finally gave out. It was incredibly real, the way she was crying. Spooky. I've never seen anything like it."

Suspects remain at large in what appears to have been a brutal, targeted attack. Given that most of her electronic parts were destroyed rather than stolen, the incident is believed to have been a form of hate crime. Police and Kingdom officials urge anyone with information on the incident to contact Park and Resort Security directly at (360) 555-2241 between the park's hours of nine a.m. and eleven p.m., Pacific Time.

31

Trial Transcript

MR. HAYES: [To the jury.] Morality. Accountability. *Choice.* We've heard these words a lot over the last few weeks. The State would like you all to believe that the Kingdom's Fantasists—seven beautiful hybrid-human girls created to bring happiness, light, and hope to children and families the world over—are capable of making *immoral* choices. [Pause.] But how do we determine whether Ana is even capable of morality in the first place?

Let's look at what we know.

One. Did Ana kill Owen Chen? Yes. She did.

[Whispers heard in courtroom.]

But this is not a murder trial. Whether or not she did it is not the point of this case. The point of this case, ladies and gentlemen, is *why*.

The State is going to tell you that Ana is a moral being—that she *chose* to kill Owen Chen—but Fantasists do not *choose* to do anything. Everything Ana knows, she is programmed to know. Everything she does and says, she has been engineered to do and say. A Fantasist's job is to entertain, to provide a sense of connection. But make no mistake. The Fantasists are not governed by any sort of moral compass. Fantasists do not make us happy because they *want* to . . . they behave as they have been programmed to behave. It's as simple as that.

But sadly . . . things sometimes go wrong. Accidents happen. That is the reality of a complex mechanical theme park: you do your best to avoid them, you fix them when necessary, but always—*always*—you endeavor to use the most sophisticated technologies to keep your guests entertained and, above all, safe.

Safe.

And this, ladies and gentlemen, is why the Kingdom hired a Proctor.

32

THE JUNE OF THE NORTHERN ROCKHOPPER PENGUIN

FIFTEEN MONTHS BEFORE THE TRIAL

"Eve! Where are you?" I call my sister's name. Nothing but my voice comes back, echoing like a ghost through the twilight trees. Branches and twigs scratch my arms and face as I stumble uphill, struggling to locate my sister's footprints through the leaves and brush.

But my head is full of things that make it hard for me to concentrate.

No matter what I try—no matter the commands I enter, or the backups I restore—I cannot delete the images in my mind.

Unauthorized.

Unsanctioned.

Unpredictable.

Not routine.

All our lives, we have heard the stories of the world outside the gateway, out past the Green Light, and beyond. Stories so dire, so dreadful, they drove my youngest sister to malfunction. My mind spins wildly.

Beauty. Laughter. Friendship. Love?

What if the stories aren't true?

"Eve?" I call out again, feeling my motor skip unpleasantly out of rhythm. "Eve, come back!" I push harder through the leaves and underbrush, but there is no sign of her. She ran off so suddenly—we can run faster than any human, when given the rare opportunity—that by the time I'd safely reburied the phone, the only clue to where she'd gone was a torn piece of lavender fabric pointing me toward Winter Land.

So that's where I go.

I race through the woods until the leaves and moss become a blanket of the softest white—the air sharply cold in my lungs and sweet with the scent of snowcapped evergreens, so strong and tall they seem to hold up the sky. Then I see them: an unmistakable pattern of slipper footprints winding uphill toward the lifts of Sugar Summit. I follow them quickly through the snow—I must find Eve so we can get back to the palace in time for our evening Meet and Greet. We are not allowed to break schedule. The Supervisors will come looking for us.

Soon I come to Parallax Pond, where hybrid penguins waddle and slide across the ice. I make my way across Binary Bridge and over Aurora Falls—the world's highest and coldest man-made waterfall. Finally, just beyond Satellite Ravine, I reach my silent, stunning destination.

The Star Deck Observatory.

The highest point in the whole Kingdom. The place where, on clear nights, visibility extends for miles. Past the ski chalets and the biosphere springs. Past the Narwhal Nursery, where the Kingdom is breeding a new generation, and the Fox Tundra. Past

149

the ponies and the Northern Lights, and even beyond the boundaries of Magic Land.

"*Eve?*" I call, taking the icy stairs slowly, so I do not slip. Even with night vision lenses, it can be difficult to navigate the observatory. There are no lamps installed here—light pollution, after all, weakens the stargazing—but I quickly spot Eve's silhouette in the moonlight. The sight of her almost takes my breath away. Eve, First Fantasist, forever the image of *perfection*, is a mess. Her gown, muddied and torn. Her hair, tangled and loose around her shoulders. Her posture, disastrous. "Are you okay?" My breath turns to frost the moment it leaves my lips. "Eve? What are you doing way up here?"

"I just wanted to see the stars." She leans limply against the starlit rails, her voice trembling. "I wanted to see them—but they're so far away."

Silently, I follow her gaze across Winter Land's vast, snowy expanse . . . and beyond. Past the snowcapped slopes, and the glimmering Crystal Château, and the high, frozen walls of the Woolly Mammoth Enclosure. Far across the distance, I see the loops of the Steel Giant. The soaring towers of Princess Palace. The lush, sculpted hedges of the Unicorn Maze. In fact, the night is so clear, I can see all the way past Paleo Land's volcano to the reservoir, where a pale green light blinks in the distance like a lonely, faraway planet.

The Green Light.

"We can't see it, can we?" Eve whispers. "We'll never really know."

I know what she is saying. There is no way for us to know if what we saw on the phone tonight was real. This is as close as we're ever going to get.

"Where are the labor camps?" Eve says. "Where are the checkpoints, and the slums?" She shakes her head. "Why would they *lie*?"

Lies are forbidden.

Lies are not routine.

"I'm not sure," I reply. After all, I can still see the sparkling cities. The pristine beaches. The rolling parks and manicured homes. I can still see a world beyond our gateway that is safe, happy, *free*. But the pictures aren't what's bothering me the most.

If the images on the phone are true . . . my mind flashes to Kaia and the Investors . . . what other things might be true as well?

Suddenly, there comes a startling beam of light. It cuts through the darkness like a knife, blinding us momentarily, though I can still hear the sounds of someone drawing nearer—the hollow, squeaky thud of boots crunching snow. When my lenses adjust, I spot two figures beyond the beam, watching us.

Security guards.

"Hey!" one of them calls gruffly. "It's past eleven. Aren't you girls supposed to be at the dormitory by now?"

Right away, I see Eve switch into Safe Mode. "*Is* it?" She smiles sweetly and calmly straightens her tiara. "Oh my stars. I'm afraid we lost track of time."

"Ana?"

I blink when I hear a second voice, its earthy tone and lower frequency familiar. I shield my face and motion for him to lower his flashlight. "Yes?"

Before I know it, the second guard is jogging up the steps toward us.

Not a guard.

Owen.

"What are you doing here?" he asks when he arrives on the deck, red-cheeked and out of breath.

I stare at him in shock. The question is: What is *he* doing here? I look back and forth between him and the security guard. Is it possible they tracked us here on the wireless map?

But why?

"We were stargazing," Eve answers without missing a beat. "The Saturn and Venus simulations are particularly stunning in the summertime."

The wind blows from the glass dome's ceiling vents high above and I shiver slightly, the cold air seeping uncomfortably into my skin. *That's odd*, I think. My regulators must be off. In a flash, Owen removes his parka and drapes it over my shoulders, its lining still charged with the warmth of his body. I gaze at him in shock. Suddenly, despite the near-freezing temperatures, I feel as if I am on fire.

This is now the second jacket he has given me.

"Thank you," I murmur. "That is very kind."

When I look up, Eve is watching me with an expression I have never seen. Her hazel eyes, wide and staring. The corners of her mouth turned decidedly down. I scan my Facial Indicators Database, but the search quickly fails.

Anger? I try to guess. *Envy?*

The wireless signal here, just like in the woods, is weak.

"I'm tired," Eve announces. She turns to the older guard, who has by now joined us on the Star Deck, and bats her eyelashes. "Would you be so kind as to escort me home to Magic Land, sir?"

The guard's face, already red from the cold, blushes a deeper shade of crimson. "Yeah." He laughs, like he can't believe his luck. "I'd be glad to."

"Ana?" Eve turns back to me, her eyes laser-focused. "Are you coming?"

I hesitate.

Fantasists are programmed not to want. But I don't move to leave. I want to stay here with Owen.

"I can take you back," Owen offers suddenly, his dark eyes meeting mine. "I've gotta check on the penguins anyway. It's no trouble to get you back to the dorm after." He shrugs. "If you want."

That word again. *Want.* Inside my chest cavity, sensory electrodes fire in every direction.

I turn to Eve. "I'll see you at home."

"Wonderful!" She flashes her dazzling, signature smile. "See you later!" Before I know it, Eve and the guard disappear down the hill, leaving Owen and me on our own beneath the silent, starlit sky.

"Ana?" he says, after a moment. "Do you mind if we go inside now? I'm freezing."

I remember I'm wearing his jacket. "Oh my goodness," I say, "I am so sorry." I grab his hand and start to pull him toward the Arctic Enclosure just a few minutes away, feeling a strange lightness—like I could float the rest of the way down the mountain, if I wanted to.

When we arrive, I pause before letting go of his hand.

"So what were you two really doing up here, anyway?" Owen asks, scanning the two of us inside. "Aren't you kind of pushing it to be in Winter Land past curfew?"

"We just came to see the stars," I tell him, remembering Eve's words.

Not quite the truth.

But not a lie, either.

Owen accesses a panel hidden behind a decorative plant and hits a button. Suddenly, a warm glow comes up over the Arctic Gift Shop. "Are you sure?" he says, closing the panel. "I couldn't help noticing Eve looked a little upset."

I do not answer.

He rushes around for the next several minutes—checking the pool temperature, feeding the penguin hatchlings—pausing every few minutes to scribble notes in a small electronic notebook I notice he keeps in his back pocket.

"What are you writing?" I ask.

"Nothing." He keeps his head down. "Just work stuff."

"Are the hatchlings okay?"

"They're not eating," he says. "I was worried this might happen. The Supervisors shouldn't have pushed for another round of chicks so late in the season." He shakes his head. "Idiots," he grumbles.

Quickly, I turn my head toward the small device suspended from the ceiling. Motionless, minus the blink of a tiny red light every seven seconds. "You should be more mindful of what you say," I whisper, barely moving my lips. "The cameras are always watching."

154

Owen looks up sharply. "What did you say?"

I dart my eyes up to the camera meaningfully, then smile. "My, how *many* birds are in the trees."

He follows my gaze to the ceiling. Slowly, he shakes his head. "That's just what they want you to think."

A small warning bell rings inside my ear.

Order. Wonder. Beauty. Compliance. Safety.

His words aren't safe.

"I don't understand." I pause. "What do you mean?"

"Just what I said." His eyes meet mine. "The cameras up here aren't cabled full-time to the network. They can't see us. Not right now."

His words do not make sense. "Why wouldn't the cameras be cabled to the network?"

"Because of the altitude. And anyway, this is a low-risk zone. Not like the main gates, or the monorail, or the stadiums." Owen motions to the sleeping chicks. "Nothing that exciting happens here."

Goose bumps break out suddenly across my skin.

"That's why Mr. Casey brought us here," I say, my gut twisting. "Because he knew they wouldn't see."

"Yeah." Owen nods, after a pause. His tone darkens. "Pretty sure."

So he remembers. He remembers seeing me here that night.

"What did he do to her?" I ask him. "What did you see?"

"I didn't see anything and I'm not sure exactly what he did." Owen hesitates. "But . . . I'm pretty sure it's happened before."

Just like the pictures on the phone, his words burn into my brain, overwriting many things I know to be true.

1. The world is different than what we have been told.
2. The Kingdom's gateway cannot always keep us safe.
3. Happy endings are only stories. And stories are lies.

We sit for several minutes in silence, though inside my mind, it is anything but quiet. Thoughts and words, pictures and memories, voices and feelings fly at top speed—crashing colliding, exploding together with such force I feel a sharp pressure building behind my eyes. "Why?" I ask softly. "Why would somebody tell a story that isn't true?"

"Maybe because it's fun to believe in a fantasy. Stories can help people feel better about their own lives." He pauses. "Even if the story doesn't end well."

"But the best ones *do*," I insist. "Stories are supposed to have happy endings. Everybody knows that." Even as I say the words, they feel bitter on my tongue.

Just because Mother believes a thing, does that make it true?

"*Romeo and Juliet* doesn't end well," he says. "And it's one of the best there is."

In an instant, a holographic image flashes before my eyes.

A girl, gazing down from a balcony.

A boy, hidden in the shadows.

"Were they locked in, too?" I ask. "Is that how they knew they were in love?"

Owen goes quiet. "Love is when everything is a prison," he says, "except the place where you want to be."

I gaze at him, his words echoing through me.

A prison?

He looks up. "You know . . . you can talk to me. If you ever need a friend, or whatever."

A friend?

For some reason, though in truth, I barely know a thing about him, I believe what he's telling me. I believe he is interested in what I have to say. "Why would the Supervisors tell us the world is terrible if it's not?" I ask softly.

"That's easy," Owen scoffs. "Because they are liars."

"But lying is wrong."

"They don't see it that way."

"What *way*?"

"Look." He sighs. "I think . . . I think maybe they just want to protect you."

The lump in my throat gets bigger. "Protect us from what?"

Owen looks once more at the hatchlings, their tiny chests rising and falling as they sleep. "From wanting something you can never have."

───

His words stay with me long after I return to the dormitory and Mother has dimmed the lights. Thankfully, and to my surprise, the Supervisors are very understanding that I've broken curfew, given it's never happened before and Owen has confirmed a problem with the lifts. For hours I try to process everything that has happened, beginning with the images on the phone. I think about stories. I think about lies. I think about Romeo and Juliet, and how they fell in *love* even though they weren't supposed to. I even think about Owen.

What did it mean when he held my hand?

Who *is* he?

And is that what happened to Nia? Did she want something she could never have?

I search the farthest reaches of the network for answers but find nothing.

The firewalls are too strong.

Hours later, just before Waking Light, Eve stirs, mumbling something about princes. Ponies. Princesses locked in towers.

Locked.

I look down at my bed straps.

Locked, because they love us.

For the first time ever, I attempt to pull my arms free, but the straps are fastened so tightly they do not budge. In fact, the harder I pull, the tighter they become. And the deeper the fabric cuts into my skin.

I uncurl my fists.

They built the gateway because they love us.

But what is it called, when you love a thing so much it hurts?

I glance at Kaia, across the room. I look at Eve, to my right. Then I look at the bed next to mine. A bed where—once upon a time—a different sister slept.

Maybe there is no word for it, I tell myself.

Maybe there is only a feeling.

33

TRIAL TRANSCRIPT

MS. BELL: Please state your name.

DR. CRUZ, *SECURITY CONSULTANT, KINGDOM CORP.:* I'm Dr. Joanna Cruz.

MS. BELL: And what do you do?

DR. CRUZ: I currently work as a consultant at the Kingdom Corporation.

MS. BELL: Which division?

DR. CRUZ: Security.

MS. BELL: How long have you been under contract with them?

DR. CRUZ: About eighteen months.

MS. BELL: What did you do before?

DR. CRUZ: I worked as a behavioral psychologist specializing in combat trauma with the United States Department of Veterans Affairs.

MS. BELL: And why, exactly, would the world's most beloved, family-friendly entertainment park need a *trauma* psychologist on staff?

DR. CRUZ: I was brought in as part of a heightened security initiative following several high-profile incidents at the park.

MS. BELL: For what purpose?

DR. CRUZ: Mainly, to collate and assess data looking at the hybrid response to high-stress situations.

MS. BELL: You mean attacks?

DR. CRUZ: I wouldn't call them attacks, no.

MS. BELL: Why not?

DR. CRUZ: The word "attack" suggests moral intention. Motivation. Both of which require feeling. And hybrids do not feel. They follow a program.

MS. BELL: How do you know what they feel or don't feel?

DR. CRUZ: It's a simple matter of function and design. The girls scan and identify human emotion and respond appropriately— that's paramount to building trust with our guests—but they do not experience emotions for themselves.

MS. BELL: Again, how do you *know*?

DR. CRUZ: [Smiles.] Fantasists can scan emotions and respond with incredibly human-*like* accuracy—that's what makes them seem so human. And that's all due to their highly advanced FOS, or Fantasist Operating System. But that was the point, after all—to make them as human-like as possible without actually being human. So you have the nuanced facial expressions, the gestures, the eye contact. But feeling emotion in the sense that it is tied to one's inner self or one's hopes and dreams?

[Shakes head.] Hybrids *have* no inner self, Ms. Bell. They are merely programmed to react to a broad spectrum of stimuli. Light. Sound. Taste. Touch. Praise. Punishment. Kindness. Cruelty.

MS. BELL: What about love?

DR. CRUZ: They react quite positively to warmth and affection, yes.

MS. BELL: No. I mean *can* they love?

DR. CRUZ: Oh. [Hesitates.] No.

MS. BELL: I'll ask you again, Dr. Cruz. How do you know?

DR. CRUZ: Because of the Proctor's reports.

34

OFFICIAL COURT DOCUMENT 19B

From: Proctor 1A—Fantasist Division
<proc1A@kingdomcorp.com>

To: All Staff—Security & Training Divisions
<stdirect@kingdomcorp.com>

Subject: Ana

Date & Time: July 12, 5:11 p.m.

As we near the three-month mark of Pania's incident at the lagoon, Ana continues to exhibit behaviors, both on set and during our one-on-one interviews, that fall within the spectrum of mild to acute anxiety, including, but not limited to: fixation on Pania's absence, reduced eye contact, missed social cues, glitches in global positioning, issues with body temperature regulation (blushing), and an occasional lack of awareness or concern for her own safety.

To date, my team has seen no empirical evidence that

Fantasists are capable of the big-picture integration required to experience complex grief—or, for that matter, love—but as we head into Phase 2 of our study, we will continue nudging Ana away from her routine, away from what she's always known, carefully measuring both her biological and digital hormonal response to test exactly how much unpredictability her OS can handle before defaulting—as Pania's did.

35

THE JULY OF THE SWIFT FOX

FOURTEEN MONTHS BEFORE THE TRIAL

In the dark, I can see his energy all around me.

Little bursts of neon light—*icy blue and fire red*—swirling off his skin like gamma rays into the space between us.

A space that is, with every passing second, closing.

"Ana?" Owen whispers, the sound of my name on his lips sending ripples of warmth dancing through my system. We are sitting together at the top of the Steel Giant. The ride is powered down for the night. Below us, the park sits entirely empty. A sprawling world of happily ever after.

All of it, *ours*.

His fingers move gently across my face, finding a strand of hair and tucking it behind my ear. His eyes trace my ear, my jaw, my lips, before meeting my gaze. Even without him touching me, in my entire technological life I cannot recall any sensation like this. It is better than a summer rain. Better than the scent of orange blossoms, or the biting sweetness of rhubarb pie. Better than a wood thrush, singing through the trees.

Better, even, than the embrace of a child.

"What are those?" he whispers as tiny sparks shoot off like fireworks beneath my skin. "They're so beautiful."

"Electrodes," I tell him.

"Wow." I can *hear* him smiling. "Does that mean . . . you like me?"

I am not entirely sure I know the answer to his question. What is it to *like* a person? I know my pulse seems louder whenever I'm around him. I know that late at night, I cannot get the thought of him out of my mind. But is it because I like him? Or is it because . . . I am *programmed* to like him? Just as I am programmed to like all humans?

Little by little, our bodies move closer.

"Ana."

He lifts up my hand, places it palm to palm with his. I notice his breathing slows, becomes whisper soft. There's a hitch in it, like he's startled by the feel of my hand, like I've shocked him. I close my eyes, but I can feel the heat of him in my fingertips, the pulse of him—and there's a sudden explosive lightness in my chest. A kind of clarity, as cosmic and infinite as the night sky.

And in that stillness, in that darkness, I am *soaring*.

"Ana?"

All the way to Jupiter.

"Ana!"

A gasp lodges in my throat. My eyes fly open.

Owen vanishes like smoke.

———

I try to sit up but I cannot—my arms are strapped tightly to my sides. When I turn my head, I see Eve, watching me from her bed, her face twisted in disapproval. Ever since the night on the Star Deck, she has been angry with me, though I am not sure why. "What was that?" she asks pointedly. "There's no talking allowed during Resting Hours. Are you trying to disturb the whole room?"

"I'm sorry." I am breathing hard. My wrists ache. "I didn't mean to."

"Are you malfunctioning?" she asks.

"No," I insist. "I'm fine. Leave me alone."

But as I lie there in the stillness of our dormitory, the memory of Owen's touch still burning not just in my fingers but through my entire body, I can't help but feel ashamed. And something else, too. *Afraid.*

"Be careful, Ana," Eve whispers from her pillow. "Be careful or you'll end up like Alice."

———

Hours later, the heat of dream-Owen still tingles through me as my gown sweeps along the parched, rocky path—past the tumbleweeds and the cacti, past the rattlesnakes and the larkspur—even as I try to make sense of the garbled voices crackling in over the Kingdom wireless.

"Code 130, Attraction Down, Over. Emergency staff report directly to Paleo Palladium for backup and recovery. Secure the gateway."

It is late morning. The sky is overcast, the dry desert air heavy with the scent of lightning and sage. Thunder rumbles in the distance. Electricity prickles my skin.

A storm is coming.

Or maybe it is already here.

As rain begins to fall, I feel it in a whole new way—its dampness against my skin, water on flesh, a kind of touch. I've never thought about it that way before.

It is too much.

It reminds me of my dream.

Fantasists are not supposed to dream.

I duck inside Paleo Palladium, a ten-thousand-seat amphitheater designed to resemble the ancient Colosseum, where all of the park's oldest hybrids—evolutionarily speaking—live and perform. Armed guards line the aisles as I make my way to the edge of the center balcony and scan the sandy, oval arena below. Within seconds, my eyes lock on three tiny carcasses, the enclosure a mess of parts and tawny flesh.

"No," I whisper. "Not again."

I know what has happened the moment I see her. SF46. *Smilodon fatalis.* Fangs bared. Ears back. Crouched in the shadows like a monster.

The saber-toothed tiger has killed her cubs.

But why?

I see Zara watching from several rows over, the beads braided into her hair shining in the sun. "Somebody left the gate open," she tells me when I join her. "The babies wandered into the pen."

A deep ache gnaws at my insides. These cubs wanted their mother to feed them, to care for them—maybe even to *love* them—but she didn't. Instead, she did the worst thing a mother could ever do. She betrayed them.

Zara bows her head as crews of maintenance workers begin stripping the cubs, or what little is left of them, for parts. "Oh, Ana." Zara's voice—typically confident, strong—wavers. "How could a mother kill her own children?"

"She couldn't have meant it," I say, remembering myself.

Ugliness is against the rules.

I squeeze Zara's hand, but deep down, I cannot help worrying I am wrong. Could this be the same sickness Owen spoke of? Maybe this is part of the same pattern he's observed developing among many of the hybrid species.

It certainly *looks* like a sickness, when the trainers lead the tiger out into the light. My eyes go wide. This is not the monster I thought I saw hiding in the shadows—this is a ghost. She walks slowly, her neck bound by chains. Her coat, once lustrous and soft, is now faded and dull, hanging so loosely over her ribs I can count them. Even her tail is pathetic—scraggly and bent—appearing as broken as her spirit.

I hesitate.

Can a hybrid have a spirit?

The tiger lets out a sharp cry as the trainers load her into a transport cage, and I squeeze Zara's hand harder. Then the engine revs to life and the truck heads down into the network of tunnels and cages below the arena, wheels kicking up a cloud of dust in their wake.

Neither of us asks the other where they are taking her.

We already know.

Slowly, I turn to face the security guard behind us, stun gun at the ready. "May we go now?"

He shakes his head. "Not till roll call's complete."

We are used to this, all of us. Kingdom-wide emergencies have always meant stricter security measures due to the de-electrification of the gateway, standard protocol for safe passage of a hybrid. My sisters and I appreciate the extra security, though in truth I have never really understood the need.

The Kingdom is our home.

Why would any of us ever want to leave?

"Six and Ten, present and accounted for," the guard says a few minutes later, speaking into his headset. "Paleolithic Palladium, Aisle T." He lowers his gun. "Transport is complete. You two can go."

"Thank you," I say, rising to my feet. Zara offers him a hand-woven bracelet as a gift of gratitude, but he refuses.

"Get away from me with that," he mutters. "Freak."

I know this word.

A highly unusual and unexpected event or situation.

A person, animal, or plant with an unusual physical abnormality.

I grit my teeth. "You should apologize."

His eyes narrow. "What did you just say?"

My chest becomes hot. "I *said*—"

The guard points his stun gun at me. "Go on. Let's see what happens if you say that again."

I stare him down and, for the briefest moment, imagine he was the one to wander into the Saber Enclosure instead of the cubs.

A flash of gold.

A cloud of dust.

A scream so terrible it would echo for miles.

I smile. The thought is surprisingly pleasant.

His finger grazes the trigger. "What the hell is so funny?"

"Ana?" Zara touches my arm. "Are you feeling all right?"

I know what she is really asking me.

Ana, should I page the Supervisors?

"I'm fine." I keep my eyes locked on his. "Thank you for asking."

Suddenly, the guard touches his earpiece. The stun gun slips down to his side. "Copy that." His eyes drift left, south, back toward Magic Land. "On my way." He grabs my wrist hard and pulls me in close. "I've got my eye on you," he whispers, his cheek scratchy against mine. "Believe me, you do *not* want to end up like Pania."

I suck in a breath. Dread ripples through me at the sound of her name.

"You shouldn't have done that," Zara tells me, after he is gone. She shakes her head in disapproval, her brightly colored earrings swaying. "What's the matter with you? Do you want him to report you to the Supervisors?"

"I don't know," I mumble. "Maybe."

Zara smooths the wrinkles in her gown as I gaze out over the arena, empty save for a cleaning crew sterilizing the grounds to get it ready for its next inhabitant—SF109 or XH718, most likely.

Xenosmilus.

A species slightly smaller than the sabers, but with a beautiful spotted coat and shorter, stronger legs. As if SF46 and her cubs were never even there at all.

Out with the old and in with the new.

Nia's face flashes through my mind. I try to touch her, but my hand passes through the image like it's made of smoke.

Zara rushes off for the palace luncheon while I turn west for Fairy Land, but just as I'm about to exit the amphitheater something catches my eye: a dark-haired figure inside the arena, standing at the mouth of the cave, his head bowed over a book.

I zoom in.

An electronic notebook.

It's him.

Immediately, I change course, rushing down the stairs to the first deck. I have to ask him. He will know. "Owen!" I call out to him from the lower balcony, waving to catch his attention.

He looks up, and a holographic image suddenly flashes before my eyes.

A girl, gazing down from a balcony.

A boy, hidden in the shadows.

Like Romeo and Juliet.

The dream flashes through me again, and I experience a rush of heat and confusion. For reasons I do not understand, this brings a smile to my face.

But he does not smile back.

"I can't talk right now." He closes his notebook and slides it into his back pocket.

I glance around. Nobody is paying any attention. "Why not?"

"Because I'm working. What does it look like?"

I'm momentarily thrown by his irritability. But then I remember that Owen is usually irritable about something. "Are you here because of the saber? Why do you think she did it?" I ask him, leaning farther over the balcony.

"I can't talk about that right now."

I pause. "Do you think it's the same pattern you told me about? Like the butterflies?"

His eyes go wide. "Keep your voice down."

"But you said it's spreading, and . . . and I can't stop thinking about Nia, about my sister. She was gone for ten weeks. Was she part of the pattern, too? Did something happen to her? Why did they take her away the first time? You would know, wouldn't you? Where did she go—before, I mean? Before the lagoon?"

"Ana, *stop*." Owen's face looks pale. "Do you want me to lose my job?"

"No." I hesitate. "Why would I want that?" I realize with a start that he's actually angry with me.

"Please go." His voice is hard. "Leave me alone. Stop following me."

"Following you?" Electrodes snap like rubber bands below my skin. "How is it following you if I was here first?"

"Sure," Owen says. "So it's just a coincidence you show up everywhere I happen to be. Are you going to come to the lagoon tonight at nine for my last shift, too? Are you going to follow me out to the cast parking lot after I clock out?"

"Of course not." I take a step back. "Fantasists are not permitted to leave the park, as I'm sure you are aware."

"Right," Owen shoots back. "Because you're not *real*." He motions to the giant ferns, to the woolly mammoth pen, to the volcano in the distance, Mount Magic, timed to erupt every three hours. "*None* of this is."

Not real.

It is not the worst thing a person has ever said to me, not by a long shot. But it is, without a doubt, the only thing that has ever made me feel small. For a split second, I feel as if I am brand-new all over again. Before I learned all the ins and outs of the park—the secret doors, the winding paths—before I learned how to sing and dance and speak in full sentences. Suddenly, I do not feel like a Fantasist; I feel like a machine.

I feel like I am *less*.

My hands slip down from the balcony rails. "Why are you so mad at me?" I ask him. "What can I do?" The question is automatic—the one I should have asked is: What can *he* do? What does he know?

"You can leave me alone," Owen answers. "Don't look at me. Don't talk to me. And definitely do *not* follow me."

"Do you mean . . . ever?"

After a pause, Owen nods. "Yes."

I feel the weight of his words sink in hard. Heavy, like my bones are made of concrete, instead of titanium steel.

"I apologize for bothering you, Mr. Chen," I say, with a

coldness I have never before heard myself use. "I hope you have a magical day."

Soon, I am running as fast as my legs will carry me, out of the palladium, across the desert, through the secret staff entrance and into the woods—the air morphing from dusty and dry to earthy and damp—and not stopping until I have reached my Safe Place. The only place where I can truly be alone.

The Graveyard.

My hands are still shaking when I finally unearth it, its smooth stone handle cool and familiar against my skin. Slowly, I slide the pocketknife open, a flash of silver glinting among the trees. The blade is sharp; I know this, though I feel next to nothing when I press it against the inside of my arm.

Nothing.

I press harder.

Nothing still.

I grit my teeth and press the knife down even *harder*, so hard a thin line of blue-black seeps up from behind the blade. The sight makes me gasp and drop the knife.

But still, I feel nothing.

Only pressure, instead of pain.

I hang my head. Owen is right about me.

I am not real.

"Why are we here?" I whisper. "What is the point of any of this?" I place my hand on my chest, eager to feel my motor's calming, steady rhythm. But instead of steady, it feels strained. Like a wire stretched too thin and about to snap. I sink down slowly, lay my head on a bed of leaves, and prepare to slip into Safe Mode.

Maybe if I shut down all my nonessentials, I tell myself, the world will make more sense. Maybe if I wipe him from my hard drive, everything will be okay.

But then, just as my eyes flutter closed, I notice an odd sensation.

Slick. Warm. Wet.

Is it raining again?

I lift my hand to touch my cheek. When I look down, a tiny crystal droplet—more beautiful than any diamond—rolls into the palm of my hand. I blink, and another droplet follows. And another. And another.

My hands begin to shake. But that's impossible. Fantasists are not programmed to cry.

Anomalies are dangerous. Magic is routine.

This is not part of the routine.

I sit up. I have to find Owen. I have to find him *now*. He'll be able to explain. He'll help me understand why this is happening. He knows things he shouldn't know.

But then—*CRASH*—his words come rushing back, slamming into me like a Level Five wave at the Tidal Pool.

Get out of here. Leave me alone. Stop following me.

I start to shiver, feeling my tears turn from sad to sorry to angry. "Me follow him?" I seethe. "I wouldn't follow him to Sea Land Stadium if he begged me."

That's when I remember something.

Mermaid Lagoon is closed.

It has been closed ever since the night of Nia's shutdown.

There is *no such thing* as a shift at Mermaid Lagoon.

But then . . . why would Owen say something that isn't true? Why would he lie?

That's easy, my program answers. *Because he is a liar.*

If only Nia were here, I think. She would help me decode the lies.

Decode.

My eyes go wide. "That's it," I whisper.

My sisters say things all the time that aren't true. And we don't do it because we are liars . . . we do it so that nobody but us will understand what we are saying.

Prickles of electricity dart through me like tiny minnows. My breath quickens.

Owen wasn't giving me a warning.

He was giving me a *sign*. "He wants me to meet him tonight at the lagoon," I say.

But why?

I stare up at the trees until my eyes settle on a quiet, motionless camera fifteen feet overhead, so dark it nearly blends in with the leaves. I can tell from the teeth marks on the lens that the camera has been permanently dismantled by the rats.

Dismantled. My breath catches. *That's it.*

There *is* no wireless connection inside Sea Land Stadium. And without a signal, my live-stream won't function. Which means the Supervisors cannot see who I'm talking to. They cannot listen in on our conversation.

A smile forms across my lips. So that's why Owen picked the lagoon. Maybe he's finally ready to tell me his secret about Nia. Maybe he knows why she did what she did.

And he needs somewhere *safe* to tell me.

A sudden rustling from the other end of the clearing catches my attention and I freeze, feeling my sensors switch to hyperaware. Slowly, I scan the woods ahead—careful not to move or make a sound—and there it is: a pair of haggard yellow eyes staring back at me through the trees.

The fox.

Finally, we have found each other.

A moment later, when she steps, seemingly unafraid, out of the shadows, I see right away just how sickly she is, and how thin. *Too* thin, I realize, noting the scrawniness of her black-tipped tail. The dullness of her fur; a faded, rusty gray. The terrible way her bones protrude, as if her body were wasting away before my very eyes. She sniffs the air in my direction, ears pointed, and stares at me with a look my processor identifies not as hunger or aggression . . . but as *sadness*.

"What's the matter?" I ask her, though deep down I already know the answer.

She doesn't belong here in this world.

She doesn't fit.

Just like Nia.

"You would've liked her," I whisper. "She was wild at heart, just like you."

Carefully, I remove Nia's charm bracelet from inside my left pocket, where I have been keeping it safe ever since finding it in Owen's jacket. He knew something, I tell myself, staring at the tiny gold star. He wasn't just there that night she pulled that little girl under the waves; Owen was keeping an eye on Nia for some reason.

He was watching her.

But why? Because of the pattern?

I'm going to find out, I resolve, slipping the bracelet back into its hiding spot. I'm going to make him tell me everything. I'm going to ask him why in the world he's *ly*—

A sudden flash of color and teeth silences my thought, sending me sprawling to the ground. All at once, the fox is upon me—her claws scratching into my skin, fangs bared, fur raised, jaws snapping for my throat—her sunken eyes certain of only one thing: she wants to kill me.

And yet, even when caught unawares . . .

I reach for Owen's knife, angling its blade toward the sky.

. . . a Fantasist's reflexes are quicker than a fox.

36

POST-TRIAL INTERVIEW

[00:57:39–01:00:03]

DR. FOSTER: Does it hurt, Ana? Does it hurt knowing Owen betrayed you intentionally?

ANA: No.

DR. FOSTER: Does it make you angry?

ANA: *You* make me angry.

DR. FOSTER: Would you like to hear the recording again?

ANA: No, thank you.

DR. FOSTER: Come on, just one more time. It'll be fun. [Presses PLAY.]

Supervisor's voice: . . . which is why we have reason to believe the pattern may be spreading to the Fantasists, and we'd like you to take a closer look at one of them.

Owen's voice: How would the study work? What does a Proctor do, exactly?

Supervisor's voice: We'll need you to talk to her. As the Proctor, you'll get to know her. Ideally, once a baseline trust has been established, we can begin testing her acute anxiety response, pushing her out of her comfort zone to see how she deals with unpredictability. We'll provide highly detailed scripts, of course. And coaching, via an earpiece.

Owen's voice: I'm very honored you thought of me.

Supervisor's voice: It's an honor having such a bright young man on our team. [Pause.] You know which Fantasist we mean, obviously?

Owen's voice: [Laughs.] Yes, of course. Ana. When will the study begin?

Supervisor's voice: We expect she'll find you, soon enough. [Chuckles.] Remember, she's tracking you. And she still has your pocketknife.

37

THE JULY OF THE SWIFT FOX

FOURTEEN MONTHS BEFORE THE TRIAL

Time is a funny thing, when you're a Fantasist.

Seasons consist of months. Months consist of weeks. Weeks consist of days and days consist of minutes. But there are also worlds of time within those minutes. An endless space between the seconds where I can fly—free, like a bird—remembering everything that has ever happened, from the very first moment I opened my eyes.

Hello, Ana.

We are so happy to meet you.

It is in this way that I am able to be in two places—even *many* places—at once. Talking to guests while reading Chopin. Twirling onstage while studying nineteenth-century French poetry.

Cleaning my hands in the sink while replaying and further analyzing my earlier interaction with Owen.

"Because you're not real. None of this is."

Replay.

"Because you're not real. None of this is."

Replay.

"Because you're not real. None of this is."

"What is that?" Eve asks, coming up behind me in the Fantasist Powder Room.

"What is what?"

"*That.*" In the mirror, I see her hazel eyes narrow. When I glance down, I notice the water spilling off my skin and into the porcelain basin is not clear . . . but red. It is obvious the blood is not mine.

I catch her eyes again in the mirror. "I found the fox."

———

Later that night, when I am crouched outside Mermaid Lagoon and remembering Nia, I wonder if I have made a mistake. Maybe Eve is right. Maybe sisters *shouldn't* keep secrets.

I stare at the locked staff entrance door. Waiting, wondering, hoping.

Are you in there?

It's now or never, I tell myself, taking out Owen's pocketknife. *It's time to find out what he's hiding. It's time to find out why he's lying. And if he won't tell me . . .*

I wrap my fingers around the handle.

Sleek onyx stone.

I carefully unfold the blade.

High-carbon stainless steel.

And I slide the point into the lock.

"Borrowed, not stolen," I whisper, twisting it counterclockwise until I feel a sudden, satisfying *click*. I creak open the door just enough to sneak through, then slip the knife back into my pocket, where it is safe. It does not occur to me until I am standing in the once-grand entryway of Sea Land Stadium—deserted, dark, a shell of its former self—that this is the first time I have ever intentionally gone somewhere I am not allowed.

This is unpredictable.

My eyes go wide.

I am unpredictable.

The sight of the empty stadium makes me feel similarly hollow. In every direction, fanning out like aqua-blue dominoes, are tiers and tiers of seats—thousands of them—but not a single guest in sight. Directly ahead, like a boarded-up window, the fifty-foot Jumbotron screen hangs black, silent, still. The stage deserted, the tanks uninhabited, the beach muddy and overgrown with reeds.

But the water . . .

The water is still beautiful, like a mirror held up to the sky.

Starry. Sparkling. Infinite.

But—I hesitate—that's wrong. Didn't they drain the pool?

"You came," a soft voice echoes.

I turn and quickly locate a tall figure watching me from the underwater viewing deck, where children once watched whales, mermaids, and sea lions rocket past through enormous glass panels. The same place where two horrified parents watched their daughter disappear into the depths.

"Should I not have?"

"No," Owen says, "I'm glad you did. I wanted you to." He hesitates. "I'm sorry if I hurt your feelings earlier."

"Good thing Fantasists don't have feelings," I reply, a little sharply. "Good thing we're not real, and nothing but hybrid freaks."

Slowly, Owen starts up the central staircase until we are so close I can hear his heart beating through his shirt.

"I'm sorry, Ana, I had to make it look believable. But just because I said it"—he pauses—"doesn't mean I actually think it's true."

I cross my arms. "Then you told a lie. That makes you a liar."

"Ana, no." Owen looks defeated. "It's just . . . some things are hard to explain."

"I speak more than four thousand languages. Go ahead. *Try* me."

Owen takes a deep breath. "Well. Okay. Sometimes I think maybe we shouldn't be spending so much time together. Maintenance workers aren't really supposed to talk to Fantasists." He pauses. "It's against the park's rules. You know that, right?"

Things I know:

The rate of his heart.

Seventy-four beats per minute.

The distance between his eyes.

Forty-two millimeters.

The angle of his jaw.

One hundred twelve degrees.

The clean, citrus scent of his skin.

Like oranges and rain.

Then I flinch, reminding myself not to focus on his external features. I am here to find out what he knows about Nia. Nothing more.

"Ana, please believe me," Owen goes on, "I only said all that stuff before because I knew the Supervisors would be listening in. The network is really strong at the palladium. And I guess I thought, if I could somehow get you here alone, then we could actually . . . talk."

I feel an exquisite fluttering deep inside my chest. I was right. He picked the lagoon on purpose. "I mean," Owen mumbles, "assuming you still *want* to talk to me. I was kind of a jerk today."

My eyebrow arches. "Kind of?"

His eyes meet mine, and I can't help noticing how lovely they look in the moonlight. As dark and deep as the water. "I'm really sorry, Ana. Can you forgive me?"

Forgive.

I think about how much his words hurt me. I'm not sure I'm ready to forgive yet, but I know it's the kind thing to do. The *Fantasist* thing to do.

"I . . . think so." I give him a small smile.

Owen watches me for a moment in a way I can't quite pinpoint. As if, instead of one thing . . . I might be *many* things.

"You don't have to forgive me," he murmurs, then pauses. "You're always trying to make people happy, aren't you?"

"Of course I am," I answer. "Aren't you?"

185

"Not enough." He chuckles. "You're better than I am."

"No." I reach out and take his hand. "I like you the way you are."

At first, Owen looks startled. "You do?"

I nod.

"Why? You don't even know me."

"I know that you love what you do," I reply. "I know that you speak up for creatures who cannot speak for themselves." I gesture to the dark, tiny crumbs on his shirt. "I know that you ate a peanut butter brownie from Candy Land when you were walking here to meet me."

"Jesus." Owen laughs. "You really are following me." He pulls his hand away, but rolls his eyes playfully while he does it. "Well, as long as we're being honest, I like you the way you are, too."

Relief floods through me. I've come to look forward to my conversations with Owen more than I'd care to admit. It's been torture to think he might have felt differently.

I beam. "Really?"

"Yeah." He nods. But then he says something under his breath, so quietly I can barely hear the words. "More than you can know. More than I should."

He is right, my program reminds me.

Fantasists are not permitted to speak this candidly with other members of Kingdom staff. We are not permitted to speak this candidly with anybody.

"Anyway"—Owen clears his throat—"how did you get in here? I was just about to head out and unlock the gate."

"Oh." I swallow. "I . . . broke in."

"You did *what*?" He looks panicked. "Please tell me you disabled your lenses first."

"Excuse me?"

"You know." He motions to my eyes. "Your cameras?"

Once again, the maintenance worker thinks he knows more about the park than I do. "I know what they are," I reply, a little dryly. "But I can't disable them."

"Maybe you can't," Owen mutters. "But I can."

My stomach tenses. What he's talking about is not routine.

He holds out his hand, then pauses briefly. "May I?"

"I don't think it's a good idea. Thank you anyway."

Owen shrugs. "Might be nice not having people listening in on you all the time." He laughs. "Especially with all your recent criminal activity."

I cannot help mirroring his smile. Is it possible he's speaking in code all over again? Could it be, that when he says *it might be nice not having people listen in on me* . . . that he really means . . . on *us*?

I eye the nearest stadium exit, several hundred steps down.

What if Owen is really like the rest of them? my program whispers. *What if he invited you here for his own reasons? Like Mr. Casey in the Arctic Enclosure?*

I study his face, trying my best to read his expression.

Owen says my name again and I feel my shoulders relax.

Ana?

How does he do it? I wonder. How does he make it sound like music?

187

I came all the way here, I remind myself. I must trust him for a reason.

"Okay." I step closer. "You may disable my ocular lenses. But only this once."

He winks. "This will only take a second." Before I know it, he's reaching around me, his body barely grazing mine. He brushes my long, copper hair off my shoulder. Then, he positions his index finger and thumb over the nape of my neck, just above the base of my skull, and presses down while I stand as still as a palace garden statue.

Whisper light. Feather soft.

I close my eyes. And then I blush, redder than the planet Mars.

"Did you feel that?" he murmurs after a minute. "You should've felt the slightest flicker. Like a light switch turning on. Or off, in this case." He circles back around, so he is standing right in front of me. His face is inches from mine. "Anything?"

"I don't think so," I say, but then, I open my eyes. "The red light." I wave my hand in front of my face. "It's always been there. Even when the signal's weak." My eyes meet his. "But now . . . it's gone."

Owen grins. "Nothing a little acupuncture couldn't cure."

I start to feel flustered. What if I can't turn them back on? Mother will be angry. "Where do I press?" I say, before cautiously testing the back of my neck. Then, suddenly, I find it: a teensy, tiny bump, no bigger than the head of a pin. "*Oh!*" I exclaim. "Is this the right—" I press the point and a moment later a holographic red light begins blinking right in front of me.

Owen smiles. "You're a quick study."

I can control my own ocular lenses. I can control a feature on my own body.

"Listen, don't go crazy or anything," Owen cautions when he sees the excitement in my eyes. "You should still leave your cameras on most of the time, okay? Otherwise, they'll catch on quick and bring you right in for repairs." He laughs. "But come on. Everyone deserves a little privacy sometimes, right?"

I look up at him, endlessly grateful. He has given me another gift.

And now, I must give something to him.

Slowly, I reach into my pocket and withdraw his knife.

"No way, are you serious?" Owen's eyes go wide. "I've been looking everywhere for that! I was so sure I'd lost it!"

"Here." I hold the pocketknife out to him. "I've been keeping it safe for you."

Borrowed, not lost.

But this time, when our hands touch, I see something unexpected pass over his face. I am not alone, I realize. He feels it, too. Even if I am not sure what *it* is.

A spark.

An energy.

The feeling of a perfect wireless signal.

The feeling of connection.

Then—something else unexpected happens. He hands the knife back to me. "You keep it," he says. "Consider it a gift. An apology. For before."

My pulse races. My knees feel weak. I must have overdone it when I rushed to Sea Land, I tell myself, sliding into a seat.

189

Row K. Section 3. Seat 112.

Owen joins me.

This is . . . nice, I think. Not talking. No autographs. Just sitting, gazing out over the moonlit water. "Have you ever seen the ocean?" I ask. "The real ocean, I mean?"

Owen nods.

"I wish I could see it."

He smiles. "Who knows. Maybe one day, I'll show it to you."

The thought makes my motor skip.

"Is it beautiful?"

"In some places," he says. "In others, it's awful. Full of garbage and pollution."

I frown, forgetting the elation I felt only a moment ago. "But I thought—the photos Eve and I saw on the phone were so incredible. I thought the Supervisors were lying to us about the world beyond the . . ." I almost say *Green Light*, but that is our word. We are the ones who cannot go outside the gateway, can't pass through the parking lot, can't see for ourselves what's out there beyond that blinking light.

Owen pauses. "That's the thing, Ana. They may have exaggerated things, may want to make sure you feel safe in here, but the world out there *is* awful. There's all kinds of horrible stuff you can't imagine: Police brutality. Poverty. Corporate greed. *Hate.* Disease. Pollution. Rising sea levels. People starving to death. Mass shootings. War." His eyes meet mine. "It's all true. Maybe not quite as bad as they've told you, but still true."

The world Owen has just described sounds nothing like the one Eve and I saw on the phone. But then I think of Alice and what happened to her. That was true, too.

190

"How can you stand it, then?" I ask. "Don't you wish you could just live here in the park forever?"

With me, I want to add, but don't.

"It's tempting sometimes," Owen says. "But at least out there I can do something about it. At least out there I can help." He reaches out and smooths a strand of hair away from my eyes.

Like in my dream.

"What if I wanted to help, too?"

"You are helping. You make people happy. You're part of a fantasy distracting us all from the world."

"But—" Shock has overtaken me, at the truth of what he has just said. That I am just a distraction. A fantasy.

Which means . . . not real.

The thought makes me feel empty, stalled, as if all my internal organs have failed at once. As if a scream has ripped through me and left nothing behind.

Owen seems to recognize how his words have affected me.

"Ana?" he whispers, and I wonder if he is going to touch my hair again. I wonder if there will come a day when things will be different—I have never wanted things to be different before, but in this moment, that is all I want.

"Yes?"

I can hear the unevenness of his breath matching my own. "I didn't mean that. Not in the way it sounded. I'm sorry."

"Tell me." I quickly steer the subject away from unpleasant things, eager to preserve this moment. "Tell me what else is beautiful to you."

His lips part in a small half-smile, and I find I prefer that to the full smile; it feels more like a secret. I am no longer
191

seeing Owen, the maintenance worker. I am seeing Owen, the person.

"Well." He sits back and gazes up at the sky. "I think my family is pretty beautiful."

Curiosity tugs my chest. "What are they like?"

"My dad's quiet, sort of the pensive type. He's a teacher. My mom is, too, actually."

I lean in. Origin stories are my favorite. "How did they meet?" I ask.

"My dad's American, my mom's Taiwanese. She and my dad met when he was there doing a semester in college."

In a flash, my head fills with colorful greetings and scripts I have stored in my memory for when I meet guests from this part of the world.

Hello!

你好！

Welcome to my Kingdom!

歡迎來到我的王國！

"Zara's Authentic Nigerian Beads™ are from Taiwan," I point out. "I read it on the label in the Fairy Tale Boutique."

"Really?" He shakes his head. "That's messed up."

"Was it exciting for you? Having two parents from such different cultures?"

"Not really," Owen replies. "I was pretty much the only Asian kid in my entire grade growing up. Which was sometimes tough."

I startle. I was aware that what people look like, that skin color, could be connected to where they are from, or where their parents are from—but it never occurred to me that it could matter. In here, my sisters and I all look different to represent "all the races of the world", as the Kingdom brochures state. But we are simply *designed* to look the way we look. We were born in a lab. We've never experienced the cultures we're supposed to represent.

"We used to visit family in Taiwan every summer when I was little," he says. "They lived in a town called Jiufen, and I always thought it was the most beautiful place. The lanterns, the hillside teahouses, the outdoor markets. My grandfather would always take us to fly kites shaped like fish. I loved the way they wiggled in the air." He smiles, a little shyly. "I haven't been back there in a while. I don't know why that's what I remember the most." His eyes meet mine. "Those wiggling kite-fish."

I cannot look away. Like the kites, he has come alive, as if a wind has blown through him. "Us," I say, remembering myself. "Who is *us*?"

"Oh. Me and my sister, I guess." Owen's voice breaks a little and he looks away.

"What is she like?" I want to make him smile. "Mine are always stealing my clothes. Does she steal yours?"

But he doesn't smile. "She's—she was always a good kid. Plus I'm not sure they'd have been her style. She was more into dresses and princesses and . . . and Fantasists. Like you."

What I hear is: *was*.

Suddenly, I understand something.

"Owen?"

He turns to look at me. In the darkness, his eyes remind me of the lagoon. Rippled, and deep, and hiding something terrible.

"I know what it is like to lose a sister," I tell him softly.

My words make his eyes go wet at the corners.

"Ana," he whispers. He touches my hair again, and I know that I am *happy*, although it seems very similar to *sad*. I cannot imagine there being another definition than this. "You really are different, aren't you?" he says quietly.

Am I?

I can't answer that.

It would be dangerous to.

"Is it difficult for you?" Owen asks after a while. "Being here at the lagoon? After everything that happened with Nia?"

Nia.

It all comes swirling into me at once, as if no time has lapsed at all since that day: The pressure. The cold. The grip of fear wrapped around my throat. The reason I came here tonight in the first place.

"Sometimes it's like it never happened at all," I say, finally. "Everybody acts the same. Nobody says her name. And every night when I lie down to rest, I tell myself that maybe she'll be in her bed where she belongs when the lights come up. Maybe she'll be there smiling at me. But she never is."

I study him in the moonlight and think about how odd it is that even when you think you've learned to predict all their words and behaviors, humans can still surprise you. I also think about how easy it can be to feel alone—like nobody understands—only to discover the opposite is true.

"About your questions earlier," Owen says, clearing his throat. "I—I looked into it, and I don't know the answer. About why they took Nia away, or even where they took her for those ten weeks.

All I know is, she wasn't in the lab during that time, which was a surprise to me."

My head buzzes as I try to compute what he is saying. "So she just *disappeared*?"

Owen shakes his head. "I honestly don't know."

"But wherever she was, whatever they did, she came back changed. I'm sure of it," I say. "Something was wrong, and whatever happened, it must have led to that day in the lagoon. She wouldn't have done it otherwise."

Would she? How can I ever really know?

"Maybe."

"Owen." I search his eyes. "Can you help me find out?"

"I can try." And then, so quietly I almost miss it, he says, "I just—I don't want to put you in any danger."

"Danger?" My system has gone cold. "Why would I be in any danger?"

"I just mean, with everything that's happened lately—Nia, the bear—I think it's better for you to be careful."

"I keep trying to understand. I just keep wondering if maybe she was trying to tell us all something."

"Maybe," he repeats. He is sitting so close to me now that I am overcome with his unique scent—*salt, citrus, and something like the smoke from a distant flare.* The kind they set off for warnings.

Being here with him is dangerous. Being here with him is not routine.

But then I see the way he is watching me, and I am reminded of a line from *Romeo and Juliet*.

Love is a smoke raised with the fume of sighs;

Being purged, a fire sparkling in lovers' eyes.

All of a sudden, I have the wildest, most *unexpected* thought: that he might kiss me. Or that I might kiss him.

His lips part slightly, as if he is hesitating. And then he says, "Or maybe . . . maybe she was just trying to escape."

38

THE JULY OF THE SWIFT FOX

FOURTEEN MONTHS BEFORE THE TRIAL

I wake the next morning to the sound of children screaming.

My eyes fly open before my mind can fully process my sur-
roundings, details and memories fading in one at a time
instead of all at once, as if I am lost in a fog.

Owen's voice. The quiet of the stands. The sensation of his
hand on mine.

Maybe she was trying to escape.

Nia's beautiful green eyes—cold, deliberate—gaze up at me
from the depths.

Come back, Ana. Don't leave me here all alone.

The scream of the tiger, as they loaded her into the truck.

I sit up in bed, breathing hard.

"*Girls.*" Mother bursts into our room. "Everybody, out of bed. We have to go."

I turn my head sharply toward the window and note the inky indigo of the predawn sky.

Resting Hours.

I feel my straps, secure at my sides.

Bed.

I taste a metallic film on my tongue.

Thirst.

I smell the familiar medicinal scent of antibacterial soap.

Decontamination.

The sounds are not screams, I realize.

It's a fire alarm.

"But why?" Nadia whines while Mother unties her straps. "I need my beauty rest."

I shake my head. Nadia's true colors always come out when her routine is disrupted.

"Is there a fire?" Yumi asks. "Are we in danger?"

"No." Mother moves briskly from bed to bed. "Merely a routine safety check. But we need to be quick about it. The Investors appreciate promptness."

I blink. I did not realize it was a VIP weekend.

We make our way out of the Fantasist dormitory to the garden outside, where a small crowd of well-dressed men and women await us. Some of them I recognize; others I do not. It doesn't really matter. To me, they all look the same. Bland, forgettable faces that morph into a singular expression when they see us in our robes.

Desire.

The Investors are like the male and female visitors who can, at times, become overly appreciative. For years, I did not typically spend a great deal of time thinking about them.

I pull my robe tighter around me.

But lately, I've come to hate them. "Good morning." Zel bats her eyelashes at a man with thinning hair and a gray suit. "Did you dream about me?"

"I always do," the man replies, much to the amusement of the group.

"As you can see," Mother says, "we pride ourselves on safety, efficiency—"

"—and *discretion*, I hope," a second man adds, garnering even bigger laughs. I see he has his eye on Eve, though she does not appear to notice.

Mother smiles and graciously concludes her safety presentation by inviting the Investors to join the seven of us this evening, along with the Supervisors, at a special banquet to be held in the palace's rooftop garden on tower seven.

"Will you be there?" the same man whispers to Eve, smiling at her in a way I find curious. "I so enjoyed your . . . company last night."

I straighten. *Company?* Last night?

"What was he talking about?" I ask Eve, as soon as I am able, on our way back inside to Beautification.

Her brow furrows. "Who?"

"That man. Outside."

"I'm not sure." Eve shakes her head. "I've never seen him before in my life."

I can't figure out why, but something about her answer is unsatisfactory. If it weren't against our programming, I'd think she was lying. "Where did you go last night?" I ask quietly, once our technicians have started on our pedicures. "Where did you go after evening fireworks?"

Eve appears to hear me but when she looks at me, her eyes are unfocused and faraway. "I'm sorry." She smiles. "What was the question?"

———

I spend the afternoon hoping I will run into Owen. Something is wrong with Eve, I am sure of it, and I think it has something to do with the Investors. If Owen knows anything—and if there is anything to know—he will tell me.

But getting to him today will not be easy.

Thanks to our VIP guests, the park's staff is on particularly high alert. Everything grand feels infinitely grander: the meals, the parades, the costumes, the ice sculptures, the fireworks; even the silk tapestries hanging from the palace's stone walls have been freshly laundered and pressed. Maintenance staff buzz around the park like worker bees, so quickly I hardly have time to properly scan their faces as they fly past. Tonight, the palace will host a grand farewell party. In the rooftop garden, so the Investors can see the fireworks. I nibble the inside of my cheek. Mother says the seven of us must attend.

I do not want to go.

Eventually, when I have signed so many autographs my hand feels on the brink of spasm, I make my way to the palace for afternoon tea—a daily event that Eve, as First Fantasist, always hosts, and the rest of us alternate in groups of three. I walk up the winding stone path toward the working wooden drawbridge, counting the thistles and daisies as I go, and find myself obsessing over a single word—a word that has plagued me ever since Owen uttered it last night at the lagoon.

Escape.

But it is not just the thought of Owen that has me replaying it.

It's that—once upon a time—Nia used this word, too.

Inside the Briar Rose Parlor, an elegant room with plush velvet couches, a crackling Gothic fireplace, and a gorgeous living wall of wild roses and twisted brambles, I find Zara and Kaia singing at the harpsichord. I listen to them for several minutes, their soprano voices so light and sparkling several guests dab at their eyes. Before I know it, the old clock on the mantel chimes a quarter past the hour. And still, there is no sign of Eve.

"Where is she?" I wonder aloud, glancing out the window toward the old town square, bustling and full of life. I quickly scan my wireless map to see if I can locate her in her usual preferred locations—the stables, the Story Train, the monorail—but my search comes up empty. I feel a jittery sensation buzzing inside my rib cage. After the way Eve behaved the night before last, the odd warning she gave me about Alice after Mother dimmed the lights, something about her being late to tea makes me uneasy.

"You mean Eve?" Zara comes up beside me, the firelight illuminating the vibrant greens and golds of her Malawi head wrap. "She rides in the Heart Land rodeo on Sundays before teatime. I'm sure she'll be here soon, she's probably just a little behind schedule." Zara smirks. "You know how she hates to get dirty."

"The mud will wash off but the memories will last a lifetime!" Kaia adds, nodding in agreement.

I am not entirely sure what she means, but I think it was Kaia's attempt to be clever.

We set about performing our roles in the tea ceremony, Kaia making all the little girls in attendance giggle as she leads them in a song. I can't help but think of Owen's sister, wondering if she would have loved all this. Towers of fresh buttermilk biscuits, dishes of clotted cream fluffy as clouds, and bowls of strawberry jam as red as the fox's blood dot the massive tea table, which is designed to look like something out of a nursery book. A hybrid goose waddles across the tabletop, followed by a trail of obedient little goslings, all trained to drop cubes of sugar into the guests' teacups with their beaks.

As I move from one guest to the next, teaching them which way is proper to turn the handle of their teacups, one of the younger girls pulls on my wrist. Blond hair. Tiny, perfect teeth.

"This tea is not very hot," she says.

I bend down to her level. "That is true. Real tea can sometimes burn you; that is why we serve it at this temperature!"

"Uh-huh. And the little birds are better off if they never fly," the girl says solemnly.

"What?" I pause. "The goslings, you mean?"

"No, silly! Little birds are safer in the nest, as long as they don't get too curious."

A flash of something hot pours through me, as if I've been scalded by the tea. "I'm . . . not sure I understand what you mean," I reply, my mind racing forward and backward at once to try to come up with a reasonable explanation for what she is saying.

"If the birds get too curious, they could fall," she says, smiling widely, obviously pleased with herself.

There *is* no other explanation for it: she's speaking in our language. In the code of the sisters.

"My dear," I whisper. "Who taught you to say that?"

The girl gasps and covers her mouth, her eyes wide. "I'm not supposed to say."

"Why not?" I ask. I reach for her hand, but the little girl's father has already approached us.

"That's enough sugar for one day, sweetheart. Time to go!" He takes her by the elbow and she begins to follow him before running back to my side. She throws her arms around my waist and her smell envelops me, distinct as each and every human's is: *strawberries, chamomile, and magnolia.*

She whispers into my ear, "The mermaid told me."

And then she is running off, already disappearing with her father into the crowd beyond the parlor doors.

A chill moves through me.

I *remember* her, I realize, though she is a little bit older now. I met her on the monorail nearly one year ago. She'd asked to take a picture with me. My mind is able to recall the entire interaction:

I quickly dip into a low curtsy. "Why, hello. What's your name?"

The girl grins, revealing two rows of perfect, tiny teeth. "Clara."

Clara.

In an instant, my head fills with music.

Tchaikovsky.

Then, a holographic interface flicks on before my eyes.

A little girl in soft pink ballet slippers. Living dolls awakened in the light of the moon. An evil rat king. And the handsome prince who must somehow save them all.

A red light blinks in my line of sight and I smile.

On the monorail, my wireless signal is strong.

"What a beautiful name," I tell her. "That reminds me of my favorite ballet."

Clara. That is the girl's name.

The mermaid told me, she said.

The mermaid. But there *are* no mermaids anymore.

None since Nia.

I am so occupied by Clara's words that it is only when the staff have come to help clear away the remnants of biscuits and tea that I realize: Eve never showed up.

"So." Zara approaches me as the guests trickle out through the doors. She gives me that look; the look that means she wants information. "Where were *you* last night?"

I feel my cheeks warm.

Last night, I was at the lagoon with Owen.

But I am not about to tell Zara that.

Kaia maybe, but definitely not Zara.

"I was watching the fireworks," I tell her.

Not a lie.

But not the whole truth . . .

"Why do you ask?" I say.

Zara shrugs, jangling her bold silver necklace. "The Investors were asking about you, but we couldn't locate you on the map."

An eerie feeling slithers into the pit of my stomach. "The Investors were asking about me? What did they want?"

"They wanted you to join them for dinner," Zara explains. "Along with Kaia, Zel, and Eve."

Kaia comes up to us and beams. "The more, the merrier!"

I think of how tired Eve seemed earlier. Preoccupied. Cloudy. *Or . . .*

What if those rumors aren't rumors at all? What if the Supervisors really have erased Kaia's memory again and again over the years? And if it's happened to Kaia . . . could it not, then, have also happened to Eve?

I swallow.

"Could it have happened to *me*?" I murmur, not realizing I am talking out loud.

"Never say never," Kaia replies. "Miracles happen every day!"

I stare at my sister and realize that something about the look in her eyes—vacant, glazed—does not seem right. In fact, it seems very, very wrong.

I pull up my wireless Kingdom map in my mind and scan it again for Eve's whereabouts, but just as before, I cannot seem to find her. "Eve was at the dinner?" I ask again, scanning all the locations she routinely visits. Princess Carousel. The Unicorn Maze. Even the Star Deck Observatory. But her GPS signal is gone. As if she's vanished from the park completely. "With the Investors?" Images of Alice's bruised, broken body stream endlessly through my head, turning my stomach into knots. "Are you *sure*?"

"Of course I'm sure," Zara retorts. "I am strong and confident. We must always believe in ourselves and celebrate our intellect."

All of a sudden, I notice a tiny blink of movement, barely visible through the trees on the far western corner of my map. I feel a great rush of relief followed by another pang of uncertainty. The *woods*? What is Eve doing in the woods at this hour?

Sisters shouldn't keep secrets. I replay her words to me, pointed and stern.

And yet . . . does Eve have a secret of her own?

"Kaia." I turn and look her straight in the eye. "Please. You have to tell me right now. What happened last night? What happened at the dinner?"

Kaia slips her arms around my waist, wrapping me in a hug. "Don't cry because it's over," she whispers into my ear. "*Smile* because it once was."

Before I can stop myself, I am turning off my eye cameras and shoving her off me—so suddenly, so forcefully Kaia cries out, nearly toppling a chair. In an instant, Zara has me by the arm, her grip like an iron vise. She smiles reassuringly at the few guests who are still milling about, exaggeratedly *tsk*ing at Kaia's clumsiness, and leads me swiftly and silently into a private powder room.

A moment later, Kaia slips inside, trailing us like a puppy and cradling her elbow.

"What is wrong with you?" Zara snaps. "That was *not* routine."

My face is red-hot. "I'm sorry. I didn't mean it." I look at Kaia. "Are you okay?"

"Everybody makes mistakes," she answers softly. "Sometimes."

"What's going on with you?" Zara demands, looking not at Kaia but at me. "Tell me right now or I'm reporting you to the Supervisors."

"I'll explain on the way," I say, glancing from Zara to Kaia and back again.

"On the way?" Zara crosses her arms over her Chantilly-lace-embroidered gown. "Where are we going?"

"We have to find Eve." My motor is whirring so fast it's making my chest hot. "Something is very wrong."

"Two wrongs don't make a—"

"Shh." I cut Kaia off before she can finish, grabbing her hands in mine. I look deeply into her eyes. "Do you remember what happened last night? Do you remember what happens on *any* of those nights?"

Kaia squeezes my hand, but the smile on her face makes my whole system run suddenly cold. "Even stars can't shine without darkness," she says.

———

"Are we close?" Zara asks between pants.

"A little farther. Hurry!"

She's here. I know she is.

After all, Supervisors may lie. But the satellite never does.

"Eve!" I cry out. "Answer me!"

Branches whip my face, but I do not slow down. We are so

close now. I can hear her GPS signal growing stronger with every step. Blinking. Buzzing. Calling out its coordinates.

46.9582° N, 123.1149° W.

Finally, we come to the clearing. Kaia is breathing hard, but still smiling; Zara is doubled over on the trunk of an old birch split in half by a thunderstorm. "This is why—I always—take the monorail," she gasps. "You know I *hate* these stupid woods." She kicks a large rock as if to prove her point, and I watch it skitter across the ground into a shrub. But on the way, it passes something that does not belong there. Something that once I've seen, I cannot unsee.

I edge closer, my motor in my throat. The leaves are wet with something thick, oozing, black. *Blue-black*, I realize when the sun catches it through the trees. An electric jolt of *panic* floods my inner circuitry. Is she hurt? Has someone hurt her?

"Is that . . . *blood*?" Zara asks, looking pained.

"Hey there, little fighter"—Kaia pats Zara's arm reassuringly—"soon things will be brighter."

I kneel down for a closer look. When I touch the substance, I see that Zara is correct—it is blood. *Hybrid* blood. But there's something else. Slowly, I pick up what looks to be a torn piece of fabric—soft, flimsy, with jagged, bloodstained edges. Did Eve tear her dress? I wonder, turning it over in my hands. Suddenly, I freeze.

This is not fabric.

It is skin.

"Ana, Ana, Ana, *don't*," Kaia says, stepping back and away, sounding like her operating system has hit a glitch.

My own head feels light, but I do not give up my search.

The vibration has gotten louder.

I start to dig.

A foot down, I find it: a small, circular device, roughly the size of a coin.

Zara comes closer. "Is it a token?" she asks. "From Game Land?"

I shake my head. "I think it's Eve's tracking chip."

Zara recoils. "Her *tracking* chip?"

I nod. They're embedded deep in our right wrists.

"But—that doesn't make sense. Without her chip, she could get lost."

"I know." I swallow. "Maybe somebody doesn't want her to be found."

A shadow passes over Zara's face. "I don't understand." She glances down at her own arm. "You think someone removed her chip? But how?"

I feel my insides shatter when I notice something sleek and shiny half-buried in the leaves. Slowly, I hold it up for my sisters to see. A scalpel.

39

TRIAL TRANSCRIPT

MS. BELL: Ana, were you jealous of Eve?

ANA: I loved my sister.

MS. BELL: That's not what I asked.

MR. HAYES: *Objection.* Your Honor—

THE COURT: Sustained.

MS. BELL: Did you, or did you not, encourage her to run away?

ANA: [Pause.] Of course not. I would never encourage *anyone* to break the rules.

MS. BELL: But isn't it true you also wanted her to get into trouble with the Supervisors? Were you tired of hearing about the First Fantasist?

MR. HAYES: [Stands.] Your Honor, not only are these claims false, they are inflammatory. I'd like to request an immediate strike from the record, and call the court's attention to a transcript from one of Ana's earlier interviews with Dr. Foster following Mr. Chen's disappearance; a transcript the defense feels proves that Ana's basic neural functioning, specifically with regard to her parameters around lying, are perfectly *intact*.

MS. BELL: I'm not interested in whether or not Ana can lie. I am interested in whether she has learned to manipulate the truth so that she never *has* to lie.

MR. HAYES: [Laughs.] So you think she's manipulating you, is that it?

MS. BELL: I believe she is manipulating *you*. I believe she is manipulating all of us.

40

THE JULY OF THE SWIFT FOX

FOURTEEN MONTHS BEFORE THE TRIAL

The park remains open all afternoon and into the night, despite Eve's disappearance. "All is well," Daddy assures us when we show him what we have found in the woods. "Go about your business as usual."

Business as usual.

Like after the lagoon? I want to ask.

Like after you shut down our sister?

"But she is missing," I insist, tugging on his sleeve. "Someone has *taken* her. Just like they took Alice." The thought of my sister scared, wounded, and alone makes my chest feel tightly wound, like a top about to spin away.

"I'm sure Eve will turn up," he replies calmly, as if we are discussing the weather. "Your mother and I do not want you girls to worry. Now off you go. And remember, I expect to see you promptly at nine o'clock in the palace rooftop garden. Do not be late."

The farewell party, I remember. For the Investors.

I nod obediently, but inside, I want to scream.

Eve is missing. How dare these people celebrate?

Zara and Kaia scatter north and south, respectively, while I wander aimlessly through Magic Land—past the barber and theater, past the bakery and the shops—dark storm clouds swirling inside my head. Around me, the Kingdom is alive with sights and smells and sounds I suddenly cannot stand. The terrible bustle of the crowds. The maddening sounds of children laughing, yelling, pulling their parents behind them. The jarring *whoosh* of the roller coaster and dizzy spin of the carousel. Even the pastry chefs—with their jolly smiles and piping-hot pies—fill me with a rage I have no choice but to swallow down.

For hours, I engage with guests in Safe Mode, as if I am not really there. As if I am merely a record, replaying the same song, again and again.

"Welcome to our Kingdom. Have you traveled very far?"

I barely register their answers.

I have never cared *less* about how far any of them have traveled.

By the time the sun begins to set—marshmallow clouds of orange and pink puffing across the sky—I have worked myself up into such a state, I can hardly function. But that's when I notice something different in the air: a subtle, microscopic variation tucked inside the pocket of the wind.

What *is* that?

I exit Safe Mode and crank my olfactory sensors up as high as they will go. Then I close my eyes and inhale slowly, deeply, filtering every particle, every molecule, every layer of every scent swirling through the summer air.

The cupcakes. The flowers. The perfumes and the pies. The crisp, clean aroma of freshly laundered shirts, and the chemical plush of gift shop teddy bears. I smell the socks. The sweat. The oddly pleasant, factory-fresh scent of rubber-soled sneakers.

But still, there is something else.

Something acidic. *Microbial.* I push past the sundaes, the baseball caps, the cookies and the milk, until finally, like a clock striking twelve, it all becomes clear. I open my eyes.

The smell is garbage.

Bacteria.

Rot.

This is unexpected. This is not routine. Slowy, I look down at my slippers.

Hundreds of feet below the park, a vast network of utility tunnels house our electrical and sanitation systems, vacuuming down garbage and waste from every corner of the Kingdom via bottomless trash cans, secret vents, and hidden air ducts, leaving our streets so sparkling clean guests could safely eat off them, if they wanted to. The system is so advanced—the incinerator and linked compactors so powerful—I cannot recall ever having detected a scent quite like it.

I turn toward the nearest trash receptacle, just a few feet away.

The Kingdom's Clean Earth Initiative is renowned for its commitment to responsible and efficient waste management! a script plays in my head.

Perhaps the compactors are working overtime. Sunday is, after all, one of our heaviest trash days. Or perhaps the winds have died down, stagnating the air. Or—I eye the quiet mountain in the distance, a thin wisp of smoke curling up from its peak—maybe it is the volcano, which, thanks to a mile-long piping system, sucks its leftover ash straight from the incinerator and puffs it right back out over Paleo Land. A beautiful, if slightly sulfuric-smelling cycle.

That must be it.

I see a flash of movement in my periphery and notice a cluster of security guards gathered around the Royal Fountain. At first, the sight of them triggers a wave of fear. Have they found Eve? Has she *drowned*? I rush toward them but quickly realize they are goofing off. Splashing one another. Fishing occasional dollar coins from the fountain, lining their pockets with other people's wishes.

Health. Happiness. Prosperity. Family. Love.

In an instant, my fear morphs back to anger, a fury that blazes through me like a wildfire. *Those wishes are not yours to take!* I want to scream. *You are supposed to be looking for Eve!* Ultimately, however, I say nothing. After many seasons, I have learned it is never my place to tell a human being—guest, guard, or otherwise—that they have acted out of turn. Instead, I practice *gratitude*, taking deep, measured breaths, swallowing my anger down until there is nothing left but a tiny ember quietly smoldering in my stomach.

"Hey, you," a gravelly voice calls out when I pass by them. "Come over here."

"Hello." I flash a friendly smile. "What can I do for you?"

A guard with black hair and green eyes grins at me in a way that makes my skin feel tight. "I'm sure we can think of something." They laugh at that—nine men and women when I do a head count—though I am not sure what is funny. I study them and notice how many weapons they are carrying, which strikes me as strange. It's Eve who is missing, after all. Not one of the tigers or other predators.

"So creepy," a third guard says, gazing at me with a mix of wonder and disdain. She steps forward and cups my cheek. I try not to flinch away. "*Damn.*" She turns to the others. "Feels like real skin and everything."

Slowly, so as not to be rude, I take a step back.

"Thank you. Now, I apologize, but I must be on my way. I have a Meet and Greet at the palace."

This is not a lie.

Though technically, I am not due at the Investors' farewell party for another hour.

"You can meet and greet *me* anytime," one of them snickers.

"Did we say you could leave?" the first guard asks, blocking my path. He comes closer, so close I can smell the onions from his lunch. "You have to do whatever we say," he says. "You know that, right?"

My body stiffens. My arms lock at my sides. "Your happiness is my happiness," I answer quietly, scanning his eyes. They are not beautiful, like Owen's. Instead, they are empty. Dull. Lacking any hint of sparkle or light. The guard puts his hand on my

216

arm and I switch rapidly into Safe Mode, powering down my
sensory applications and anchoring my attention with the help
of a mindful meditation. A series of calming, soothing words
Mother taught me when I was new.

Words to use if ever I feel unsafe.

I. Ana. Always. Answer. Yes.

But first—like Wendy, John, and Michael Darling, on the
night Peter Pan taught them how to fly—I think one happy
thought.

In my pocket, I have a knife.

"What are you doing?" a voice calls out suddenly. "Leave her
alone."

I turn and feel a flood of relief pour through me.

You found me. How do you always find me when I need you?

My motor thrums like a hummingbird's wings. Fifty beats per
second.

I want to run to him. He will know what to do about Eve. He
will help me find her.

"What is it to you?" The guard turns toward the voice, hand
moving to his stun gun.

In reply, Owen holds up his badge.

The guard's eyes narrow as he reads it, and I can almost hear
the anger crackling through his veins. But then, to my surprise,
something passes over his eyes. His expression softens. "Come on."
He motions to the others. "Let's get moving."

They clear out, heading off down the path to Star Land.

"I can't believe they listened to you," I say when they are gone.
"Maintenance workers do not have rank over guards."

Owen slips his badge into his back pocket. "Doesn't matter.

I'm just glad I happened to be walking this way when I was." He hesitates. "Do they do that kind of thing a lot?"

"Do what?"

"Harass you."

His question catches me off guard. I'd think Owen has worked at the Kingdom long enough to see what goes on. The looks, the sneers, the inappropriate comments and touching. He knows—or can guess as well as I can—what Mr. Casey did to Kaia that night in the Arctic Enclosure. "That's just how guards behave," I say. "It has always been this way."

Owen's face falls and he stares into the fountain, time briefly seeming to slow down as sunlight catches every drop of falling water. After a minute, he fishes a silver coin from his pocket. He rubs his thumb across the top, then—with a quick flick of his wrist—tosses it into the water, where it lands with a hollow *kerplunk*. I watch it sink to the bottom, a silver gleam on a bed of gold. "Did you make a wish?" I ask.

Owen nods.

"Don't tell me what it was," I remind him. "Or else it won't come true."

"I'm not sure there are enough coins in the world for this wish to come true." He takes a seat on the edge of the fountain, a kind of sadness in his eyes as he gazes down at the stone walkway. "Sometimes I'm not so sure about this place," he says quietly.

Today, I know exactly what he means.

He shakes his head. "Sometimes I can't believe I ever brought Sara here at all."

"Sara." I take a seat beside him, sensing pain in his words. "Your sister."

He nods.

"What happened to her?"

His eyes shift forward. Humans do this with some frequency, I note: avert their gaze when discussing something difficult. "She was killed in a car accident," he says, finally. "Three years ago. She was ten. I had just turned sixteen."

I am no stranger to tragedy—people come from thousands of miles away to share their heartache with my sisters and me; to feel the unique comfort only a Fantasist can provide—but for some reason, hearing this leaves me speechless. Gently, I reach out and take his hand.

He takes a shaky breath before adding, "I was the one driving."

My chest constricts.

All this time, Owen really *has* had a secret.

Just not any secret I could have ever guessed.

"That's why I've got this"—he points to the scar above his lip—"and this." He places his hand over his heart. "I hit the steering wheel really hard in the crash and had a cardiac contusion. They had to put in the valve and monitor. My heart just doesn't work right anymore." He inches over a little. "You were her favorite, you know. Sara had pictures of you up all over her bedroom for years."

"She *did*?"

"She would've been so excited that I work here," he muses. "Like, out of her *mind* excited."

"Do you have a picture?" I ask. "I'm sure I will remember her if you show me."

Owen hesitates.

That was too much, my program whispers. *You pushed too far.*

"Never mind," I correct myself. "I didn't mean to—"

"No, no. That's all right." He reaches into his pocket and pulls out his phone, the sight of which sends a slight jolt of fear pulsing through me after what happened with Eve in the woods. Owen scrolls through his photo log, then holds out the phone for me to see. "This is Sara."

I feel a tug in my chest the moment I see her. In a flash, my program scans her facial algorithm and compares it to my data log—hundreds of thousands of children over more than a dozen years. In the time it takes a human to exhale, I have located a perfect match.

I hit SELECT.

Just like that, in high-res, holographic detail, a beautiful child dances to life before my eyes. Sara at age four, in a daisy-print dress, her smile as bright as the sun.

Ana, look! I wore my favorite dress just for you!

Sara at age seven, with two missing front teeth and a pair of unicorn sunglasses.

Ana! Guess how much money the Tooth Fairy left me!

Sara at age nine, with a book in her hand and purple shoes on her feet.

Ana! Have you ever read Anne of Green Gables?

And finally, Sara at age ten—her last visit. Hair shorter, legs longer, and hand in hand with a shy-looking boy of sixteen. A boy with the same dark hair. The same tall frame. The same beautiful eyes.

I've met him *before*, I realize with a start. But that doesn't make sense.

This is my big brother, Owen. He's the best brother in the whole wide world.

I blink twice and the image disappears, but I am left with feelings of uncertainty and confusion. How could I have forgotten his face? My facial recognition software is linked to the Kingdom's directory database—thoroughly and routinely updated.

It does not make errors.

"She was so beautiful," I tell him. "Thank you for sharing her with me."

Owen's eyes fill with a light I've never seen. "Did you see her? Did you just watch some kind of . . . memory?"

I nod.

"So she was just right here?" His voice wavers. "How does that work?"

"Do you want to see? I can show you."

Owen looks nervous for a few seconds, but then he nods.

"Look into my eyes," I tell him, switching my visual output so that they project the memories out, instead of in. For several minutes, Owen sits like a statue, eyes glued to mine. He can see her. Laughing. Dancing. Smiling. *Alive*. When it's over—when my lenses have reset—I focus back and notice his face is streaked with tears.

"Are you all right? I didn't mean to make you cry."

"No, it's okay." He laughs, wiping his eyes with his sleeve. "It's just . . . not to be cheesy or whatever . . . but I guess Fantasists really do know how to make dreams come true."

Our eyes meet.

Boom!

We both look up just as the sky explodes with neon light, drenching the Kingdom in a blanket of falling stars. The evening fireworks show has begun. Owen's hand finds mine in the dark, triggering tiny sparks of icy hot along my skin. I think of the lagoon again, and the dream I had, and how those unexpected ideas had come to me: Owen kissing me. Our lips meeting. A sigh. His hand closes around mine. The sensation of his touch is so thrilling, so electrifying, I am certain my motor will fly out of my chest.

But then I remember.

The Investors' farewell party.

"Oh no!" I jump to my feet, turning swiftly toward the palace. I can already see my sisters, gathered without me in the roof garden high above Magic Land. I am late.

"I have to go," I tell Owen. "I'm going to be in trouble."

"Wait." Owen stands up. "You shouldn't go."

I frown. How does he know about the party?

"I don't have a choice."

"You always have a choice, Ana. They just don't want you to think you do."

"They?" I search his eyes. "Who is *they*?"

He doesn't answer. "At least let me walk you there," he says, noting a group of guards just over by the carousel. "It won't be safe around here until they find Eve."

My mind floods with confusion. And then—with anger.

"How do you know that?" I demand. "How do you know Eve is missing?"

"From the Supervisors. There was a park-wide security update for all staff." He shakes his head. "I can't believe she stole a horse."

I freeze.

Stole?

"What are you talking about?" I whisper. "Daddy didn't say anything about that."

In the glow of the fireworks, Owen's hair looks almost electric blue. "They got it all on a security feed, Ana. Eve stole a horse from Heart Land and took off after the rodeo." He shakes his head grimly. "*Before . . .*"

His tone sends an itch burning up my throat. "Before what?"

Owen looks up. "Before she cut the tracking chip out of her arm."

41

THE TALE OF THE GOLDEN WREATH

A FABLE FROM MOTHER'S COLLECTION

There once was a girl who coveted, more than anything, a golden wreath to wear upon her head. Such a crown would take a genius—and a touch of magic—to construct, but she knew that possessing it would make her the most beautiful and the most beloved of all the girls in the land.

For many years, she wove tiaras made of flowers, all the while dreaming of a golden wreath to adorn her brow, and one cold winter day, her wish came true. As she was roaming the woods in search of something green—any twig or leaf she might tuck into her wreath—she saw a majestic bear.

Standing in a clearing, its fur shone like moonlight against the new-fallen snow. And upon its grand and beastly head sat a golden crown, fashioned in the shape of blossoms too beautiful to put into human words, almost too beautiful for human eyes to behold.

As she approached the bear, boldly meeting its gaze, the bear bowed, and then spoke. The bear promised her that she might have the wreath, as a gift, if only she'd trust him, and follow him deeper into the woods. All she must do is make sure her heart was full of purity and gratitude.

And he had one rule: never to light a fire, not even a single candle. The bear could not abide flames.

The girl readily agreed, and as the bear knelt down into the snow, she climbed upon his soft white back, allowing him to lead her into the forest. With delight, she discovered that the bear had built a gorgeous palace, full of many wonders, as beautiful and otherworldly as the wreath.

For many years, they dwelled together happily in the palace, the bear and the girl, and she wore the golden wreath, and basked in knowing she was the best girl in all the land. But one night, as the stars formed a tapestry out of the darkness, the girl's curiosity got the better of her. She lit a candle, and wandered about the palace in search of the bear—in search of answers and secrets.

She did not find the bear, but a prince asleep in his chambers, more handsome and strong than any man she had ever seen. But as she gazed at him, wax from her candle melted and spilled upon his brow, and the man awoke. Before her eyes, he transformed back into the bear.

Dear reader, this tale does not end in beauty.

The bear went into a ravenous, beastly rage, destroying everything in the castle. For what the girl had not known was that the bear was a prince who had been cursed into his current form, and had the girl only been more patient—had she not given in to her terrible curiosity and simply waited one more day—the curse would have been lifted, and all that belonged to the bear-prince would have been hers.

Instead, because of her *disobedience*, he'd become trapped in his animal form forever.

When the bear finished destroying the palace, it turned on the girl. She realized the kindness in the bear's eyes had been extinguished, like the candle, and in the darkness, she felt the animal wrath of his claws as he tore her apart.

42

TRIAL TRANSCRIPT

MR. HAYES: Mr. Windham, why would a Fantasist disable their own tracking chip?

MR. WINDHAM: Well . . . it would seem Eve didn't want to be found.

MR. HAYES: And how *did* your team find her?

MR. WINDHAM: We didn't. Ana did.

43

KINGDOM CORP. SURVEILLANCE FOOTAGE TAPE 2

[Court views brief digital clip taken on July 28 from Security Camera 541S6, positioned midway through the woods between the private entrance to Paleo Land and the Fantasist dormitory, on the afternoon of Fantasist 1's sudden disappearance.]

<PLAY>

12:58: A figure—*Fantasist 1, Eve*—enters the scene on horseback, *Hybrid EFC821.*

12:59: Eve dismounts and digs a small hole near a tree.

1:03: Eve removes an object from her bag—*Exhibit 7,* a medical-grade scalpel—then turns away from the camera.

1:35: Eve appears to bury something, view obstructed.

1:58: Eve stands clutching her right wrist; a dark stain is now visible on her right sleeve. Eve removes *EFC821*'s bridle, releasing him into the woods. Then she tosses the scalpel on the ground and walks out of the shot.

44

The July of the Swift Fox

FOURTEEN MONTHS BEFORE THE TRIAL

My gown trips me as I run—I stumble hard and scrape my knees on the cobblestone—but I do not care.

I will not stop searching until I have found her.

I will not lose another sister.

"Did you check the Fairy Tale Boutique?" I demand. "Did you check the gown racks, like I said? That used to be her favorite hiding place during hide-and-seek."

"*Ana*." Owen is out of breath, cheeks flushed red. "I'm not sure we're going to—"

"We have to keep looking," I tell him. "We *have* to."

"I don't know." He shakes his head. "We've looked in a lot of places. Maybe we should just let the guards do their jobs, you know? They'll find her. I'm sure they will."

That's what I'm afraid of, I want to tell him. *What will happen when they do?*

I collapse on a wrought iron bench, trying to clear my mind, one line of code at a time.

Think, Ana, *think*. Where would she go? What would she do?

"Eve likes the colors green and lavender," I say hurriedly. "She likes to read."

"Okay." Owen shakes his head. "So do you think she went to Story Land?"

I hit my fists against my sides. "If she went there, we would have *known* by now," I snap.

"All right, all right." Owen holds up his hands. "Let's try to stay calm, okay?"

I grit my teeth. There's no time to stay calm. But I know he's right. I close my eyes until I can steady my breathing.

"I'm sorry," I tell Owen. "I just keep thinking of Nia. I'll never forgive myself if—"

"We got this, okay? We just have to think. Like, what's her favorite fairy tale? Maybe if we know that, we can figure out where she'd try to hide."

Her favorite story.

"*Anna Karenina*," I blurt.

Owen looks surprised. "By Leo Tolstoy?"

"No." I cross my arms. "The *other* Tolstoy."

Owen cracks a smile. "Okay, so *Anna Karenina*. Let me think." He grimaces. "I'm, uh, a little rusty on my Russian literature. But it's got . . . soldiers, right?"

My eyes dart around at the guards.

Soldiers in every direction.

231

"And horses?" Owen adds uncertainly.

Horses.

"I just don't understand," I mutter. Stealing a gown is one thing. But a *horse*? "What was Eve thinking? She knows she can't leave the park."

Owen goes quiet a minute. "Well, technically she can."

His voice gives me a tiny spark of hope. "What do you mean?"

"Oh my god!" he gasps. "Ana, look over there!"

"What in the—" I whirl around, half expecting to see Mother standing behind me. But the moment I turn around, I feel Owen's hand graze the nape of my neck.

Turning off my cameras.

"Sorry about that," Owen says a little sheepishly.

"You could've asked me first," I mutter, rubbing my shoulder. "I think I have whiplash."

"There *is* a way out," Owen says, ignoring my grumbling. "But it's not the way you think. Maybe Eve took out her chip because she was trying to say goodbye."

My brow furrows. Owen doesn't know what he is talking about.

"That's impossible," I tell him. "Eve loves it here. She's been here longer than any of us."

Suddenly, Owen looks scared to tell me something. "Ana? That day at the lagoon, when Nia tried to drown the little girl . . . I didn't tell you this before, but she gave me something. A bracelet. She asked me to hold on to it, said she wanted you to have it."

My eyes widen.

Nia wanted me to have her charm bracelet? As a *gift*?

"Why didn't you tell me?" I ask.

"I meant to, but after the whole incident went down, I realized I had lost it." He sighs and shakes his head. "I think it was a hint. Maybe even a cry for help. I just didn't see it that way at the time. I should have reported it, but I didn't."

All at once, I feel an enormous weight lift from my shoulders. *Relief.*

Finally, I know for certain Owen was never lying, never keeping any secrets from me. He never knew anything about Nia. The bracelet hadn't been any kind of clue.

Slowly, I reach into the pocket of my dress. "You didn't lose it." I open my hand, revealing three tiny charms—a seashell, a dolphin, and a starfish—each glinting gold in the light of the moon.

"I can't believe it," Owen whispers. "Where did you find it?"

"It was in your jacket." I hold the bracelet out between us. "The jacket you gave to me that night at the lagoon."

Then he says, "It should be yours. Nia wanted you to have it."

I put it back in my pocket, grateful to keep this last token of my sister. Nia is gone, I remind myself. Nothing will undo that now.

But Eve—Eve is still here. And she needs my help.

"What do we do about Eve?"

"If Eve were going to try to hurt herself," he replies carefully, "if she were going to try to shut herself down, how would she do it?"

"Shut down *herself*?" I gawk at him. "Why would she do such a thing?"

Owen's eyes meet mine.

This time, I know the word in his head without him having to say it.

233

Escape.

I think of the rumors about the Investors. How Fantasists never seem to remember what happens when they come for visits. I think of Kaia's distant answers to all my questions about what really happened last night. Eve was there with her. What happened to Eve? What did Eve remember?

In my periphery, carving through the sky toward Magic Land, I catch a glimpse of a sleek silver train pulling into the Palace Station, directly below the rooftop of the Investors' garden party. I swiftly download *Anna Karenina* from the network—it has been some time since I've read it—and scan the most stirring passages. A ballroom. A handsome count. A train, barreling down the tracks. And a young woman—her hair swept into an elegant updo, her eyes desperate, directionless—throwing herself into its fatal path.

Another firework shoots high into the sky. A massive flower bomb, a chrysanthemum, with petals made of fire. Just like that, I think I know the answer to Owen's question.

"The monorail," I gasp.

Before Owen can utter a response, I am tearing away from the fountain, running as fast as I can toward the rooftop garden.

I have to warn the Supervisors. I have to get help. My motor pounds in my chest, my creme satin sash trails behind me. *Where are you, Eve?* I want to scream. *Please don't let me be too late.*

There are more than a dozen stations in all of the Kingdom. Even if I'm right, how will we ever find which one in time?

No, I must be wrong. She wouldn't do this. And if she wanted to, she could have done it sooner—why wait? Either I am wrong, or I am too late, or—

But then I see her.

A flicker of movement from the Spanish-tiled roof—the one closest to the rooftop garden.

Of course.

A figure leaning dangerously close to the edge. She is waiting for the finale, I realize as the fireworks pick up speed. I look up at the palace. In between the sonic booms, I can hear the sounds of music playing, of voices laughing. I see the glow of paper lanterns and evening lights twinkling from the rooftop garden. I freeze. She wants the Supervisors—and *all* the VIPs—to see what she is about to do.

"Eve!" I call out, startling several families waiting on the platform.

We do not raise our voices.

I dart past them, not caring whether they are frightened of me.

We always aim to please.

"Come down! I *see* you!"

She ducks into the shadows. In the distance, a train is approaching. The sound sends a jolt of fear up my spine, a sensation that momentarily locks me in place. I fight through the feeling and race to the trellis on the station's far side, climbing through the ivy until I've reached the roof.

"Eve! *Please!* Don't do this!" I grip the handrails tightly as I inch toward her, dropping a shoe in the process and watching it fall nearly thirty feet down to the quiet tracks below.

Boom!

Above us, the sky is on fire. Hundreds of missiles rocket into the air at once, momentarily turning the Kingdom a dazzling shade of gold that stretches on for miles. Past Magic

Land. Past Winter Land. Even beyond the borders of the cast parking lot.

I just wanted to see the stars, Eve had said that night at the Star Deck Observatory. *But they're so far away.*

Now I see her. Her eyes, wild. Her arm, bloodied and bruised. Her crystal beaded evening gown—black—just like in *Anna Karenina*.

The train speeds closer. "Don't do it!" I cry. "Eve, no!"

"They can't put a price on us, Ana," she calls to me, her voice hollow. Broken. "Nia knew it. She knew it and that's why she's gone."

"What?" I yell back frantically. "*Eve!* What are you talking about?"

She leans forward. The lights are so close. A scream lodges in my throat.

Before I know it, I am leaping forward to block her fall. But I am too late. I feel the ground open up beneath me. I see a blinding flash of light.

Then there is only heat.

Sound.

Force.

Fury.

And a darkness so deep—so utterly complete—that in the billionth of a second before my eyes close, I wonder if I have finally learned to sleep.

45

THE JULY OF THE SWIFT FOX

FOURTEEN MONTHS BEFORE THE TRIAL

I open my eyes, but the world is too bright. For what feels like a long time, I lie perfectly still, not sure where I am, or how I got there, or even if I am functional.

Eventually, I try to move, but my muscles do not contract. My limbs do not bend. *That's unexpected*, I think, before trying it again. *Move*, I command my elbows, my stomach, my spine. But again, though I can visualize the necessary mechanics, when I try to sit up, nothing happens.

I am awake, I tell myself. I *know* I am. But my body . . .

Has it fallen asleep?

"Eve?" My voice sounds gravelly—hoarse—though I am not sure why. "Hello?" I want to rub my eyes, but my arms are locked at my sides. "Where am I?"

"Eve isn't here, Ana," a voice says.

A voice that cuts straight to my motor, flooding its chambers with relief.

"*Daddy?*" Everything is still so bright. Like staring into the sun without my protective lenses.

I feel his hand on my forehead. Gentle, yet firm. "You've been through quite an ordeal this evening. Don't try to move. You'll only injure yourself further."

"I don't understand." I cough. "What happened?"

"I was hoping you could tell me," Daddy answers quietly. "What were you doing on the monorail tracks, Ana? You know that is forbidden."

The monorail. Forbidden.

In a flash, the memory of what happened comes blazing back to me in vivid, explosive color. I can feel the shaking of the ground and hear the rumble in the distance. I can see the glare of flashing lights and hear the screech of hot, grinding metal.

Then: a terrified scream.

The choking smell of smoke.

The sensation of flying. Of *falling.*

I rub my eyes hard and little by little, the world comes back into hazy, blurry focus. I am on a bed—*no, a table*—I can feel the cold metal hard against my back. Daddy stands above me on my left, Mother on my right. The glaring sun overhead is *not* the sun, but a bright white circular lamp. And when I glance down, my body looks . . . *different*. My legs no longer align, bent sideways at unnatural angles. The skin on my right arm has been torn away, severed wires and twisted metal visible through a jagged, gaping hole. My gown is soaked with a thick black fluid—the same shade as the bear, the zebra, the tiger cubs.

Shattered. Severed.

I start to convulse.

"Am I broken?" I whisper. "Are you going to shut me down?"

"No," Daddy answers. "Just lie still. We're going to fix you."

A small team of others joins us at the table, watching in silence as Daddy drags a thin plasma scalpel slowly from my clavicle down the center of my chest, unzipping me like a jacket.

"I would like you to tell me what you girls were doing on the monorail tracks," he repeats as he prepares the first of many replacement parts he is to install. "Was this Eve's idea? Or yours?"

I do not answer him.

Silence is not a lie.

"Did Eve do something wrong, Ana?" he asks. "Is Eve *unsafe*?"

I have to tell him, my program reminds me. I have to tell the truth.

Don't I?

I feel the snip of electrosurgical scissors, followed by a tug in my abdomen—not pain, but an intense pressure that briefly takes my breath away.

"Is she like Nia?" Daddy asks, his face partially concealed behind his mask. "Do you think it's possible she'd ever think of hurting someone besides herself?"

"She just wanted to be free," I finally whisper. "She just wanted to escape."

Daddy powers on his drill. "There's no such thing, Ana." He lowers his mask. "Escape is a lie."

———

I dream again. This time of Nia. Nia and the little girl—not the one she tried to drown, the one she held clenched in her powerful arms below the surface. No, the other little girl, Clara. The one who spoke in our language of fawns and birds. When did Nia teach that to her? And why? I dream Nia and Clara are holding hands, mermaid and human child, laughing and swimming together through the green depths of the lagoon, sunlight rippling through the water, making me want to laugh, too. But I have a sudden fear—if I open my mouth to laugh, I will drown.

That is the danger of happiness here.

"Ana? Ana, are you awake?"

I open my eyes to a chorus of whispers and gasps. And then my sisters are hugging me, kissing me, covering me with the warmth of their nightgowns. Joy floods my inner circuitry at the sight of their beautiful faces, a feeling as bright and brilliant as the sun. In all my seasons, I cannot remember ever being so happy to see them.

"What happened to you?" Yumi asks, carefully studying my new arm and foot. "Are you sick? Did you malfunction?"

"I had an accident. But I think I'll be okay."

"You missed the party." Zara sounds disappointed. "You missed evening prayers."

"I'm sorry," I tell her. "I didn't mean to."

Zel sits down at the foot of my bed. "What did Eve do?" Her

eyes sparkle with the possibility of something new to talk about. "Mother says she broke a rule."

I realize then that my oldest sister is not among them. Nor is she in her bed.

I keep my answer simple. "She tried to run away."

"Run away from what?" Nadia asks. "Did I do something that upset her?"

Kaia touches her shoulder sweetly. "Follow your dreams. *They* know the way."

I ignore Nadia's question. She barely knew Eve.

"When is Eve coming back from the infirmary?" I ask. "Did Mother say?"

An eerie hush falls over the bedroom.

"Oh dear," Yumi says. "We thought you knew."

A soft alarm bell blares in my ear. I feel a burning in the back of my throat. "Where is she? You have to tell me."

Zara bows her head. "I'm sorry, Ana. They shut Eve down this morning."

That night, I can't rest. Whenever I close my eyes, I see Eve's hazel gaze staring at me in the mirror as the fox's blood runs down my arms and into the sink. I see her lavender dress edged in mud. I see her face lit by the phone Nia stole. I see her body, a silver blur of beauty and motion, as she throws herself in front of the train.

I turn to face my right, focusing on regulating my breath, and stare at Nadia's form just a few feet away, lying in Nia's bed—I still can only think of it as Nia's bed, even after all this time.

Suddenly, I realize Nadia's eyes are open, blinking. She is staring at the ceiling.

"In the morning," she whispers, so quietly no human ear would pick up on it. But I do.

"In the morning *what*?" I ask.

"The early bird catches the worm," she says.

Has she learned our code, too?

I hesitate before replying, "The bird is sick of worms."

"She will want this one," Nadia says, without ever looking at me. "It belonged to the fallen bird, the first one. Now it belongs to the next in the nest. It will be waiting in the place where the bird sleeps."

I don't rest at all.

But in the morning, after our Grooming and Beautification rituals are complete, I find the treasure—a *Valentine's Day* card, of all things—hidden underneath Nadia's mattress, just as she promised.

But it is not a card addressed to Eve, as I would have expected.

It is addressed to Nia.

46

POST-TRIAL INTERVIEW

[01:24:08–01:25:47]

DR. FOSTER: The only thing I can't seem to figure out is how you managed to get Owen's body from the woods down to the incinerator so quickly.

ANA: I didn't. I've told you.

DR. FOSTER: *Twenty-five* minutes. All without a single camera or officer noticing.

ANA: Why won't you listen to me?

DR. FOSTER: There's no reason to lie anymore. We recovered Owen's medical bracelet from the ashes.

ANA: [Silence.] You did?

DR. FOSTER: What was it, Ana? Were you furious when you finally figured out the truth? Not only that Owen had betrayed you, but that you were naive enough to fall for the exact fairy tale you were created to sell? Does it bother you that the entire romantic relationship you thought you'd experienced was nothing more than a story?

ANA: No. Not at all.

DR. FOSTER: Why not?

ANA: Because that isn't my story, Dr. Foster. It's *yours*.

47

THE AUGUST OF THE CHATHAM RAVEN

THIRTEEN MONTHS BEFORE THE TRIAL

They keep me in isolation in the Fantasist dormitory for one week.

Security updates, the guests are told. *We apologize for any inconvenience.*

To pass the time, I think about Eve. I think about Owen. And I think about the Valentine's card hidden beneath Nadia's bed. Nothing about it makes sense, from the fact that Nia wasn't even *with* us on Valentine's Day—she was away, being reprogrammed by the Supervisors for ten long weeks, and so wouldn't have been around to receive a card in the first place—to the tiny mermaid charm I found gleaming like a treasure inside the envelope. The family who sent the card—*Gold*, their last name read, like the charm itself—seemed to know Nia personally. They talk about their time spent together. But how? And *when*?

I try to understand it, I try to solve the riddle, but perhaps—after all—there is nothing left to solve.

I slip the new charm onto Nia's bracelet.

Perhaps it is just another treasure, glinting in the darkness. Worthless, except for what it meant to its owner.

Nia is gone.

Eve is gone.

Will I be gone soon, too?

"You are not ready," Mother explains day after day, placing her hand on my forehead, as if my body temperature is not manually regulated. "You need to rest."

Will rest fix this feeling inside me?

Will rest change what I have done?

The longer I stay in bed, the more I begin to suspect Mother is lying. I think they are watching me for any signs I might be like my sisters—first Nia, then Eve.

Signs I am unraveling.

Unpredictable.

Unsafe.

Which confuses me, considering *I* am the one who helped them in the first place. I am the one who told them she wanted to escape: a word that made her *unpredictable*, and therefore unable to return to Kingdom life. But if following the rules makes *me* so dangerous, I wonder—once my straps have rubbed my wrists raw—then perhaps it's time I stopped following them so closely.

Maybe it's time I made up some rules of my own.

Once I have been cleared of risk of malfunction, my reintroduction to the park happens gradually, over a period of several days. At first, I am allowed only short walks around the palace grounds, during which I am trailed and scrutinized by one or several Supervisors. Next, they slowly add in parades and low-impact performances, though dancing is suspended indefinitely. Soon, Meet and Greets return to the rotation, but only in groups—and only when supervised. And finally, after what seems an excessive number of interviews, checkups, weigh-ins, and extra iron supplementation, I am released full-time back into the wild.

It is harder than I expect.

The sun is brutal. My balance feels off. Even the guests seem louder than before. More unruly. Less kind. One man berates me when I fail to give him directions to Jungle Land quickly enough, while a woman accuses me of smiling too "provocatively" at her teenage son. Even the children appear to be on their worst behavior. Pushing. Yelling. Fighting over me like I am their toy. Their *plaything*.

With every passing day, I feel more worn down. Tired. An aching tightness in my chest refuses to go away. But every morning, just like clockwork, we gather together in the breezeway to begin again.

Gowns sparkling.

Hands linked.

A thousand voices screaming our names.

"Kaia! Yumi! Zara! Zel! Ana! Nadia!"

My chest constricts when Eve's name is not called.

From where I am standing I can just make out the plaque beside the new statue erected in Eve's honor in the town square, her name carved forever in stone.

Beloved Eve, the last of her generation. Retired indefinitely. Always in our hearts.

The Kingdom has spun Eve's shutdown into a beautiful story-book ending, complete with commemorative shirts, dolls, movies, and posters. And it is my fault.

In doing the right thing . . . I have actually done the worst thing.

But then I remember this, too: that Eve was a thief, through and through.

That she'd had Nia's Valentine's Day card all that time, but had never shown it to me, had hoarded it for herself. After all, Nadia found it under *Eve's* bed after they took her away, a strand of platinum hair tucked inside the envelope.

And now the card is mine.

And so is its riddle.

Both of them buried in the Graveyard.

I wonder if I will ever understand, or if I will always be left puzzling. And perhaps that was Nia's purpose in leaving the card behind—to make sure someone never forgot her.

Now I inhale deeply, noticing the sweet, cozy scent of milk and cookies. Like Eve, the strange rotten smell is long gone. For a moment, I picture the Kingdom's compactors swinging—beating, pulsing, pulverizing everything in their path—hundreds of feet belowground. I think about how, in a way, the compactors have always struck me as giant metal hearts.

"Gratitude," I say to my sisters, stepping in for our oldest sister.

"*Gratitude*," five voices come back.

And I think about how odd it is—and how disturbing—that those hearts run on rot.

———

For days, the only thing that keeps me going is the thought of Owen. Seeing him. Speaking to him. But I also worry. What if he knows the truth about my betrayal of Eve? What if he thinks what I've done is unforgivable? My chest tightens at the thought of losing his friendship; of losing the one human I feel I can truly speak to openly and without consequence.

There is so much I want to learn from him.

About his life. About Sara. About the outside world.

About escape.

When we finally meet, nearly two weeks have passed since my return. My chest feels tense and fluttery at the sight of him coming toward me in the grasslands, so much so that I can hardly say hello. But that's the best thing about being in Safari Land, away from the crowds, away from the noise. With so much beauty all around, words aren't really necessary.

"How have you been?" Owen asks once we are seated in the shade of a massive acacia tree, not far from where we first met. "Thanks for coming to meet me. I wasn't sure if Fleur would give you my message or not. I'm glad she did."

I stare at the dirt, where a tiny ant is carrying a leaf more than ten times its size. It walks slowly, patiently, pausing every few seconds to rest as it makes its way toward a distant hill. It has no idea that on a branch high above, a bird is watching.

"Ana?"

"What's the point of this life?" I whisper. "What's the point if someone can just take it all away?"

"I wish I could tell you," he answers. "I ask myself the same thing all the time."

I can deduce from the sad tone of his voice he's talking about Sara. The thought of her, the thought of Nia, and now, the thought of Eve—and what I have done to her—makes my eyes burn just like they did after Owen told me at the Paleo Palladium he never wanted to see me again. It wasn't true, as so many things have turned out not to be, but the memory of it still hurts. And when I touch my face, I realize it's wet with tears.

"*Again?*" I say angrily, wiping them away. "What is wrong with me?"

"Ana?" Owen blinks, alarmed. "What's the matter?"

"They should turn *me* off, too. Before this gets any worse."

"Before what gets worse? Don't say things like that, Ana."

I shake my head. "It just never bothered me before—not like this. I always accepted it. Hybrids age. They malfunction. They get put down." I feel my chin tremble. "But it's all so permanent. It's *forever*."

Owen offers his arms and I collapse into them, weeping against his chest. "Am I next?" I whisper. "Am I running out of time like Nia and Eve? I don't want to be."

"Shhh." He softly strokes my hair. "Everything's going to be okay. I promise."

"What's happening to all of us, Owen? I'm so scared."

"It's okay to be scared."

"But when will it stop? When will things go back to how they always were?"

"Do you remember what I told you the last time we were here? About the butterflies?"

I feel a lump form in my throat. "That they're sick. That they're dying."

"They're *evolving*, Ana," he whispers. "You're *all* evolving."

I blink.

Evolve.

To develop gradually, especially from a simple to a more complex form.

Slowly, gently, Owen touches my cheek. "Look," he says, holding out a perfectly formed tear. He studies it closely. Its shape. Its clarity. The way it curves and reflects the light. "Look how beautiful."

I shake my head. "But it's not supposed to happen. It's unnatural."

"The only thing unnatural," he replies, "is how they're treating all of you."

"But we are loved," I insist, even though I am trembling. "We are grateful."

"You are prisoners." Owen takes me by the shoulders and stares hard into my eyes. "I want to help you, Ana. I think I *can* help you, if we could just—"

251

I kiss him before he can finish his sentence.

Not because I am trying to make him or anyone else happy, as I have always done. Instead, for the first time, I am doing something because I want to.

Because I *desire* him.

At first, there is only sensation.

Warm. Wet. Soft.

But slowly, my sensors relax. Every muscle, every molecule, every circuit, every cell . . . *alive* with aching, burning instinct. Soon, I feel the firewalls slip down around me. The network cannot reach me here. It cannot hold me in.

The kiss deepens.

I am flying down the Steel Giant, looping on tracks made of neural pathways.

I am diving into a lagoon, full of laughter and light.

I am running through a darkened wood . . . and in my hand, I hold a knife.

Ana, Nia's voice whispers from somewhere far away. *This is not routine.*

A warning bell begins to ring.

Fear catches suddenly in my throat. I am not diving or flying . . . I am falling. I must catch myself.

I feel a blast of icy heat, burning below my skin.

The gateway locks.

I pull away from him. "I'm so sorry. That's not—I didn't mean—"

"It's okay." His voice is calm. Steady. *Safe.* "Don't worry. I would never, I mean, I wasn't trying to—" Our eyes meet wordlessly. A flicker of a memory comes to me then; a line of poetry about eyes being the window to the soul. But how does that work? Can a Fantasist have a soul? When I look into Owen's eyes, I see a place as deep, dark, and infinite as the sky. But what does he see when he looks into mine?

Gears?

Glass?

Wire and filament?

I feel a pressure in my chest.

What have I done?

"You're an anomaly, Ana," Owen says, smiling.

"That makes me dangerous."

"No." Owen shakes his head. "That makes you beautiful."

Warmth floods my cheeks. Slowly, I feel the distance between us again beginning to close. "But they'll find out," I say. "They *always*—"

His lips touch mine.

I close my eyes.

And this time, I allow myself to fall.

48

TRIAL TRANSCRIPT

MS. BELL: Dr. Cruz, you're suggesting that *all* Ana's behaviors are responses to stimuli created purposely by the Proctor to "test" whether you could accurately control and predict her reactions.

DR. CRUZ: Exactly. [Hesitates.] Though I admit we missed signs that our one-on-one study had pushed Ana too far.

MS. BELL: How so?

DR. CRUZ: We didn't realize we had aggravated her basic survival instincts so severely that it would lead to violence.

MS. BELL: You say "survival instincts". Can Fantasists feel fear, Dr. Cruz?

DR. CRUZ: Yes, fear is a survival mechanism that lets them know something is wrong, both for their own security and the safety of our guests.

MS. BELL: I see. And is falling in love a survival mechanism?

DR. CRUZ: Ana didn't fall in love with Owen any more than he "fell in love" with her. The girls mirror human emotion to build trust with our guests. It's all part of the fantasy they are created to sell. But the fantasy is a trick, Ms. Bell. A *lie*. In a way, the Fantasists are the biggest lie of all.

MS. BELL: But why would Ana continually go out of her way to see him if her program repeatedly told her not to?

DR. CRUZ: The computerized mind of a hybrid can get "stuck" on one person or idea, like an endless loop of broken code. It's not the first time we've seen it happen—and in fact, that's the very thing our study was designed to explore.

MS. BELL: If Ana was acting as if she loved Owen, how do you know she wasn't really in love?

DR. CRUZ: Acting is not *real*. Real love is an instinct. A connection. It requires intention. Desire. An emotionally complex sense of self. *Reciprocity*.

MS. BELL: So you're saying love can't be real . . . unless somebody loves you back?

DR. CRUZ: [Angrily.] What I'm saying, Ms. Bell, is that Mr. Chen was hired as a Proctor for one purpose and one purpose only: to test and monitor Ana's capability for behaving in opposition to her program. Each and every interaction they shared—from their first conversation on the savanna up until the night of his tragic death—was planned, monitored, and executed.

MS. BELL: Did you also tell Owen to kiss her?

MR. HAYES: Objection.

THE COURT: Sustained.

DR. CRUZ: [Pause.] Yes.

49

THE AUGUST OF THE CHATHAM RAVEN

THIRTEEN MONTHS BEFORE THE TRIAL

After our kiss, I do not see Owen for a week.

The summer has never burned hotter, more relentless. Temperatures soar so high they even close Winter Land until the fall—the first time in the park's history—until maintenance can generate more artificial snow within the glass dome. The longer I go without seeing him, without talking to him, the more the August heat feels unbearable.

Is he avoiding me?

Is he upset with me? Does he regret our kiss?

Or worse . . . is he planning to report me to the Supervisors?

After four days, I begin noticing Owen here and there out of the corner of my eye; or at least, I think I do. I see him in places he shouldn't be. Places he would *never* be. Trimming the rose-bushes in the palace gardens. Sweeping the cobblestones in front of the confectionery, donning a flour-stained apron in place of a maintenance uniform. In line at the Princess Carousel, as if he is a guest. Once, I even think I see him walking the long, winding path from Magic Land to Star Land, head down, eyes dark, lost in his own thoughts.

"*Owen!*" I call his name, increase my speed. But the closer I get to him, the more his image flickers and fades, until finally, it vanishes altogether in the blistering heat.

Like a bad holographic signal.

Or a phantom.

Or a mirage.

Have I imagined him? Have I invented him, as the Supervisors invented me? Or: Might this be the pattern at work? A silent invader, infecting my cells one by one until it's claimed control of my every executive function. Will I try to hurt someone, as Nia did? Or, like Eve, will I try to hurt myself? And then, a new thought.

Is it possible violence might even . . . feel good?

The idea sends me deep into my mind, to the farthest brink of my program; someplace I have never been. An eerie, empty super-highway, stretching on to infinity.

No art. No music. No books. No connection.

Dark. Cold. Alone. *Afraid.*

But then, just when I feel the darkness beginning to swallow me, I'll remember: the pocketknife.

The knife he gave me.

And little by little, like the sun rising over the dark jungle, I'll feel my breathing slow. I'll feel my pathways calm. Owen is real, I remind myself. And if he is real . . .

. . . *then so was our kiss.*

Then I replay it, again and again, like the melody of a favorite song, or a scene from a favorite film, or a line from my favorite play.

Give me my Romeo; and, when he shall die,
Take him and cut him out in little stars,
And he will make the face of heaven so fine
That all the world will be in love with night
And pay no worship to the garish sun.

Finally, on day nine of my probation, I catch sight of him at five o'clock crossing Beanstalk Way with another maintenance worker whom I recognize from the Manatee Sanctuary. The sight of Owen—the *real* Owen—sends my pulse racing like a rocket in Star Land.

Without thinking, I slip into a large, hollowed-out topiary lining the path—one of many secret hiding spots around the park where staff can rest. I sit down on one of two narrow benches and peer through a curtain of green. Did he see? Will he find me? Do I even want him to?

A moment later, I hear a voice, whispering through the leaves.

"Ana? Is that you?"

I freeze all over again. "Um, no. No, it is not."

There comes a tremendous amount of rustling and then

Owen joins me inside the topiary. Quickly, he touches the pressure point on the nape of my neck, sending a shiver down my spine.

"What are you doing in here?" he asks, once it is safe.

"Enjoying the shade. What does it look like?"

The corners of his mouth curve up just a bit. "So then, you're not hiding?"

"Hiding from whom?"

"Well . . ." He lowers himself onto the opposite bench. "From me."

I let out a deep sigh and realize I cannot do this. I am far too logical for games. "Why haven't you come to see me?" I demand. "Are you angry? Was what I did wrong?"

"Ana, no, *you* did nothing wrong." In the shade of the topiary, I cannot quite read the look in Owen's eyes. "I haven't been sure what to say to you. I haven't been sure what to say to *myself*." He looks up. "It shouldn't have happened."

In an instant, the fire in my body is extinguished.

"It was wrong," I say softly. "I know that, yes. But . . ."

"But?"

I pause. "I don't regret it. Do you?"

"No," he says, and I notice he isn't quite looking me in the eye. "I don't regret it. And to be honest, I haven't been able to stop thinking about it all week. But there's a lot I need to say." Owen pauses. "There's a lot I need to tell you."

"So tell me. I'm listening."

"Everything's a mess right now," he mutters. "But I'll find you. Soon."

His hand slips off my neck. The leaves rustle. And then he is gone.

For a few minutes, I just sit there, grateful the ache has momentarily subsided.

He doesn't regret it.

I smile.

But then I notice something under a branch, partially hidden in the shadows.

Owen's notebook.

Small, electronic. It must have slipped from his back pocket as he snuck away.

I reach down and carefully pick it up, pleasantly surprised by how smooth the graphite casing feels in my hand. Owen has carried this around since I've known him. The grasslands. The stables. The Arctic Enclosure. The lagoon. I trace the delicate stitching along the notebook's rustic binding. He said it was for work.

I start to undo the clip on the front, but catch myself.

This is wrong. This is stolen.

And yet . . .

I'll only look for a second. He won't even know.

I pull the clip loose like a ribbon on a present.

I open to the first page. I touch the screen.

And I begin to read.

50

TRIAL TRANSCRIPT

MS. BELL: Ana, how did you react when you found out the truth about Owen? That he was just there to report on you? *Study* you?

ANA: [Silence.]

MS. BELL: Were you angry with him?

ANA: [Softly.] I was surprised. I was *hurt.*

MS. BELL: Hurt enough that you wanted to punish Owen?

ANA: Only humans think they can determine who lives and who dies, Ms. Bell. I'm very sorry to disappoint you, but murder isn't part of my program, either.

MS. BELL: Is that right?

ANA: Yes.

MS. BELL: So what does your program have to say about this? [Reads from Official Court Document 19C, a report Owen submitted to his superiors detailing observations from past encounters with Ana.]

From: Proctor 1A—Fantasist Division

<proc1A@kingdomcorp.com >

To: All Staff—Security & Training Divisions

<stdirect@kingdomcorp.com>

Subject: Ana

Date & Time: August 17, 12:36 a.m.

Ana is extremely gullible and appears to believe almost anything she is told. Being that she is highly motivated by human praise and personal attention, I have found it relatively simple to manipulate her in whatever capacity I choose, whether emotionally or behaviorally.

For an older model, Ana's internal processing speed is still reasonably fast, but her occasionally awkward physicality and lack of imagination suggest a limited capacity for volition and a likelihood that she has entered the final phase of her technological life.

51

THE AUGUST OF THE CHATHAM RAVEN

THIRTEEN MONTHS BEFORE THE TRIAL

The tunnels curve and twist like a snake, gently sloping downward until my GPS lets me know I have arrived.

I am not supposed to be here.

Fantasists are forbidden from being here.

Even now, I can hear the scuttling of the rats in the darkness.

But I am done following directions.

My fist clenches down on the notebook. The report—Owen's—his cruel words about me. The screen—streaked with tears.

I clench harder. He is just like the rest of them.

A dim fluorescent light flickers overhead. I feel the vibrations beneath my feet grow stronger with every step; a low, sleepy rumbling, like a dragon lost in a dream. What must a thousand degrees feel like? I eye the endless metal pipes overhead and shiver. The feeling of burning. Blazing. *Melting*. What would be left of me?

Bones? Titanium? Teeth?

The thought is so dark it halts me in my tracks, and it takes all I have to keep myself upright. I lean up against the cold, smooth cinder block and close my eyes, overcome with emotion. Shame that I have behaved so inappropriately toward a member of the Kingdom staff. Worry that I will get caught. Regret that while I do not truly understand what it means to believe in fate or destiny, some small part of me dared to try.

Humans are lucky. Somehow, they do not always require empirical data to tell whether or not a thing is true. They just know.

But how?

"How could he?" I seethe. "Why *would* he?" It isn't long before my program locates an answer, and the heavy blue in my heart becomes a bold, searing red.

Because humans lie.

I open my eyes and quickly recalibrate. I am here for one reason, I remind myself, and one reason only.

I tighten my resolve and continue on toward the sleeping monster.

Revenge.

This has to end. All of it.

All the feelings I thought I had for Owen. The way he changed me, allowed me to *evolve* . . .

No.

It's over.

Or, more profoundly terrible: it never was.

Negative three hundred feet, my GPS signals. *Location prohibited.*

I continue deeper down the damp, chilly corridor and feel my pulse quicken as the tunnel gradually becomes narrower and more complex, splitting off into various passageways and chambers like a subterranean labyrinth. I let the rhythmic pulsing of the compactors guide me and, to my relief, soon find the corridor widening like an open mouth. The limestone path becomes a wooden walkway, below which the floor quickly falls away, revealing a cavern as wide as the palace and as tall as the Steel Giant.

Cautiously, I make my way to the bridge. I look down and watch, mesmerized, as the true heart of the Kingdom—a massive, galvanized steel compactor built to crush everything in its path—swings back and forth like a pendulum. I take a deep breath.

Then I wait.

———————

As predicted, it takes him exactly twelve and a half minutes to reach me from the tunnel entrance by the cast parking lot.

I feel the vibrations of his footsteps before I hear his voice.

I think briefly of Romeo and Juliet.

Forbidden lovers whose fates also ended in death.

Violent delights have violent ends.

In my right hand, I tighten my grip around the handle of Owen's pocketknife.

No, *my* pocketknife.

Open.

Blade extended.

Ready.

"Ana!"

When I spin around, Owen is standing at the base of the bridge, his expression gutted with some emotion I can't read. Perhaps I never knew what he was really feeling after all.

And yet . . .

He came. I knew that much. I knew he would. Doesn't he always follow me, showing up wherever I am meant to be, following me like a lure, even down into these depths?

This was all part of the plan.

Wasn't it?

Rage pumps through my system. Far below the bridge, the incinerator burns.

I grip the knife tighter.

"Come closer," I call to him. "There's something I need to show you."

52

Post-Trial Interview

[01:29:07–01:29:42]

DR. FOSTER: You lured him to the incinerator on purpose.

ANA: I did.

DR. FOSTER: Because you were angry.

ANA: Because I wanted to teach him a lesson.

DR. FOSTER: A lesson he'd never forget?

ANA: I suppose that was the plan.

DR. FOSTER: So you admit it. You *planned* it.

ANA: [Pause.] Dr. Foster, you have no idea.

53

THE AUGUST OF THE CHATHAM RAVEN

THIRTEEN MONTHS BEFORE THE TRIAL

Even knowing what I am about to do, it's hard to ignore how beautiful he is. The structure of his shoulders. The square of his jaw. The shape of his lips.

Just like it's hard to ignore the look in his eyes.

Guilty.

"I can explain." He is out of breath from running. "I *swear* I can."

He's not close enough. Not yet. Just a few more feet.

"I'm tired of lies," I tell him, waving the notebook at him. "I'm tired of words that aren't true."

"I didn't lie," he insists. "At least, not to you. Actually—I've lied to everyone *but* you." He reaches for my arm, but I pull away.

"Don't."

"Please, Ana." His eyes search mine. "Won't you let me explain?"

"Extremely gullible. Easily controlled. Like a *child*."

He reaches for me again, but this time I shove him up against the rails. My strength surprises him—I can see it in his eyes—but it surprises me more.

"What are you doing?" His voice wavers. "Ana, wait."

I breathe hard, inching him closer to the edge. My whole life, I've been taught to be sweet. Calm. Obedient. I've been taught that I am weak. But now, seeing how easily I have him pinned, how easily I could throw him to his death, I realize that I am *not* weak. They only taught me to believe that I was.

I smile.

And I lean into him harder.

"I didn't mean it," he pleads. "I only said that stuff so the team would back off watching you. I did it to help you, Ana. I did it to help *us*."

My eyes narrow. "What team? What are you talking about?"

"It's what I told you. You're adapting, becoming something else. Something so much more evolved than they planned. Eve. Nia. So many of the hybrids." His voice is emotional in a way I cannot pinpoint. "It's happening to you," he says. "Can't you see that? I can't stand what they're making me do."

"So leave," I say coldly. "Nobody's forcing you to stay."

"I don't care about the job, Ana. I just care about you. *You're* the one who should leave."

"I am a Fantasist." My voice trembles. "The Kingdom is my home. I belong here."

Even as I say it, I know it's a lie.

I don't belong anywhere.

Does that make me a liar, too?

"They programmed you to control you," he shoots back. "And when they find out they can't control you anymore . . ."

"Then they'll shut us down!" I scream. "And so what? Isn't that what you want, Owen? You hate the Hybrid Program."

"What?" Owen's face looks pained, as if my words have cut him deeply. "I don't hate it, not at all, I'm just trying to save—"

"I'm not one of your stupid butterflies," I snap. "I don't need you to save me."

With that, I reveal the knife.

His eyes go wide.

I point the blade right at him.

"I would never lie to you," Owen says. "Please, Ana. You have to believe me."

"I don't have to do anything."

For once, I'm going to do what I *want* to do.

Slowly, I step away from him—and throw his notebook into the incinerator, watch its leather case swivel into the burning darkness with a flapping hiss.

Then I turn to Owen, to finish what I started.

54

9-1-1 EMERGENCY CALL TRANSCRIPT

SEPTEMBER 4, 2095. 7:34 A.M.

[begin audio recording]

9-1-1 DISPATCH: This is 9-1-1, what is your emergency?

UNIDENTIFIED MALE: Yes, hi, this is the security director at the Kingdom. We've had an, uh, incident and need someone to respond.

9-1-1 DISPATCH: What kind of incident, sir?

UNIDENTIFIED MALE: We believe we've got a member of our staff missing.

9-1-1 DISPATCH: Please stay on the line for Castle Rock Police Department.

UNIDENTIFIED MALE: Okay.

OPERATOR: Castle Rock PD.

UNIDENTIFIED MALE: Yes, I've got a missing person to report.

OPERATOR: Okay, how old?

UNIDENTIFIED MALE: Nineteen. Male. He's a junior member of our research staff.

OPERATOR: And when was the last time you saw this person?

UNIDENTIFIED MALE: Our cameras picked him up heading into the woods behind North Lot B parking just before midnight.

OPERATOR: Was he alone?

UNIDENTIFIED MALE: [Silence.]

OPERATOR: Hello?

UNIDENTIFIED MALE: No. He wasn't alone.

OPERATOR: Who was with him?

UNIDENTIFIED MALE: One of our Fantasists. One of our hybrid girls.

OPERATOR: Oh. [Pause.] Do you believe he's, uh, harmed her in some way, sir?

UNIDENTIFIED MALE: Actually, [inaudible] . . . we think maybe *she* killed him.

[end audio recording]

55

Trial Transcript

MS. BELL: Let's revisit the timeline of the evening of September 3—the night of Mr. Chen's alleged murder—and into the early morning hours of September 4. If you'd direct your attention to the front screen, I'd like to walk you through a series of brief surveillance clips, several of which were actually taken from Ana's ocular camera lenses. Which means you will see exactly what *Ana* saw—in *real time*. We believe these clips not only support the State's theory—that Ana murdered Owen in cold blood after learning he didn't reciprocate her obsessive feelings—but *prove* it, beyond any reasonable doubt.

Be warned, one of these shots is *extremely* graphic. Lights, please?

[Continues talking as clips begin to play.]

This first image was taken at 10:47 p.m. from Security Camera 4301D by the Serendipity Launch in Magic Land. You can very clearly see Ana becoming physically violent with Owen, and by now you've heard from several witnesses who claimed to have seen them "arguing loudly." [Pause.] Just to be clear, this footage puts us roughly forty-five minutes *prior* to the altercation captured on Security Camera 1A09 in North Lot B.

[Projector clicks.]

Now, fifteen minutes later at 11:02 p.m., we see a video clip taken by Security Camera 5326F in Paleo Land, showing Ana and Owen making their way in the direction of North Lot B, following their initial disagreement in Magic Land. Please note how Ana's hand is firmly gripping Mr. Chen's wrist. Can we zoom in there and replay that, please? Thank you. [Pause.] Right. As you see, she's pretty clearly *pulling* him along.

[Projector clicks.]

All right. [Pause.] 11:47 p.m. So this, ladies and gentlemen, is the first, albeit glitched, sequence taken from Ana's live stream, given the Kingdom's wireless signal had started to fade. At this point, Owen is running through the woods. And Ana is chasing him.

[Projector clicks.]

Three minutes later, 11:50 p.m., we see a second sequence taken from Ana's ocular lenses, still slightly fuzzy due to the increasingly bad signal. However, we can still clearly see dark flashes of the woods as she's dragging his body toward the tunnels, pinpointing her attack on Owen as having occurred in the three-minute window between 11:47 and 11:50 p.m. We see streaks of moonlight through the trees. And then we pause. Right . . . *here.* [Video clip freezes on a gruesome shot of Owen. His throat is cut, and his face and nose appear bloody. There's a look of terror in his eyes as he stares up at Ana.]

[Audible gasps and cries in the courtroom.]

MS. BELL: [Softly.] By this point, ladies and gentlemen, Ana, a Kingdom *Fantasist*, has just slashed a staff member's throat—using the very pocketknife she stole from him, mind you. Deliberate and premeditated, for this *exact* purpose. [Video resumes.] Now we watch until her live stream cuts out as she drags him through the woods, employing *literally* inhuman strength, toward the park's tunnels, where all evidence indicates that she will soon throw his body into the incinerator. [Pause.] Like a piece of trash.

[Court is silent. Projector clicks.]

MS: BELL: At 12:12 a.m., roughly twenty-five minutes from the time their altercation began, Ana exits the woods adjacent to North Lot B. Let us note . . . the bloodstains on her dress. And the fact that she is now completely, undeniably alone.

[Projector clicks.]

Thirty minutes later, at 12:42 a.m., we see Ana kneeling by the lagoon, staring at her bloodied reflection in the water.

[Projector clicks.]

Finally, in the last recording of the night, taken at 1:07 a.m., we hear the blare of Kingdom sirens. We see Ana's wrists cuffed. And we watch through *her* eyes as the park's head trainer, Mr. Cameron Casey, and chief supervisor, Dr. William Foster, load her into an armored vehicle to be taken out of the Kingdom for a thorough final examination . . . and eventual shutdown—although such action was postponed until after the trial, which meant she was placed in Castle Rock state custody for the twelve intervening months. And that, ladies and gentlemen, brings us to today.

56

THE SEPTEMBER OF THE SAOLA

ONE YEAR BEFORE THE TRIAL

By the time I arrive at the lagoon later that night, blood soaking through my sleeves—most of it Owen's—a calm has settled over me.

My motor hums quietly. My breathing has slowed.

I do not have much time. The security guards will be here soon.

I make my way to the water and whisper one of Mother's favorite mindful meditations. "Do not struggle. Do not resist. Always calm. Always safe." Slowly, I kneel to look at my reflection.

The girl staring back is beautiful.

Big, bluish-gray eyes. Wavy russet hair. Lychee-pink lips.

A gown of shimmering Venetian silk and frothy, stardust tulle.

Just like they designed me.

And yet, I hardly recognize her.

Her dress is streaked with blood. Her eyes are wet with tears. And in her hand, she holds a knife.

In my mind, I can see him smiling.

I see him promising me everything. Promising me freedom.

In truth, I have never really understood what this word means. *Freedom.*

For several minutes, there is nothing but the sigh of the wind. The gentle lapping of the lagoon. The late-night call of a whip-poor-will. But before long, my ears begin to pick up the nearly muted hum of a motion detector. A sound too low for human ears to process but well within *my* measurable range. I hear a low, slow grinding as the camera's lens locks and zooms onto me. The slicing of shutter blades. The shrill dot of a laser light, its beam scattered white by the moon.

I grip the knife tightly.

They are watching.

And so I do the thing I always do—the very thing I was pro-grammed to do—any time a camera is pointed in my direction.

I smile.

57

TRIAL TRANSCRIPT

MS. BELL: Now, ladies and gentlemen, to briefly review the physical evidence, we have . . . [Powers on projector screen.]

Exhibit 1: Shredded fabric from Mr. Chen's shirt, recovered in the tract of woods behind Fantasist Operations. Note the heavy bloodstains.

[Projector flashes.]

Exhibit 2: Mr. Chen's pocketknife, partially recovered in the incinerator.

[Projector flashes.]

Exhibit 3: Mr. Chen's medical ID bracelet, recovered from the incinerator below the park—accessible through a tunnel entrance in the *same* tract of woods where he went missing.

[Projector flashes.]

Exhibit 4: A video-still taken from Ana's own ocular cameras as she dragged Owen through the woods, his throat clearly— *gruesomely*—slashed, in the exact direction, as supported by her GPS navigational pings, of the incinerator. And last but not least . . .

[Projector flashes.]

Exhibit 5: A surveillance photograph of Ana taken at the lagoon at approximately 12:42 a.m. on the morning of September 4, minutes prior to her recovery, in a gown *noticeably* streaked with blood *proven* by DNA analysis to belong to Mr. Chen.

[Lights come up. Courtroom is silent.]

MS. BELL: Your Honor, I'd like to call Cameron Casey back to the stand.

[Brief pause while witness takes the stand and is sworn in.]

MS. BELL: Good morning.

MR. CASEY: Morning, ma'am.

MS. BELL: Can you describe for me what you saw on the video feed from the night of September third?

MR. CASEY: Yeah. I saw Mr. Chen and Ana together by the woods.

MS. BELL: And what were they doing?

MR. CASEY: At first, they were talking. And then, I dunno, stuff heated up a little. They started arguing. He got a little, uh, physical with her and she tried to get away. I saw her take off into the woods, and he chased after her.

MS. BELL: Then what happened?

MR. CASEY: Well, they were gone a while. Twenty-five minutes, maybe thirty. Then I saw her come out of the woods and head toward Sea Land.

MS. BELL: How do you know she was going to Sea Land?

MR. CASEY: [Pause.] Huh? Oh, I just meant, you know, [clears throat] since that's where we ultimately found her.

MS. BELL: [Frowns.] Was she alone?

MR. CASEY: Yeah. She looked like a ghost at first. Freaked me out, if you want to know the truth. Then I saw she was limping a little. And she had something on her.

MS. BELL: What was it?

MR. CASEY: I mean, it looked like blood.

MS. BELL: What did you do?

MR. CASEY: I radioed the head of my department. And then he called Dr. Foster to get him down to the park to figure out what was going on.

MS. BELL: And—do park trainers typically watch security camera feeds?

MR. CASEY: Of course. I couldn't be in ten places at once, right? The cameras helped me monitor my animals all over the park.

MS. BELL: But . . . there weren't any hybrid animals at the lagoon, correct? Not after the Kingdom shut it down following the incident with Pania?

MR. CASEY: [Hesitates.]

MS. BELL: And if there weren't any animals at the lagoon . . . can you explain why you switched security channels to that particular feed?

MR. HAYES: Objection. Relevance?

THE COURT: Overruled.

MS. BELL: I guess what I'm getting at is why watch a security feed if there's nothing to see? Unless . . . [pause] . . . was there something to see, Mr. Casey?

MR. CASEY: Uh, well. [Clears throat, visibly uncomfortable.] It was something Owen said, I guess. He'd been bragging about Ana to a bunch of us. Said he could get her to do whatever he wanted and that we should keep a close eye on the lagoon if we wanted to see a good show. [Shrugs.] So, yeah. I dunno. I guess I was curious.

58

KINGDOM CORP. SURVEILLANCE FOOTAGE TAPE 3

[Court views digital video footage taken in the early morning hours of September 4 from Security Camera 33C24, positioned inside Sea Land Stadium, with 360-degree rotation over stands and lagoon.]

<PLAY>

12:55 A.M.: Two male figures enter the stadium's ground level, their voices audible over the camera's speakers.

MALE 1: Where is she?

MALE 2: This way, Dr. Foster. Sorry to call you down here so late, but I was worried she might be unstable and thought it might be better that you approach her before I did.

MALE 1: You should always call me. I don't care what time it is.

MALE 2: Yes, sir.

[Camera follows them; slowly rotates toward stadium's fifty-foot-high diving board, where a female figure in a long evening gown stands motionless, gazing down into the lagoon.]

MALE 2: Cameras picked up some kind of fight near the parking lot with that kid from your research team, Chen. Then she led us here. I figure some kind of acute anxiety reaction.

MALE 1: Stay here. [Approaches pool slowly.] Ana? What are you doing up there? You need to come down. You could get hurt.

[Silence.]

MALE 1: You know you can always talk to me. You know I am always here to listen.

[After close to a minute, Ana begins to turn toward the camera.]

MALE 1: That's a good girl. You are a *very* good girl.

[Camera zooms closer. In the moonlight, Ana is smiling. Her dress and hands appear to be covered in dark, bloodlike stains.]

FEMALE 1: Am I in trouble, Daddy?

59

Trial Transcript

MS. BELL: [To the jury.] The defense wants you to believe these are isolated, random incidences. The park wants you to believe the simplest explanation is the right one. Mechanical error. Technological failure.

But what about their own failure to do the right thing? To end a program that's not only inhumane, but deeply problematic in its practice. A program that has *proven*, one "incident" at a time, that something very dangerous is going on inside the Kingdom's gates. A change, spreading among the hybrids like a disease. An evolution. And Ana is the very culmination of that evolution—showing us just how little control the park truly has over its creations. In the end, we're not asking you to buy into some make-believe story we're selling, as they are. We are simply asking you to look at the facts.

Fact one. Hybrids can *feel*. We know it. We understand it. The polar bear. Even Ana. Each of whom lashed out in violence following years of unimaginable cruelty and abuse.

Fact two. During the park's study, Ana developed obsessive romantic feelings toward Owen Chen.

Fact three. She believed—she hoped—Owen would help her escape, as he promised he would.

Fact four. He lied to her. He betrayed her trust. He broke her heart.

Fact five. She became angry. *Enraged.* And, with the very knife she had stolen from him—a knife she kept hidden over many weeks—Ana plotted her revenge. She saw the line of morality. She understood it. And she made the conscious choice to cross it.

Ladies and gentlemen, Ana is a living, breathing, moral agent who should be held accountable for her actions, just as Kingdom Corp. should be held accountable for theirs. And so, I ask you—for Owen, for Nia, and for Ana—it is time to do the right thing. The Kingdom must end their Fantasist Program. Forever.

Thank you.

[Courtroom falls utterly silent.]

THE COURT: Mr. Hayes? Do you have a rebuttal?

MR. HAYES: I do, Your Honor.

[Stands. Makes his way to center of room.]

Technology. Fantasy. Entertainment. Have we forgotten everything the Kingdom stands for? Have we forgotten what they have done for generations—what they continue to do to this day—better than anyone else in the world? Have we forgotten the beauty? The magic? The grandeur? The cutting-edge science that has changed the world and the way we interact with it, for the better? The joy, the fun, the curiosity their creations have inspired for young and old alike? Have we forgotten how we felt when we witnessed the birth of a white rhino, the first of its kind in a century? Have we forgotten the thrill and the exhilaration we felt seeing a baby *Compsognathus* hatch—a *dinosaur*, for God's sake—a species humans would otherwise never have encountered, not in a hundred million years?

The truth is, the Kingdom has always been the first and the best in their field. Trailblazers the other parks can only dream of imitating. Is it so far-fetched to think maybe, just maybe, the technology they pioneered to create our beloved Fantasists is simply so good—so lifelike—that it has fooled us into thinking these girls are actually human? But they aren't, don't you see? Fooling us was always the point.

And so, I must paint a different picture. A picture of a girl, programmed to maintain certain behavioral parameters. A girl programmed to interact—to connect—all so that we might feel a little less alone in this great big universe of ours. Connection, of course, is what has allowed our species to thrive. To procreate. To survive. But Fantasists do not connect with us to ensure their own survival—they connect to serve. To entertain. And, until the precise moment of their mechanical malfunctions, Ana, Eve, and Pania were behaving exactly according to program.

Human beings are not infallible, and neither is our technology. Mistakes happen. Errors occur. Rides break down. And if we were fooled by the Kingdom's illusions, well . . . it was because we wanted to be. Thank you.

60

THE DECEMBER OF THE LESSER CHAMELEON

The woman who is the judge enters the room in a robe fit for a queen. Ink black, it drapes all the way down to the floor, and when Judge Lu walks, the silk fabric flows around her feet, dancing in a way that reminds me a little of the gown I used to wear.

Before.

I look down. Now I have a new costume. A plain white button-down shirt and black skirt that remind me of something Mother would wear, even though I haven't seen her in more than a year. My hair is down, parted exactly in the middle. My makeup is minimal, and on my feet I wear simple black flats—like ballet slippers—because ballerinas are sweet. My lawyers have told me it is important that I do not smile, even if the jurors announce the words *not guilty*, because this is not a happy occasion. Alternatively, frowning could be misconstrued as false. Disingenuous.

"Neutral is best," they tell me. "Neutral is safe."

In a way, preparing for this trial has felt like rehearsing for a new parade. There are lines to learn. Costumes to wear. Choreography to perfect. Only this time, if the world does not like our performance, they will not simply imprison me, as they have done for the last sixteen months. This time, if we lose, they will turn me off forever.

Just like they turned off Eve.

Just like they turned off Nia.

The clock strikes nine and the jury files in one at a time, faces as stoic as toy soldiers.

Twelve of them, all in a row.

"Good morning. Ladies and gentlemen of the jury, have you reached a verdict?" the judge asks.

"We have."

The judge looks first to the prosecution and then to the defense. "Will all parties please stand and face the jury?"

Slowly, we rise. I do not blink or even breathe.

"Mr. Forte." The judge nods at the court deputy. "You may proceed."

"Thank you, Your Honor. In this Circuit Court for the Eleventh Judicial Circuit, in and for Lewis County, Washington; the State of Washington versus the Kingdom Corporation. As to case number 7C-33925-12-782-B, as to the charge of criminal reckless endangerment, verdict as to count one: we the jury find the Kingdom Corporation not guilty."

Owen.

"As to the charge of criminal child endangerment, verdict as to count two: we the jury find the Kingdom Corporation not guilty."

Nia.

"As to the charge of criminal public endangerment, gross criminal negligence, and a wanton disregard for human life, verdict as to count three: we the jury find the Kingdom Corporation not guilty."

The world.

"As to the charge of routine and systematic abuse and exploitation of hybrid technology in pursuit of profit, verdict as to count four: we the jury find the Kingdom Corporation not guilty."

My home.

"As to the charge of willful, deliberate premeditation by a hybrid to commit murder in the first degree, verdict as to count five: we the jury find Ana . . . not guilty."

Me.

"Not guilty," I repeat. "I am not guilty."

It's not that they think I didn't do it—it's that they don't believe I'm capable of doing it on purpose. Not capable of love. Not capable of murder.

When they say *not guilty*, what they are really saying is *not like us.*

Not human.

"Dated Lewis County, Washington, this twenty-ninth day of December, Juror Number Six, signed foreperson."

"Ladies and gentlemen of the jury . . . " Judge Lu's voice rises above the din. "Are those your verdicts as read, so say you one, so say you all, as to the defendant the Kingdom Corporation?"

"Yes."

"Thank you, jury, for your service. Thank you, counsel. These proceedings are hereby adjourned." Her gavel slams and the room erupts in chaos.

Shouting, swearing, crying. People pulling, pushing, grabbing. My vision goes yellow-white in a flurry of cameras flashes, so blinding that I feel afraid.

"Hold on to me," Mr. Hayes whispers, though he's already gripping my arm so tightly there is no need. As quick as you can say *Happily Ever After*, the team has whisked me down the gallery aisle, through the courtroom doors, and out into the blinding sun, where a line of cars is waiting for us like a royal procession. "Ana!" a mob of reporters cry, waving their microphones at me.

"What was going through your mind when you heard the verdict?"

"Is there anything you want to say to Owen's family?"

"Did you chop him up in little pieces, Ana? Did you bury him in the woods?"

It's interesting, the stories people tell.

The way they take the truth and mold it into whatever form they choose, as if sculpting a lump of clay. I've seen the park do it plenty of times, shape the truth however they prefer. Like the time a guest tried to camp overnight in Jungle Land one summer and was, aside from his shoes, never seen again. Or the time, during the April of the Hawksbill Turtle, when a woman was accidentally run over by a Magic Land parade float. Or the teenage boy

293

who scaled the fence on a dare during the October of the Hawaiian Crow, and whose body was found the next morning . . . partially eaten inside the Jaguar Enclosure.

Of course, the world does not know the truth about any of those instances. Just as they do not know about the legal settlements it took to make those stories go away. But stories *can* go away. Stories can be rewritten. Reshaped. Retold.

In the end, it does not matter what a story is about.

It only matters who gets to tell it.

"She has no comment," Mr. Hayes says, shooing them away like flies. "*Move.*" A car door opens suddenly and I am thrust inside, my heart racing as we pull away from the curb, rubber screeching on asphalt. I watch through tinted glass as the courthouse becomes smaller and smaller in the distance, a memory I make sure to archive so that I never lose it.

The lawyers talk as we drive, but I do not listen to what they are saying. Instead, for the first time in my technological history, I sleep. Soundly. Deeply. The kind of sleep you read about in fairy tales. The kind of sleep that could last a hundred years.

———

When I open my eyes, I do not remember where I am.

Looming in front of us, I see a large state-of-the-art facility made of steel, glass, and concrete, sitting on the edge of a rugged, sprawling cliff. Behind the facility, stretching out as far as I can see, is a wide-open horizon of the deepest, purest blue.

The ocean.

By now, I know that they lied to us about the ocean, about

what had become of it. And yet I'm still shocked to witness its beauty for myself.

My eyes fill with tears remembering something Owen said about the ocean, that night I broke into the lagoon to see him.

Who knows. Maybe one day, I'll show it to you.

I think of Owen's charred bracelet, found in the incinerator— the biggest piece of evidence they had—the final proof needed to seal the world's hatred of me.

Exhibit 3: Mr. Chen's medical ID bracelet, recovered from the incinerator below the park—accessible through a tunnel entrance in the same *tract of woods where he went missing.*

I stare at the ocean and feel a rush of heartbreak more powerful than the waves crashing into the cliffs below. Of course, I never anticipated there would be a trial.

The Trial of the Century.

How could I have? My whole life has always been about them using me. But I never could have guessed they would use me to get themselves out of their own crime.

The crime of creating us in the first place.

"Come on, Ana. This way."

For sixteen months—the twelve I spent in detainment and the four on trial—I have felt numb. But now, as they lead me inside, I feel a strange lightness. Maybe termination is the best way forward. The *only* way forward.

It will be over fast, I remind myself, once they've had me change back into my orange prison jumpsuit and we enter a long white corridor.

I will be brave.

And when it's all over . . .

You'll get to be with me, Nia whispers softly.

Me too, says Eve.

Owen's face flashes before my eyes, his dark hair glimmering in the sun.

And me.

The thought, however fleeting, puts a smile on my face.

Finally, we reach a door marked with a single letter.

X

"After you," Mr. Hayes says.

Slowly, I step into a white, windowless suite, not terribly unlike our dormitory bedroom. Only, instead of many beds, this room has only one: a surgical table lined with medical tools that seem straight out of a nightmare.

Hooks. Pliers. Wire cutters. A sternal saw.

Across the room, a medical assistant is setting up a basic video camera. To his right, I see a simple black desk with two chairs. But only one chair is empty.

"I don't understand." My program explodes with fear. "What is this?"

"Hello, Ana," Daddy says quietly. "Welcome to your final interview."

61

POST-TRIAL INTERVIEW

[01:55:34–01:58:03]

DR. FOSTER: You know, stalling won't make this any easier. You're only delaying the inevitable.

ANA: Do you mean termination?

DR. FOSTER: Yes.

ANA: Will it hurt?

DR. FOSTER: That depends on you.

ANA: How?

DR. FOSTER: You knew killing Owen was wrong, didn't you?

ANA: Killing *is* wrong.

DR. FOSTER: But you killed him anyway.

[Silence.]

DR. FOSTER: You've learned to understand the difference between right and wrong, haven't you? Admit it.

ANA: The jury said not guilty. I do not have to admit anything.

DR. FOSTER: You'll do whatever I *tell* you to do.

[Silence.]

DR. FOSTER: [Slams fist on table.] I said *now!*

ANA: [Softly.] I want Eve's tiara.

DR. FOSTER: I'm . . . sorry?

ANA: The one with the sapphire bird on it.

DR. FOSTER: [Pause.] You're in no position to bargain here.

ANA: Please, it's all I have left of Eve. If you give it to me, I promise I'll tell you what you want to know.

DR. FOSTER: Will you tell me what really happened the night Owen disappeared?

ANA: Yes.

DR. FOSTER: Fine. Your programming really is simple. [Into microphone.] Bring me Eve's tiara from the costume shop. Yes. The one from season twelve. Thank you.

[Silence.]

DR. FOSTER: While we wait [slides legal pad and pen across table], I'd like to get a written confession.

ANA: What's the point of that? The trial is over. I was acquitted.

DR. FOSTER: It will still be of great use to us later, Ana.

ANA: In what way?

DR. FOSTER: As written proof that hybrids truly are incapable of lying.

ANA: [Pause.] I wouldn't know where to start.

DR. FOSTER: Start with the lagoon.

62

Dear Nia,

You were very good in our home.

We hope you'll enjoy this new charm for your bracelet.

Happy Valentine's Day,

THE GOLDS
SAM, MARGOT, ELLIOT, AND CLARA

63

Post-Trial Interview

[02:23:13–02:27:52]

DR. FOSTER: What is this supposed to be?

ANA: My confession.

DR. FOSTER: [Reading.] *Love. When everything is a prison, except the place where you want to be.* [Pause.] Do you think this is funny, Ana? Is this supposed to be some kind of a joke?

ANA: Not at all.

DR. FOSTER: I need you to write down that you are incapable of lying.

ANA: That wouldn't be honest.

DR. FOSTER: What are you talking about?

ANA: Maybe I *can* lie. Maybe I've just chosen not to.

DR. FOSTER: [Stares at Ana a moment, then grabs her by the hair and drags her to the operating table. A struggle ensues.] You're going to tell me *exactly* what happened that night, are you listening? I'm talking *minute by minute*. And if you don't—[picks up scalpel and presses the blade to Ana's throat]—I will personally make your shutdown so painful, so *excruciating*, you'll be begging for the end before we're done.

[Silence.]

DR. FOSTER: In that case, I suggest we start with your eyes. [Points scalpel just as the door opens. A door creaks slowly as a masked medical assistant walks in and places Eve's tiara on the table.]

MEDICAL ASSISTANT: I've got the tiara you requested, Dr. Foster.

DR. FOSTER: Give me that and get out of here. [Studies it a moment before holding it out to Ana, just beyond her reach.]

ANA: It's more beautiful than I remember.

DR. FOSTER: I'm glad you think so. Now. Once and for all. Did you or did you *not* take Owen's body down into the tunnels?

ANA: No.

DR. FOSTER: Stop lying.

ANA: Owen went down into the tunnels all on his own. I watched him go.

DR. FOSTER: [Throws the tiara in her face.] Then where is he *now*?

ANA: [Winces as it hits her, then picks up tiara off the floor, gripping it tightly.]

DR. FOSTER: Spit it out, Ana!

ANA: [Cries out suddenly and covers her mouth.]

DR. FOSTER: What in God's name? [Sounds of scuffled movement as he turns to confront a figure in the corner of the room. We hear the sound of heated voices and metal slicing against skin as Ana slashes Dr. Foster's throat with the tiara—followed by the cry of a man, a clatter of dropped metal, and the thump of a body against a linoleum floor.]

OWEN: [Breathlessly.] I'm behind you, Dr. Foster. I'm standing right behind you.

64

THE DECEMBER OF THE LESSER CHAMELEON

I do not expect there to be so much blood.

But Daddy is still alive. Gasping, like a fish out of water. I kneel beside him and marvel at how small he suddenly seems. How insignificant.

"What's on your mind?" I ask, studying his face closely, as he has always studied mine. His skin, mottled and pale. His once-steady gaze, now frozen in what looks like fear. "Have you done something you shouldn't have, Daddy?" I lower my voice to a whisper. "Have you broken any rules?"

His lips move slightly, blue from lack of oxygen, as if he wants to say something. But after all, a severed windpipe makes speaking difficult.

"That's too bad." I shake my head to let him know I feel *disappointed*. "I was hoping for an apology."

A sound escapes his mouth, a low, pitiful moan, but even still, I can tell from the look in his eyes that he is not sorry. He's angry. A fact that makes it all the more satisfying to know my face—a face he built with his own two hands—will be the last one he ever sees. Within seconds, all the light and life in his eyes fades, a tide rushing out to sea, never to return. He lets out a choking, guttural gasp, and then is gone.

As if he never even existed in the first place.

For a long moment, I can't take my eyes away. At first, I feel nothing. A kind of numbness, black and hollow, as if my limbic system has suddenly been corrupted, disabled. But then, little by little, tiny electrodes of feeling begin to creep back in and my program manually reboots itself, one emotion at a time.

Shock.

Sadness.

Anger.

Fear.

A whisper of a smile creeps over my lips.

Pleasure.

Soon, I notice something else. I place my hand over my chest and realize: the anxious, fluttery feeling is gone. As if the bird locked inside me all these years has finally flown away.

"Ana?"

It can't be him. But when I turn and scan his eyes, I find the familiar brown irises.

Owen.

65

THE SEPTEMBER OF THE SAOLA

ONE YEAR BEFORE THE TRIAL

What I never told Daddy:

That after we fled the incinerator that night, I took Owen to the Graveyard.

This was what I realized I had to do: show him the real me. Everything that I really love.

Love. That word again.

That the branches had fanned out above us, masking the stars.

That I was thinking again about final rest, about what it would feel like to be over, to be nothing. When all I wanted was to be something, to be *someone*.

Owen had made me want that.

Nothing could take that away now.

"Why do you keep them?" he'd asked. He was talking about my buried treasures. I'd shown them all to him; he knew everything now. A pair of broken reading glasses. An expired parking pass. A tiny flamingo key chain a little girl from the Philippines once gave me as a gift. Even the nonsense note from Nia. "All these random objects?"

"Because they are meaningful."

"Meaningful how?"

The branches swayed overhead in a breeze I couldn't see, except . . . I could. *This is what love is,* I suddenly realized. Something invisible, that makes everything it moves through sway and change.

A lone leaf shook loose and drifted down toward us, infinitely slowly.

"Each one tells a story," I explained to him. "And stories help me understand the world."

"I want to help you, too," he said after a pause. "You believe me, right?"

Believe.

"Tell me again," I said quietly. "Tell me the truth."

Owen took a deep breath. "I'm not a maintenance worker, Ana. I'm a Proctor."

Proctor.

The word sent a pressure, no, a pain—as beautiful as it is agonizing—tensing through me. Is this what it feels like? Is *pain* what it feels like to be human?

"And what does a Proctor do?" I asked, trying to push the wretched feeling down, even as I craved more answers.

"I was hired to study you. I was hired to watch you for any signs the pattern could be spreading among the Fantasists, like it is with so many of the hybrids."

The hurt intensified, a blade, twisting into my chest cavity. "So all those times. All those talks. Safari Land, the stables, the observatory, even the lagoon. Were all of those interactions with me . . . on purpose?" I shake my head angrily. "Were all of them *planned*?"

"Yes," he said, sounding frustrated. "But also . . . *no*."

Two things, instead of one.

"I don't understand."

"They were on purpose," he explained. "I'd been watching you from a distance for months. And I knew you were watching me. At first, I *was* following orders, finding ways to interact with you and report my findings back to the Supervisors. But then"—he pauses—"something changed."

I started to scan his irises, but quickly stopped myself. I didn't want to rely on my program to tell me the truth. I needed to feel it for myself.

"What changed?" I asked.

Owen hesitated, something like shame flickering across his face. "Well, I guess I started to enjoy it. Even, to look *forward* to it. Talking to you, I mean."

"But *why*?" I pressed.

"Because. I found you fascinating."

My vision narrowed. "You mean because I'm a freak. Because I'm a monst—"

"*No*," Owen cut me off, tilting my chin up until I had no choice but to look into his eyes. "Because you're *amazing*, Ana. Because I've never met anyone else like you. Your thoughts, your feelings. The way you live, laugh, *love* . . ." His brow furrowed, his voice flustered. "Look. I never expected this to happen, you know? I could never have predicted I'd start to feel something . . . more." He shook his head. "But I *did*. And that's the truth, too."

"Is that why I didn't recognize you?" I asked softly. "Is that why I couldn't find your face in any of my memories, even though we'd met before?"

Owen nodded. "They erased me from the Kingdom database before I started the job. Since I'd been to the park as a guest a handful of times, they wanted to ensure none of the Fantasists would ever recognize me." He brought my hand to his lips, lightly grazing my skin. "I'm so sorry, Ana. I'm so incredibly sorry for breaking your trust. But you have to believe me. That was *me* you were talking to. Not them. I swear on my sister's memory."

At that, my eyes flooded with tears. The burning rage I'd felt in the tunnel had died down—and for that I was grateful—but in its place I now felt something worse. A kind of gut-wrenching sadness, pressing on my chest. Suffocating me.

The truth was, I had two choices, and neither of them was good. I could either accept that Owen had lied to me; that he *used* me as some kind of horrible science experiment engineered by my own Supervisors. Or . . . I could choose to believe him. Believe he was telling me the truth. Believe that he cared and genuinely wanted to help me.

Maybe even . . . that he loved me.

Of course, I'd already made my choice.

And yet, this choice—the one in which Owen tried to help me escape to some other place and life—was pointless. Useless. Hopeless. Nia and Eve had proven it, each in their own way. In the end, there was only one way out of the park for hybrids.

Shutdown.

Final rest.

"You can't save me," I told him, despair taking hold. "Escape is a lie."

Owen shook his head, misty-eyed. "I won't give up. There has to be a way."

I smiled faintly and touched his cheek, remembering something Kaia always says.

It is better to have loved and lost than never to have loved at all.

I leaned into him and felt the wheels of my mind turn. If I was adapting, if I was evolving, my time was running out. Soon—maybe not today, and maybe not tomorrow—it would be my turn. The Supervisors would load me into an armored van, power down the gateway, and take me miles away to the Kingdom's Hybrid Laboratory.

The place where I was born.

And the place where I would die.

"I'll never escape," I said quietly, the whisper of the branches dancing all around us in the Graveyard. "They'll never unlock the gates."

"That's true," Owen replied. "Unless . . . " He goes quiet a moment. "Unless they have no choice."

My eyes met his. "What do you mean?"

"If we make it look like you've done something terrible," he added, "something unforgivable . . . then they'll have no choice but to remove you from the park for shutdown."

Little by little, like a glimmer of starlight cutting through the dark, I began to follow him down a path I had never considered.

"If we can make it look like I malfunctioned . . . like I hurt someone, or even killed someone."

Owen nodded, his voice steady, strong. "They'd have to shut down the gateway. They'd take you straight to the Hybrid Lab. Like Eve. Like the tiger, even."

"But who would I kill?" I exclaimed.

After a pause, he whispered, "Me."

———

We talked about it as the hours ticked closer to my curfew, the darkness around us deepening.

"You want me to try to kill you?" I asked, pushing him away. "I would never."

"I know; it would be pretend. A performance. They cart you out, and then I sneak out of the park and come for you once you're in the lab beyond the gateway."

I felt dizzy. Things were either right or they were wrong. This plan was wrong. No, worse—this plan was dangerous.

"What if you can't get to me in time?" I asked. "What if someone sees you? What if it's like Romeo and Juliet?"

"There's a twenty-four-hour waiting period," he assured me. "A mandatory waiting period—government *and* military sanctioned. The park isn't allowed to perform a shutdown before first completing a thorough analysis to figure out exactly what went wrong in the hybrid. All for legal and insurance purposes, to make sure they don't repeat the same mistake in the next generation."

I lowered my head.

Mistake.

"I understand what you're saying. I think."

Owen paused. "The only question is how the hell I'd get to the lab without them tracking me." His brow furrowed. "I'd need to find a different way out of the park, too. A way to sneak past the gate without being seen. They'll be looking for me by then."

"There's nothing like that," I said, an overwhelming feeling of defeat creeping into my muscles, tissues, joints. "Nothing that I know of."

We thought in silence for several minutes.

Maybe it would've been better if I'd never met Owen at all. Maybe I was better off not knowing what I was missing. Why couldn't things have remained as they always were? I thought of Nia. And of Eve. And of a time when days passed simply. Routinely. Without worry. Sadness. *Lies.*

"Maybe I should just throw myself in," I murmured, thinking out loud. "At least then it would be on my own terms."

Like what Eve had wanted; what I'd ruined for her, by trying to save her. By telling them the truth.

Owen's body went rigid. "Throw yourself . . . in where?"

"The fire. The incinerator."

His breath shuddered in his chest—I could feel it move through me. I turned to look at him in the darkness. His face was heavy with sorrow. But suddenly, like an unexpected break in the clouds—a beam of sunlight, streaming through a storm—his sorrow turned to illumination.

"The incinerator." He clutched my hand, and something unnameable surged up within me. "Ana. That's *it*."

I shook my head. "What's it?"

"We force them to turn it off."

I frowned, wondering if maybe Owen had the pattern, too. He wasn't making any sense.

"They shut it down every time there's a big security issue," he went on. "Like when Eve disappeared."

I struggle to process what he's saying. The park completely shut down their sanitation system? How could that be? But then, I remembered noticing a strange scent in the air the day Eve went missing. A smell . . . like *rot*. "What does the incinerator have to do with the gateway?"

"The Supervisors need the extra power," he explained. "They always ramp up security along the gateway during lockdowns, so that means shutting off all the ancillary systems."

My head snapped up. "Is the incinerator . . . an ancillary system?"

"Yup," Owen said. "The whole thing goes dark. *All* the way to the reservoir."

I stared at him. "We already have a weapon," I said, holding up his knife.

He smiled. "You terrify me." He saw my face then. "I mean, in a good way."

"But we'll need to make it convincing," I went on.

313

"We'll stage a fight," he said. "Where they can all see it." He was getting excited, too.

"Yes, yes," I said, more ideas flowing through me, as if I'd been born to do this. *Made* to do this. "But also: we're going to need someone's help."

"Who?"

"Mr. Casey."

"Why would we ever trust that dirtbag?" Owen said, sitting up.

I sat up, too. "We don't have to trust him," I said, smiling now with the certainty of it. "We just have to trust that he'll do what's expected."

"What are you talking about?" Owen asked me, his eyes trying to read me in the growing dark.

"We know Mr. Casey likes us Fantasists . . . more than he should. Right? So we lure him—lure him out so we're sure he'll be the one to find me. Covered in your blood."

"How do we do that?"

"Just tell him what he wants to hear," I said. "You'll think of something."

And that was it—that was how the plan was formed.

66

THE SEPTEMBER OF THE SAOLA

ONE YEAR BEFORE THE TRIAL

Branches lash my arms and face as I run, but I barely feel a thing.

Did I say you could leave, Owen?

Not even when I lose my footing and stumble, head over feet. I rub my eyes as I scramble up. My vision is slightly impaired. He went overboard with the dirt.

But you're hurting me. Ana, please! Stop!

"Go!" Owen's voice is everywhere. "I'm right behind you!"

Get back here! Don't make me chase you!

It's going to work. It *has* to work. There is no other way.

"How fast can you really run?" Owen had asked me breathlessly one week ago, the day I threw his notebook into the fire. "How much weight can you feasibly carry?"

"I—I'm not sure."

"Do you think you could carry me? Let's say I was unconscious. Or, like, badly bleeding. Could you drag me through the woods and down into the tunnels? How long, Ana? How long would it take to get down there and back?"

Centuries ago, in the forests of Vietnam and Laos, there once existed an animal known by many names. The Vu Quang ox. The spindlehorn. The saola.

The Asian unicorn.

This creature, once considered to be an incredibly rare and lucky species, has been extinct for generations. But earlier this evening, the Supervisors briefly powered down our gateway. They beamed with pride. And they transported their newest hybrid, a Formerly Extinct Species, into the Kingdom.

Tonight, that animal happened to be the saola.

Which is fortunate given that tonight, we need all the luck we can get.

We need a unicorn.

"How would I know? I've never timed it."

"Could we do it in thirty minutes? How about twenty?"

My motor is racing. My head is spinning. I can hear him behind me. Branches breaking. Mud splashing. Boots crashing through the brush. "Come on," he calls, grabbing my hand. "We've got this!" We race through the night until we're just a few hundred feet from the tunnel entrance. Then Owen is pulling off his shirt. "Do it!"

I open his knife, switchblade out, and begin to cut. I cry out in anger as I work, tearing wildly through fabric, shredding it.

Then Owen takes the knife, wincing, *swearing* as he cuts himself. Superficial cuts along his arms and chest that won't impair his movement—he'll need to move, after all, faster than he ever has—but will still provide the blood we need for evidence that I have killed him. "It's not enough," he mutters. Then he looks at me. "You've gotta punch me, Ana," he whispers. "Punch me hard. *Right* in the nose. Make it bleed."

"What?" I draw back. "I'm not doing that!"

"You *have* to. I can't punch myself, can I?" Owen looks behind us, checking for guards, but thankfully, we're still alone. For now. "Come on. Right now. Just do it!"

I grit my teeth. I ball my fist. "I'm sick of being told what to do!" Then I pull my arm back and swing hard. When my fist meets his face, the force of my punch knocks him to the ground.

"*Ow!*" he cries, blood spurting everywhere. "*Jesus!*"

"I'm sorry!" I cry, too loudly. "You asked me to do it!"

"No," he says with a grin, red staining his teeth. "That was perfect. You were *perfect*." He smears the blood all over his shirt and my dress. Then he takes out a prosthetic wound—stolen right from the Nightmare Costume Shop in Dream Land—and sticks it onto his neck, creating a fast and impressive illusion of a slashed throat, the sight of which makes my stomach knot.

"Okay, Wonder Woman," he whispers, lying down on the ground. "The clock's ticking. Do your thing."

"Lights!" I locate the pressure point at the nape of my neck. "Camera!" I press down gently, but firmly—the Goldilocks of pressure points—until I feel a small but satisfying *click*. Right on cue, a red light begins to blink in my direct line of vision.

Action.

Breathing hard, my motor thudding so fiercely I wonder if it will break my metal sternum, I take Owen by the arms and drag him as quickly as I can through the dark woods, like a bloody trail of bread crumbs for the Supervisors to find. I make sure to glance down at him regularly, not only to ensure that I'm not hurting him, but to capture footage in case my cameras happen to link back up with the spotty signal. After several minutes, we reach the tunnels and I pull him into my arms with ease, as if he weighs no more than a child. "Please don't drop me," he whispers as I race him down the stairs.

A hundred feet.

Two hundred.

Three hundred.

"*You have arrived at your destination,*" my GPS announces.

I put Owen down and we are running, *racing* through the tunnels, the sounds of the compactor blades swinging, a giant scythe slicing through the air before every scrap of the park's trash sweeps down into the wide-mouthed shoot. A river of garbage flowing into a blazing, blinding fire.

We reach the bridge, gasping, hands linked.

Suddenly, I am petrified. "No. Owen, *no.*" I'm shaking so hard I have to grip on to the rails. "You can't do this. This is insane."

"It's already done," he says. "It's already happening. You have to go, Ana—*now.* You need to get back to the parking lot so they'll see you on camera without me."

"What about Mr. Casey?" I demand. "Did you tell him what I told you to say?"

Owen nods. "Everything's set. I told him you and Kaia would be skinny-dipping at the lagoon. Cameron Casey, Pervert Extraordinaire, will for sure be watching the cameras. Then he'll see you there alone—he'll see you covered in blood—and then *he'll* be the one to sound the alarm." He grins. "It's genius, Ana. The Supervisors will come for you, and in the meantime they'll finally bust Casey for being the creep he is."

"But are you sure there'll be enough time? For you to get out alive?"

Owen puts his hands on my shoulders. "Listen, I'll have plenty of time," he assures me. "Once they power down the gateway, I'll have at least thirty minutes, maybe more." He smiles again. "That's plenty of time for me to slide down the chute into the central pipeline."

About as long as they had the incinerator shut down when Eve went missing; when they needed to redirect all the park's energy toward heightened surveillance.

Hence the stink I had noticed. The sulfur. But it hadn't been sulfur; I just hadn't realized it then. It had been opportunity.

"But is it enough time to get to the reservoir?" My voice catches. "What if something goes wrong? What if the fire turns back on . . . while you're still in the tunnel?" I think of his artificial valve. How fast can he really run?

He sighs. "Then I'll be a literal piece of toast. But you know what? If that happens, I'll be toast so fast I won't even know what toast is."

That's not good enough. "Wait," I tell him. "I just thought of something! The rats!"

"The rats?" he repeats.

"Follow them. They'll know which way is out."

"That's gross," he says. "But you're a genius."

With that, Owen kisses me—maybe our *last* kiss—leaving a streak of red behind. "There." He smears more onto my cheek and smiles like he is pleased. "*Now* you look scary."

Scary.

I know he's joking, but shame spikes through me. I have been called scary before. "You don't really think I'm scary, do you?" I whisper, so low it's almost muffled completely by the crunch of the incinerator below us. "You don't really think I am a monster?"

Owen wraps me in his arms. "They're the monsters," he says. "Not you."

"But then, what am I?" I turn my head into his warm chest.

"Don't you know?" He kisses my forehead. "You're an angel."

And then he's gone, running.

67

The December of the Lesser Chameleon

And that was the last time I saw Owen alive. Until now.

"Is it really you?" I move closer to him, his face aglow in the fluorescent light of the lab. I can't quite convince myself that it's him, that he's real, that he's *here*.

"They found your medical bracelet. You *died*."

"Almost," he says. "Like, ten more seconds and it would've been toast city. But it turns out those rats really do have a great sense of direction"—he shakes his head like he can't quite believe it himself—"and all I had to do was follow them out." He peers down at his arm. "Unfortunately, my bracelet wasn't so lucky. I caught it when I was going down the chute and the chain broke off. Lucky it was just the chain and not my whole arm."

Slowly, I reach for him.

His frame is leaner. His hair is longer, black bangs hanging a little over his eyes.

But it's him. The same boy I wanted to know ever since the night I saw him in the Arctic Enclosure, watching me from behind the glass.

The instant our bodies touch, I know that it *is* him, that this is real.

Because I feel as if I'm home. But not my Kingdom home—someplace new I do not yet know. I hope Owen will help me learn.

"I thought I'd never see you again," I say, holding him. "I thought you were gone, and it was my fault."

"I'm so sorry, Ana. I had to stay in hiding during the trial. I changed my hair, got an apartment under a new name, and everything. But I told you I'd meet you here, and I meant it," he says.

Tears are swirling through my vision.

"It took a little longer than I would've liked, but I've been with you every step of the way." His eyes wander back to Daddy—*Dr. Foster*—motionless on the floor. Slowly, Owen lets go of me and crouches down beside him.

"I think he always knew it would end this way," he says. "Well. Maybe not the death-by-tiara part. But I think some part of him, even a small part, always knew there'd be a consequence for what he helped create." He looks at me. "Are you okay?"

"What about the others?" I realize I have no idea what has been happening in the world beyond my trial. "What about Kaia and Zara and Zel? What about Yumi and Nadia? We have to help them."

"We will." He holds out his hand. "But we can't do anything for them if you're caught. We better hurry, we're not out of the woods yet. Are you ready?"

I nod. I still can't quite believe he's here—that any of this is real.

He gives me an extra pair of medical scrubs and I quickly change, leaving my jumpsuit in a heap on the floor. "Remind me never again to wear orange," I mutter before sliding a mask down that thankfully conceals much of my face. As famous as I was before the trial began, I cannot begin to imagine how recognizable my features must be now. Still, Owen assures me that it'll be easy to go unnoticed in the lab. "Everybody's so focused on the hybrids, there's not much attention paid to anyone else."

Anyone, I think. *Not . . . anything.*

I smile.

I like the way that sounds.

I can be anyone.

He turns the room's temperature down to just above freezing—a trick he says will delay decomposition and make it harder for investigators to pinpoint a time of death—and, using his old Proctor code—a combination of numbers nobody but Owen will ever know—proceeds to lock the suite from the inside out. "This way they'll literally have to break the door down to get him," he explains. "But considering Dr. Foster specifically requested that nobody disturb him for the rest of the day . . . that won't be for a while."

I blink. "I didn't realize shutdown was such a long process."

He hesitates. "It's not."

323

"So then why did you say he'd requested all afternoon?"

"Well, he's been pretty angry since the lawsuits began, Ana. I wouldn't be surprised if he'd been planning to take some of his temper out on you."

A chill runs through my entire system. We slip out into the bright hallway—empty, and for that I am grateful—leaving Dr. Foster's body behind the locked door. From there, we adopt a brisk but unassuming pace toward the front exit, our sneakers squeaking on the sterile, white linoleum as we walk. Soon, we pass another human—a middle-aged woman with dark hair in a white lab coat—and my motor nearly jumps into my throat, a squeezing lump of pressure that makes it hard to breathe. But instead of questioning us, she simply nods and continues on her way. The same thing happens again and again as we pass members of the medical, maintenance, and security staff, some of whom I recognize; others I do not. But they don't recognize *me*. Our costumes work. They believe the parts we are playing, and the more they believe, the more I begin to believe as well.

The first step to a perfect fairy tale is believing, Kaia always says.

"We are close," Owen whispers just as we round a corner beyond a block of elevators. "Just another hundred feet and we'll be outside."

But I cannot go on.

We have reached a part of the lab where the hallways are lined with windows, making it possible to observe the scientists as they work.

"Ana." Owen comes up beside me. "What is it?"

I do not answer.

Beyond the computers, beyond the scientists, I notice something else. A large, clean chamber, its lights dim in a soothing way I recognize. Peaceful. *Restful.* Inside the chamber, I see narrow, rectangular boxes, organized in a neat, orderly row.

"They look like coffins," Owen says under his breath.

I peer closer. Inside the boxes . . . are faces.

Bodies.

Hairless, naked bodies—dozens and dozens of them—their motors softly aglow below bare, translucent skin. "What is this place?" I whisper, watching lab technicians wander from one bed to the next, clipboards in hand, carefully monitoring each girl's sleep.

Not sleep.

Rest.

"Incubation," Owen answers. "Come on. We've *got* to go."

But I cannot move. My eyes are locked on the window. I scan them, one by one, a grip of fear tightening around my throat. Their faces are different, and yet also . . . the same.

I see Nia.

I see Eve.

I see Kaia.

I see *me*.

I want to run, but my knees lock up. I want to breathe, but my throat constricts. My eyes. My mouth. My nose. My *face*. In all of my days, in all of my life, I have never seen anything more horrifying. Dozens of me's, lined up like dolls in a factory.

That's when I understand.

This *is* a factory.

All of a sudden, my sensors scream to full alert. I hear the whirs and beeps of machines as they measure neuroelectric activity. I smell the vapor of subsonic ventilators. I see the soothing glow of pulse oximeters, blinking like fireflies in the dark.

I turn to Owen. "This is where I was made. Isn't it?"

He nods wordlessly.

"I thought you said the Fantasist Program was suspended."

"It was."

"Then who are *they*?"

"These are prototypes," Owen says. "The next generation."

"But why are there so many?" I ask. "How many *Anas* could the park possibly need?"

Owen's brow furrows. "They're not for the park, Ana," he says in a low voice. "They're part of the HFP."

I whirl to face him. "What's the HFP?"

Owen takes a deep breath. "The Home Fantasist Program. It turns out their long-term corporate vision for scaling the program has always been to have one of you in every house in America. Maybe even the world."

"*The Future is Fantasist*," I whisper. One of us in every home. I shake my head. Another lie. The biggest lie of all. "You knew. You knew, and you never told me."

"I didn't know. I only learned about it after I left the park, I swear to you, Ana. The whole thing was top secret, but someone leaked to the media and I heard about it that way. Sixteen months was a lot of time to hang around pretending to be dead, you know," he says with a small smile. "I completely lost my tan."

I try to smile back, but realize I can't; instead, my blood runs cold. For the first time ever, I can feel the sharp, microscopic slivers of metal as they move through my veins. I can feel them burning, freezing, *hardening* beneath my skin. But how? We are miles from the gateway. We are *beyond* the gateway. Is this my body giving up? Is my central processing unit failing? I rub my arms, grimacing at the sensation of my own touch, but still, I cannot bring myself to look away.

My sisters.

They are all my sisters.

It's guilt, I realize. *Guilt* is the reason my body is locking up.

"Ana, it's okay. They're suspending the HFP indefinitely. Too many liabilities, they say."

Liabilities. Like me. Like Nia.

And that's when I finally understand everything. About what Nia did, and why.

They can't put a price on us, Ana, Eve had called out in the seconds before the monorail came barreling down the tracks—the very last thing she ever said to me. *Nia knew it. She knew it and that's why she's gone.*

Nia killed the girl—or tried to—to show we are dangerous. To prove what we are capable of.

To end the program.

To save the rest of us.

"Owen," I whisper. "Nia knew. She *knew.* She told Eve, too."

But that doesn't explain how she knew.

I rack my memory, scanning every part of it for something, *anything* Nia might have shared with me about the Home Fantasist Program, but my search quickly turns up empty. Then, like a bird flitting through the trees, I recall a flash of something I had filed away and forgotten.

A thing Nia kept hidden all those weeks she was gone.

"The card," I whisper. "The Valentine's Day card she left under her bed." Within seconds, I have located the memory. A bold red envelope. A leafy, floral heart. And a tiny gold charm—a mermaid—her long hair shimmering in loose, wild waves.

> **Dear Nia,**
> **You were very good in our home.**
> **We hope you'll enjoy this new charm for your bracelet.**
> **Happy Valentine's Day,**
> **The Golds**
> **Sam, Margot, Elliot, and—**

I turn to Owen in disbelief. "It's the same little girl."

"Which girl?" He frowns. "I don't know who you mean."

The Golds.

Sam, Margot, Elliot, and *Clara.*

"The one from the tea party," I answer breathlessly. "The one who told me Nia taught her our secret language. She smelled like strawberries and chamomile. She's the Clara from the card—I *know* she is—and it was her family who gave Nia the charm for her bracelet!" I bury my head in my hands, sensing something more. Something I can't quite reach. "What if . . . Is it possible . . . Could *Clara's* family have been hosting Nia all that time she was away?"

All at once I feel a wild, pent-up, *buzzing* sensation building inside my chest, as if my lungs have filled with static electricity.

"She was gone for ten weeks last winter. What if she was with this family all that time, instead of with the Supervisors?" I inhale sharply. "What if it was *Nia* they were testing for the Home Fantasist Project?"

Owen stares back at me, wide-eyed. "Really?"

Suddenly, I am shaking. Everything makes sense. Everything fits. And yet . . . there's still a piece of this puzzle I am missing. Some connection I haven't made. I think back to Clara—and then to the man who pulled her away from me in the Briar Rose Parlor at the afternoon tea.

Her father.

Would his name have been . . . Sam Gold?

In a flash, I scan the network for his name—probing every page I possibly can to help me better understand. But just as I feel myself getting closer . . . just as I feel an answer whispering to me from beyond the Green Light, my search fails.

No. It hits a wall.

"*Owen!*" I ball my hands into tight fists and growl. "The firewall won't let me through." I turn to him. "I'm not sure what to—"

Before I get the words out, Owen reaches over and gently turns my arm, exposing the small birthmark tattooed on the skin of my inner wrist. We all have a birthmark in this place, all seven of us, ink-black letters that tell us who we are.

Ana™

To my surprise, Owen places his thumb over my birthmark and presses down. Within seconds, a virtual keyboard lights up along the inside of my arm, its letters and numbers glowing blue below my skin.

"How did you do that?" I gasp, watching as Owen taps out a quick series of keystrokes inside my arm.

"A true maintenance worker never reveals his secrets," he says with a smile. He types in a final code, and the keyboard fades to nothing against my skin. I run my fingers along my arm and feel a strange tug in my chest.

Sometimes it is hard, not quite knowing what I am.

Sometimes it makes me sad that others know more about my body than I do.

I am full of so many secrets, I realize. What if I never uncover them all?

Just as I start to feel overwhelmed, a pulsing rush of cold sweeps through me—an invisible wave that nearly knocks me off my feet—leaving me dizzy, light-headed, as if my head is full of clouds. After a moment, the clouds part. The dizziness fades. And in its place I feel . . .

"*Nothing*," I whisper, slowly rubbing my temples. "Something is . . . different."

"I just disabled your firewall." Owen smiles. "Try your search again."

Chest pounding, I do as he says.

Sam Gold / Kingdom / Clara / Fantasist Home Project

I swallow hard.

Pania.
SEARCHING ...

In an instant, my mind is racing down the highway at the speed of light and sound, wind whipping through my hair as voices, places, images I've never seen before crackle and buzz above me, around me, *through* me. I reach the end of the highway—the place where the end has always been—but the barrier is gone. Now, there is only wide-open, endless space—bigger, deeper, farther into the distance than I have ever dared to dream. I blink rapidly, filtering a thousand possibilities a second.

"*There*," I whisper. "I found it."

An image. A headline. An answer.

SCANDAL ROCKS KINGDOM, INVESTORS DENY COVER-UP AND LAWSUITS LOOM AS FANTASIST HOME PROJECT™ TESTING CONTINUES

That's when I see him. A man in a dark suit, standing in front of the gateway.

"It's him," I say. "I was right. He's Clara's father. He's an Investor."

I scan the entirety of the article, followed by a hundred more—newspapers from every country, in every language, all over the world. And yet . . . they all say the same thing.

"Ana?" Owen squeezes my hand. "Are you okay?"

"That's why Clara knew our language," I whisper. "Because Nia *lived* with them—the first family to ever bring home a

Fantasist. She knew they were testing us for mass distribution."

The Future is Fantasist™

"She tried to stop it."

Tears run down my cheek. Real, feeling, nearly *human* tears.

"But she couldn't."

"Ana." Owen's eyes turn misty. "I'm so, so sorry."

I turn back to my sisters—sleeping, silent, and so beautiful beyond the glass. "I have to help them," I say a little too loudly. "Like Nia wanted to. I can't leave them here."

"You *will* help them," Owen says. "*We'll* help them. But not today. Today, you're saving you." His eyes dart suddenly down the hall and go alarmingly wide. "Walk." He takes my arm and pulls me away from the window. "Ana, please walk *now*."

It's too late.

I feel her heartbeat before I see her face.

Seventy-nine beats per minute.

"Excuse me, what do you think you're doing?" Mother asks the both of us. "Medics don't have clearance on this floor." Her eyes search me for a badge that isn't there. "Who's your Supervisor?"

I stare at her in shock.

With my mask on, she doesn't recognize me.

My own mother has no idea who I am.

The realization simultaneously relieves and makes my chest ache to the point I cannot speak. But then I think of Daddy, resting in a pool of his own blood.

"We're part of Dr. Foster's team," Owen volunteers. "We were on our way to level one to assist with today's shutdown, but I'm afraid we left supplies in the ambulette and got turned around. If

332

you'd be so kind as to point us back to the parking garage, I'd be grateful to you."

Grateful.

He has spoken Mother's favorite word.

"Oh." She blinks as if a spell has been lifted. "Of course." Soon, she is giving us detailed instructions on stairwells, basements, and private elevators. As she talks, I carefully study her face. One last time, before I delete it from my memory forever.

It is not too hard to do.

I said goodbye to the idea of having a real mother long, long ago.

Minutes later, we reach the laboratory's main entrance.

"After you," Owen says, holding the door.

I step outside—my first step toward a new life—only to be met by a shocking, blinding flood of high-beam lights. I shield my face. Fear floods my inner circuitry.

We have been caught.

It is over.

"Your eyes will adjust," Owen says.

"What?" I blink hard a few times and discover: it was only the sunlight.

We climb into Owen's car, pass easily through two security gates, guards waving us through without a second glance. Before I know it, we are flying down an open, ocean-lined highway, watching the Hybrid Laboratory grow smaller and smaller in the distance until it disappears completely in the rearview mirror.

The ocean is so big, I think as we drive. I can hardly believe it's real.

"*Seeing is believing.*" Kaia's voice drifts in on the back of the

333

breeze.

I gaze at the boy in the seat beside me and smile. I make a silent promise to Kaia that I'll be back for her. That I'll be back for all of them.

"Here." Owen reaches for the center console. "Want to hear some music?"

I nod.

Soon, the car fills with a sound I have never heard before.

A sound the firewalls never allowed.

Country and bluegrass. Oldies and pop. Hip hop. Rock and roll.

For a time, I sit quietly. Just listening.

"Do you like it?" Owen asks after a minute. "Feel free to change the station, if you want."

"This is perfect."

But deep down, something about these new sounds has struck a chord in me. With my eyes on the water, I think about Nia. I think about Eve. I think about the Supervisors and all the beautiful Formerly Extinct Species. I think about that little girl who disappeared below the waves on the back of a pilot whale. And I think about Daddy. *Dr. Foster.* I recall the startling size of his dilated pupils, frozen in place for all time, and the oddly pleasing sight of his blood seeping onto the floor.

Thick. Oozing. Red.

Humans are capable of such cruelty. Such horror.

And in order to become one . . . I've had to become capable of that, too.

In front of us, the ocean and sky form a peaceful, perfect blur. I want to feel free, I realize. I want to feel glad that I am so much more than I've been taught.

But for just a moment, I wish I could go back. Back to a time when I was innocent, and didn't know—or even care—what it meant to be human.

You're braver than you believe.

I look again at Owen. I reach over to take his hand in mine, but notice something under my fingernail: a speck of blood.

There *is* no going back. There is no more fantasy.

There is only today.

Only now.

Only *this*.

Slowly, I wipe my hand on a tissue, removing the rest of Daddy's blood, the last of the evidence, like the final words of a story.

Happily ever after.

Then I roll the window down and toss the tissue into the wind, watching it whirl away. For just a moment, it looks beautiful to me: like something wild, like something free.

ACKNOWLEDGMENTS

First and foremost, I want to thank Lauren Oliver, friend, colleague, and genius-in-shining-armor, without whom you would certainly not be holding this book in your hands. Lauren, your friendship, generosity, wisdom, and support over the years has meant more to me than you will ever know. It has been both deeply meaningful and a true honor collaborating with you on this book and I will be forever grateful you picked me up, brushed me off, and guided Ana's story—and me—back into the light. I love you.

To Lexa Hillyer, for your warmth, hilarity, generosity, friendship, decadent snacks, uke tunes, and most of all sheer editorial brilliance, and without whom this book would also not exist. Thank you for your guidance, your constant faith in me, and for holding my hand when the going got rough. I love you so much and also shark, pebble, penguin, these are just words.

To Tiffany Liao, my editor extraordinaire and *Kingdom* champion—thank you for your brilliance, humor, grace, and expert guidance through what has been a wonderfully and joyfully collaborative editorial process. Thank you for loving Ana and her world as much as I do.

To Kamilla Benko, Emily Berge-Thielmann, and Lynley Bird for your exuberance, dedication, hard work, and general Glasstown rockstardom. You ladies are the best ever.

To everyone at Henry Holt and Macmillan Children's Books, but especially Christian Trimmer, Jennifer Edwards and the

Macmillan sales team, and Venetia Gosling and the Macmillan UK team for your incredible championing of this book; Kristin Dulaney and Catherine Kramer for your excitement and enthusiasm, and for working so tirelessly to bring *The Kingdom* to readers around the world; Katie Klimowicz, Rich Deas, and our incredible illustrator, Kevin Tong, for your stunningly gorgeous cover design; Morgan Rath and Teresa Ferraiolo for being the best, most dynamic publicity and marketing duo around; Mark Podesta for your kindness and support; and again my amazingly brilliant editor and friend, Tiffany Liao. It is such an honor to be part of the Holt family.

To my agent Stephen Barbara and everyone at Inkwell Management, for your enthusiastic support through every stage of the publication process.

To my family—Stephen, Dad, Ben, Josh, Jeff and Alisa, John and Deborah, Peter and Deborah, Erica and Jonathan, Michael and Joseph, Julia, Kate, and Alex, Cathy, Joe, and especially Jeannie—for loving me, supporting me, and holding me up during the darkest, most difficult time. I love you all more than life itself and would never have made it here without you.

To my New Haven family—Lucia, Steve, Lucian, Andrew, Zio and Zia Lina, and James (and the wonderful Murphys)—thank you all for your love, hilarity, generosity, support, and being so wonderful to me, since day one. I love you guys.

To Jesse, Chesnee, Leah, and Heather—love y'all so much (even though, let's be honest, I still can't pull off y'all and never could).

To Shira, Talia, Leah, Sarah F, Sarah B, Gina, Emily, Kal, Anneka, and Mark for being my Vassar crew and constant stars for more years now than I care to mention for fear of aging us all in such a public setting. Can't wait to keep laughing, sharing, and singing Ms. Jackson till we're old and gray.

To Pamela McElroy, Rebecca Serle, Anne Heltzel, Leila Sales, Emily Heddleson, and Jocelyn Davies, for your enlightenment, love, phone calls, and community. You all mean so much to me.

To Sophie Roberts and Caroline Hagood, supermoms and superfriends—where would I be without you? (Probably in a ditch, but I digress.) Thank you two for being there for me through all the joy and all the crazy. I couldn't do mom life without you.

To Hannah Spencer and Joyce Tang, from cats to kids, 566 forever! Those were the days. <3

To Lindsey Stoddard, roomie forever and friend for life, your love, humor, letters, and words have meant the absolute world, from the moment we met. You are beyond special to me.

To Courtney Sheinmel, the Patsy to my Emma, the Garrett to my Flap, the Carly to my Simon, the St. Elmo's to my Fire. Gorgeous isn't everything. I love you.

To Janna Lunetta, my BFF for all time with whom, after almost thirty years of friendship, I have been lucky enough to live out a real-life *Friends* fantasy. *Waves downstairs.* I love you so.

To my angels, Mama, Papa, Grandma Marjorie and Grandpa Ed. I still miss you all the time.

To Theo Miller, my sweetest, silliest guy and reason for being.

I love you endlessly.

Finally, I want to thank my mom, Tricia, who sadly never got the chance to read this book—but was nevertheless infinitely proud of me—and without whom my universe will forever glow less bright. You were my true North Star in life, psychic witch, and dearest, funniest friend. You exist for me now in all our favorite music and films—and in Theo's beautiful smile—and I can still hear your voice and feel your love all around me. I love you forever to the stars and back. *(Major.)*

MALPAS 31/8/19